*In the earliest days of the last century, a Florida family strives to build
a legacy in the burgeoning new city of Miami...*

In South Florida, a region that offers some of life's richest beauty as well
as some of its harshest conditions, a city is rising. Eve and Max Harjo
moved to Miami after the great freeze of 1894 wiped out their citrus grove.
Eve is busy writing for the *Miami Metropolis*, Miami's first newspaper,
while Max salvages the ships that fall victim to Florida's dangerous reefs
and violent storms.

Their nineteen-year-old daughter Eliza dives to bring up the salvaged
treasures, uncaring that it is hardly woman's work. And her stubborn
determination to educate local Seminoles—male and female—draws
the ire of the tribe's chief. But Eliza's greatest conflict will be choosing
between two men: a brilliant inventor working on the prototype for a new
motorboat, and a handsome lighthouse keeper from the northwest. When
a massive storm unleashes its fury on South Florida, it reveals people's
truest characters and deepest secrets, changing lives as drastically as it
changes the coastal landscape...

Also by Janie DeVos

Beneath a Thousand Apple Trees
The Art of Breathing

The Glory Land series
A Corner in Glory Land

The Rising of Glory Land

Janie DeVos

LYRICAL PRESS
Kensington Publishing Corp.
www.kensingtonbooks.com

LYRICAL PRESS BOOKS are published by

Kensington Publishing Corp.
119 West 40th Street
New York, NY 10018

All Kensington titles, imprints, and distributed lines are available at special quantity discounts for bulk purchases for sales promotion, premiums, fundraising, educational, or institutional use.

Special book excerpts or customized printings can also be created to fit specific needs. For details, write or phone the office of the Kensington Sales Manager: Kensington Publishing Corp., 119 West 40th Street, New York, NY 10018. Attn. Sales Department. Phone: 1-800-221-2647.

Lyrical Press and Lyrical Press logo Reg. U.S. Pat. & TM Off.

First Electronic Edition: June 2018
eISBN-13: 978-1-5161-0434-5
eISBN-10: 1-5161-0434-X

First Print Edition: June 2018
ISBN-13: 978-1-5161-0435-2
ISBN-10: 1-5161-0435-8

Printed in the United States of America

To my husband, Glen, who has been my safe port in life's storms for over thirty years. May a gentle wind always be at your back, dear one.

And to my sister, Kathy, who shares my earliest Miami memories, making them some of the ones I hold closest to my heart. Here's to those barefoot days up in the Fichus tree with the iguanas, Sis.

Acknowledgments

It not only takes people who are greatly educated about an area to help me create a novel worth reading, it also takes folks who have a great love for a place, for they are the ones who breathe life into my stories through their depth of emotion and experiences.

First, I'd like to thank Lisa Mongelia, Executive Director of the History of Diving Museum, in Islamorada, FL. Lisa's information about diving before the development of the Miller Dunn helmet was instrumental in helping me to paint a concise picture of how dangerous and primitive the world of wreck diving was at that time, and how the introduction of such a helmet helped to catapult the industry into a far safer and more lucrative one.

I'm also very grateful to Gary Bremen, park ranger at Biscayne National Park, who works hard to protect and educate the public on Biscayne Bay's history, and the importance of maintaining the health of these delicate and most vulnerable waters and barrier reefs. I learned a lot from talking with him, even though I grew up swimming and fishing in the very waters he's so committed to caring for today.

And I am especially indebted to Eric S. Martin, President of the Florida Keys Reef Lights Foundation, who is the go-to man for all things related to the six screw-pile reef lighthouses along the South Florida coastline from Biscayne Bay, down through the Florida Keys. His insight into the daily life of lighthouse keepers was invaluable in the writing of this book, and it was downright fascinating on top of it! He was most gracious about answering an endless list of questions I had, and was most generous in providing me with pictures and information far beyond what I asked of him. It's obvious these old structures are a passion of his, and because of people like him, these lighted sentinels will be cared for and preserved so that they will continue to stand majestically along Florida's southern reefs for generations to come.

Finally, a very special "thank you" to an old friend, Rich Stone. Even though he hails from the north, Rich has an uncanny understanding of the waters of South Florida, probably better than most native Miamians do, and his passion for them runs many fathoms deep. His expertise in the field of nautical mechanics was most helpful when writing about the early days of motorboats. Without Rich's guidance, my character, Striker, would have only sailed, rather than motored his way through this novel.

My friends of the deep, may there always be red skies at night for you.

Preface

Eliza

Lake Weir Area, Central Florida
February 1895

My world changed as I sat in a wasted orange tree, hidden within the branches, playing hide-and-seek with my eight-year-old brother, Dylan. As I sat silently on the tree limb, refusing to give away my hiding spot, my mother appeared below me and looked around at the devastation that surrounded us. Even at the age of seven, I knew that the amount of damage our citrus groves had suffered was enormous. Thousands of shriveled and pitted-skinned oranges covered the ground, and beyond what I could see was another hundred acres of frozen tangerine and grapefruit trees. Nothing had been spared.

Mama squatted down and picked up a ruined orange, but the sound of a wagon rolling down the road that ran parallel to our grove got her attention, as well as mine. She stood up and looked in that direction. Several rows of orange trees blocked our view for the moment, but just from the creaking, sluggish sound of the wagon plodding along, I figured it was heavily weighted down. When it cleared the trees, I could see that I was correct. The conveyance was piled high with belongings, and crowded in and among them all was Clyde Whitfield and his family. All five of his children, as well as his wife, Grace, looked as beaten down as our groves. But as Clyde turned toward Mama to touch the brim of his sweat-stained hat in greeting, I saw more than just a defeated look on his face. I could see the terrible fear in his eyes asking, *What now?*

When the first freeze slammed Florida on December twenty-ninth, the temperatures sank to nineteen degrees, and snow blanketed areas from Tampa across the state to Titusville. Even as Dylan and I were making our first snowballs, I couldn't stop thinking about the things I'd heard during the meeting at our church the night before. Another grove owner, Bob Chapman, said that Armageddon had begun, and since Reverend Short had preached about that very thing just a few weeks before, I knew what Mr. Chapman was talking about. It terrified me. Looking around at the unusually full church pews, I couldn't help but believe he might be right. We prayed together as "children of a mighty and merciful God" for hours that night, and at first, it seemed as if our prayers might actually have been heard.

Within the week, small signs of life began shooting out in green buds on the sturdy older trees. My parents, Max and Eve Harjo, knew that many of our younger trees wouldn't survive, but they felt that the older ones could, and Papa said those that did were almost guaranteed to give us the sweetest fruit we'd ever tasted. But all hope was lost when the second freeze hit us on February eighth. There was no snow this time, but after the temperatures stayed well below freezing for two straight days, there was nothing left of the trees but shriveled fruit and blown out bark from the sap that froze in the trunks. Leaves and fruit fell from the branches, leaving our once beautiful groves a dying wasteland. My father had said that if Mr. Chapman was right, and Armageddon had begun, then the Bible had gotten it wrong. We wouldn't be consumed by fire and brimstone, he said, but by an icy cold instead.

Suddenly, I heard Papa calling Mama's name. "I'm in the third row," she shouted, and a moment later, he appeared through some of the trees. I knew I should make my presence known, but there'd been too many hushed conversations between my parents lately, and I wanted an unfiltered version of what was going on, so I remained silent and still.

"Did you see the Whitfields?" he asked as he walked toward her.

"Yeah, but I didn't get a chance to talk to them. I just saw them ride by with what looked to be everything they own piled into that old wagon. Did you talk to Clyde?"

"Yes. They've had enough. Since losing most of what they had in the '86 freeze, they only had the fifteen acres of tangerines left, and most of those were younger trees. The grove's destroyed. They're heading back to Brunswick. You 'bout done here, Eve? We need to sit down and settle on what we're gonna do, and when."

"Still thinkin' about doing what we talked about last night, Max?" Mama asked.

"Yes," Papa confirmed.

"I figured you'd already made up your mind that's where we're headed." She smiled up at him. After ten years of marriage, it was obvious they knew each other pretty well. "James will be thrilled," she said, referring to her older brother.

I liked Uncle James. He always brought Dylan and me something when he came for a visit, and he looked a lot like Mama, with his dark red hair and brown eyes. He lived far away, south of us, in a tiny little town on the coast. I'd heard him tell my parents more than once that we should move down there, too, but I wasn't so sure that was a good idea. I liked living among the orange groves and swimming in the blue springs, and I saw no reason to change any of that. I had to admit, though, Uncle James's enthusiasm was contagious as he described the beauty of his new home, and the different and exciting things to do there, like swimming in an ocean of salty water. What a strange thing that would be!

"Well, I'm glad someone will be thrilled about it," Papa said, "'Cause it's a pretty rough place. But things will change fast once the railroad gets down there. It didn't freeze that far south—at least not to the extent that it did here, and I'd be willing to bet that railroad man Flagler knows it, too. Even so, we don't have to have groves again, Eve, at least not as large as we have now. There're other ways to make a living, and after what we've just been through, I'm leanin' toward those other ways. There's fishing, and, soon enough, there'll be tourists coming down on the trains. James says he's gonna help build the town up, and I have no doubt that he will. He'll prosper in a big way because of it, too. And if we get down there while the place is still young, we can do the same, Eve."

"Still, Max, there's hardly anything there, or anyone either." Mama sounded a little unsure. "Like James once told us, it's mostly dreamers of the hardiest kind or hard people of the most desperate kind that are there now, and we'd be settling our family among them. But I guess we're pretty desperate now, too," she said, forcing a smile.

I was reminded of a letter we'd received from Uncle James soon after he'd moved, six months before, when he'd gone down to help design and build a hotel. He'd written that the area had so many mosquitoes, horseflies, and sand fleas that they were thicker 'n thieves at a blind men's convention and could suck a body dry in a matter of minutes. And if that wasn't enough to make one turn tail and run, then the fact that the longtime homesteaders and Seminoles didn't take too kindly to outsiders surely was. Though

Mama had laughed and said most of that was probably exaggerated, I figured there was some truth in it, too.

My thoughts of the future were quickly replaced by the present when I heard Mama say that it was nearly dinnertime. "Are you hungry?" she asked Papa.

"I could eat," he confirmed.

"Let's find Dylan and Eliza," she said as she bent down to look beneath the branches of the trees to see if she could spot our legs down one of the rows. "We need to let them know what's goin' on."

As they headed off toward home, I didn't move from my branch. I needed to think things over for a minute or two, see how I felt about it, and see how it felt to say the name of that strange new place out loud. *"Miami,"* I whispered. I climbed down through the branches, shimmied down the trunk, and then started for home. "Miami!" I said a little louder. I decided I liked the name. *Maybe I'll decide I like the place, too*, I thought, *if the 'skeeters don't run us off before I have enough time to decide.*

Chapter 1

The Price of Paradise

Miami, Florida
April, 1906

The Biscayne Bay House of Refuge sat glistening in the noonday sun, patiently waiting for the next group of shipwrecked survivors who would need the safety of its shelter and the meager but life-sustaining supplies stocked within. Numerous houses of refuge sat scattered along Florida's eastern coastline, but the Biscayne Bay house was the one nearest to our home on the Miami River. My twenty-year-old brother, Dylan, helped to maintain the shelter whenever the usual keeper needed a break, and he'd been out at the house for the last month. My parents were bringing fresh supplies to him and I accompanied them in our single-mast sailboat. We knew that as much as he needed supplies, he needed company, too, for boredom and loneliness plagued refuge keepers. The curse of isolation was a constant with them, and lighthouse keepers as well. In many ways, those keepers at the offshore lights had to endure the worst of it for they could go days without seeing anyone other than the occasional fisherman.

After dropping off the supplies, the four of us would try our luck at some surf fishing. Mama was hoping to catch red snapper, and she'd been optimistic enough that she'd brought along a head of cabbage to make slaw, and corn meal for hushpuppies. The day was brilliantly bright and hot, and since it was Sunday, we would take full advantage of the opportunity to spend some time together.

"Eliza, throw me the stern line when I'm done tying up the bow," Papa said, startling me. We'd arrived at the refuge house's dock. Quickly jumping out of the boat, my father tied the bow line to the wooden piling as I hurried to the back of the boat for the stern rope. As I waited to toss it to him, I pushed the blowing strands of my hair away from my eyes and looked out at the bay. It was a beautiful, deep bluish-green, but there was a stiff breeze coming out of the northwest, creating white foam that topped the waves like a froth of meringue. Hurricane season was nearly upon us, and it was anyone's guess each summer which town would be struck down, or how many folks would still be alive the following day to tell about it, much less have homes to gather in for the telling.

The majority of winter tourists had boarded the train at Miami's Fort Dallas Station just the week before to return north for Easter. With the large exodus of wealthy people, our population had shrunk considerably. It would become bloated with visitors again once hurricane season was over at the end of November, taking the dense humidity and heat with it. Then the full-pocketed, well-dressed Yankee tourists would return to the place the Seminoles called "Myaamia," meaning *friends,* so they could bask in the warmth of the winter sun. And many of the northerners *had* become friends during the ten years we'd lived on the Miami River, but there were others who treated the year 'rounders as nothing more than "ignorant crackers," who were simply put on God's green Earth to make their lives as comfortable as possible.

"Rip currents today," Papa said, drawing my attention back toward the beach. I saw that my brother had posted a sign: No Swimming. Rip Currents. Just the month before, two tourists from Boston had drowned off the beach near Cape Florida, when they'd been caught up in one of the deadly currents. Instead of swimming parallel to the shore until they were out of it, they'd tried swimming through it. The current had won. It always did. There was hell to pay for living in paradise, and a wide variety of ways to make payment.

Dylan came out of the house and hurried across the sand to help us unload the boat. The wind whipped his shoulder-length chestnut-colored hair across his face. "I started to wonder if y'all would end up not coming," he said as he reached down from the dock to take a box of supplies Mama held up to him.

"It'd take more than five-foot seas to keep us in port," she said.

"No," Papa clarified, "to keep *you* in port." Laughing, he directed his attention back to my brother. "How are things goin' here, son?"

"It's been pretty quiet lately," he said as he grabbed a basket from me. "Those stronger light bulbs out at Fowey Rocks have made a huge difference in preventing wrecks. I know that's good news and bad news for you, Pa," he added, smiling.

Our father had started salvaging wrecks soon after we'd moved down to Miami, and it had been a far more lucrative way of earning a living than his other job, taking tourists into the Glades to kill gators. And my father preferred it. Though he'd always hunted, he'd hunted for a reason: to put food on the table, or to sell the meat and skins to folks who couldn't go hunting. But my father had a bad taste in his mouth about taking some over-privileged, under-worked tourist into the back country for the sake of mounting some poor animal's head on the wall and boasting about the danger he'd put himself in to capture it.

"Naw." Papa shook his head. "I'm glad for the stronger beams." He finished securing the boat's lines to the pilings, then jumped back in to help us unload. "There are already enough wrecks to work. No need to add any more to that list. Too many lives have been lost to those old reefs and sandbars. But stronger bulbs or not, those jagged rocks are still gonna create plenty of casualties. It doesn't matter whether the crews can see the reefs or not. When the winds are strong enough, they're gonna toss boats and ships around any which way they choose."

We finished unloading and started up toward the house with the supplies, but a clap of thunder sounded off in the distance, startling us, and we looked up to see ominous charcoal-colored clouds billowing up in the west.

"Weather's comin' in," Dylan said. "But Lord knows we need the rain. It's been so dry."

"Yeah," Papa agreed, taking one last look toward the sky before climbing the porch steps and seeking sanctuary in the well-made refuge house. "But you know how that goes: What Mother Nature withholds from us now, she will more than make up for in the future."

Looking off to the west just in time to see lightning backlight the rapidly building storm clouds, I wondered if the future might have just arrived.

Chapter 2

Life is Calling

I slid another stack of pancakes onto Dylan's plate, and then sat back down at the kitchen table.

"So you'll be at Fowey for just a week, you think?" Papa asked before taking another sip of coffee. We'd been forced to eat breakfast for supper since we'd been unable to fish that afternoon. The skies had opened up, chasing every living creature into shelter, including us. Now, with the wood-burning stove going, the room was cozy. It was late April, so there was still a little coolness to the air, especially on the beach in a storm, but we wouldn't have that luxury for too much longer. Within another month, heat and humidity would force us to get out of the kitchen as soon as a meal was over, and the choice of meals would be contingent on how long one would have to stand over the stove to cook them.

Once, during a dinner that was being prepared by the ladies of the First Presbyterian Church for a fourth of July celebration, I heard Elotta Aims remark that she wouldn't be at all surprised to learn that a woman who was condemned to spend eternity in hell wasn't sent to some lake of fire but banished, instead, to a kitchen in Miami, in August, with a fully fired-up wood-burning stove. "Now *that*," she'd emphasized, "is what I'd consider hell." We'd all laughed, heartily agreeing as we wiped the perspiration from our faces with our already-soaked handkerchiefs and continued frying chicken. The heavy cotton or linen blouses and wool shirts we were expected to wear in social settings nearly gave us heat stroke during the summer. As soon as I returned home, I always shed the miserable clothing for either a lighter cotton dress or a pair of canvas pants and a cotton or denim shirt, just as Mama did. As far as we were concerned, living in

South Florida's oppressive heat meant throwing the old rules of etiquette out the window and wearing clothes that wouldn't kill us.

"Pass me the sugar, Ma, would ya, please?" Dylan asked before answering Papa's question about his expected length of stay out at Fowey Rocks lighthouse. I assessed my brother across the table from me, and thought about how kind he was and how he'd make some lucky girl a fine husband. He was a good-looking man. Though he was fairer than me, we had the same angular facial structure, and his eyes were an exact copy of Papa's. They were dark blue, penetrating eyes, and when Dylan looked at you, it seemed as though he could look right through you. Truly like father, like son, I thought.

"I'll be at Fowey Light at least a week," Dylan said, stirring sugar into his coffee. "I'll man it with Striker until Adam Wilson gets back from shore leave. I appreciate y'all taking me out tomorrow. There's got to be at least two men there at all times. Adam was just getting ready to leave for the mainland when Jim Altman fell off the oil tank's ladder and broke his ribs. Lucky for Jim, Adam hadn't left yet, or Jim would have been stuck there until the next boat came by to haul him back to shore. It's tough--there's no way to send a message for help other than to hang the flag upside down and wait for a passing ship to notice it. Crews are good about keeping an eye out for it, though, and stopping when they see a distress signal. They know somethin's goin' on. But it sure would be nice to have a telegraph machine or phone line out there. Anyway, I'll stay when Adam gets back so Striker can get some shore leave, especially if Jim isn't back by then. Apparently, he got banged up pretty badly."

"Listen, Dylan, how's Striker doin' these days? And how long is he plannin' on stayin' out at the light?" Mama asked as she gathered up some of our dishes and took them over to the sink. Paul Strickland, or Striker, had become a friend of Dylan's soon after we moved to Miami. People who didn't know Striker well thought his name was just a shorter version of his surname. But he'd actually gotten the moniker because of his uncanny luck getting a "strike" almost every time he threw a fishing line into the water. He was a couple of years older than Dylan, and had lived with his parents just downriver from us to the west.

Mae and Jerry Strickland, Striker's parents, had also been citrus growers who were ruined by the freeze that had wiped us out. But their enormous groves had been south of us, in Leesburg, Florida. Just as my parents had decided that running an enormous grove was a thing of the past, so had they, and the Stricklands became involved in boat building. They mainly built glade skiffs, the flat-bottomed boats used to navigate through the marshes of sawgrass in the Everglades, but they built some small sailboats, as well. Paul, their only child, had shown a real affinity for building the boats, and before too long, he'd gone to work at the Merrill-Stevens boatyard in Jacksonville, which was considered one of the best builders in the state.

Striker was gone for about a year, and returned home with all kinds of designs and dreams sailing around in his head. He had some money in his pocket, too, for the good folks at Merrill-Stevens felt that it was a wise investment to put their money in the hands of young boat designers, and Striker opened a small boatyard on the Miami River. All had gone well the first year until Striker designed and built a beautiful small sloop as a twenty-fifth wedding anniversary gift for his parents. The couple had sailed the newly-christened *Strike One* up toward the Jupiter Inlet area, with plans to anchor overnight. But, right at dusk, they'd hit a reef and gone down. Neither Jerry nor Mae had survived.

"I guess he's okay," Dylan shrugged. "Honestly, I haven't seen much of him either—not since he went out to the light, and that's been…what… maybe eight or nine months ago?"

"He can't hide out there forever, you know," Mama said over her shoulder as she began washing dishes.

"I don't think he's hiding out," Papa said. "He's not the kind of man to do that. No, I think he's just tryin' to get some things worked out. Losing his folks the way he did—well, hell, that's enough to mess with anyone's mind. Even though it wasn't his fault, and everyone tells him that, still…I know he feels responsible for the accident. Anyway, he's got to sort through it, and he needs some time alone to do that. And where better a place to find solitude than in a lighthouse seven miles out to sea? Least he's not drownin' his sorrows in the bottle like some men would. No, he's gotta be in a place where a man can hear himself think. I hope he can put this behind him at some point and move on. He's too talented and too good a person not to."

"Has Striker ever been out to the place the *Strike One* went down?" Mama asked.

"Not that I know of," Dylan said. Papa said he didn't think so either.

"Maybe he could find some closure if he did," Mama said. "Lord, what a tragedy," she added, while drying the skillet.

"I have some news!" I volunteered, hoping to steer us away from the subject of Striker and his parents.

"What'd you go and do now?" my brother teased as he leaned back comfortably in his chair and folded his arms across his chest, as if preparing himself for a long story.

"Make light of it all you want to, but I have figured out my life's calling!"

"Lord, here we go," Dylan muttered under his breath. I chose to ignore him.

I took a deep breath and dove in. "Well, a Seminole couple came into the trading post at the end of the day last week. I'd seen 'em out on the lawn all day trading their what-nots for other what-nots. They came in right before we closed up for the day wantin' five yards of pink lace ribbon. After I'd cut the piece from a spool, I rang it up and told them it was a dollar thirty, and the Seminole woman handed her change purse over to the man so that he could count out the proper amount.

"I asked him if the woman knew how to speak English. I knew I'd seen 'em before, and I'd seen them do the same thing—she'd hand over her purse to him, letting him take what he wanted from it.

"'She speak the English a little,' the man said, 'but she not know numbers too good.'

"'Your name is Willie Factor, isn't it?' I asked him, even though I knew it was, but we'd never been formally introduced and I was just trying to be polite. He looked at me suspiciously, like I was about to make a point that he wasn't sure he wanted to be a part of. Well, he gives me this quick little nod, confirming that he was Willie Factor, and I said, 'Mr. Factor, why don't you let me help your wife with her English, and I'll teach her a little math, too—adding and subtracting? That way, if you're not around, she'll understand what's being asked of her, and she won't be taken advantage of.'

"Well, you'd think I'd just asked that man to sneak off to a thicket with me! Lord, he looked downright offended! Drew back from me like I'd just spit at him. 'She know English good enough. Plenty good enough! Don't need white lady to learn Lina nothing. White ways bad for her. Very bad'

"'Is it bad for Lina or for *you*, Mr. Factor?' I said. Well, that was it! The man latched on to poor ol' Lina's arm and practically dragged her out of the store. Then Mrs. Brickell comes up and asks me what that was all about, and was I causing her to lose good customers. And I told her, 'No, Mrs. Brickell, just ignorant ones.' Well, she didn't like that too much and told me I better watch myself. I calmly told her I would while telling myself that pretty soon I'd be watching myself walk out her store's front door for the last time. And that's when I decided!"

"Decided what?" my brother asked as though he was a little afraid to hear my answer.

"I'm gonna teach the Seminole children—*all* the children, the girls too! *And* their women!"

"Lord, Eliza." Dylan rolled his eyes and laughed, while Mama just shook her head. Papa, on the other hand, watched me with a twinkle in his wonderful eyes and an amused smile on his face.

Papa was part Creek Indian and I had his thick, jet-black hair, though mine was long and wavy like Mama's. My eyes were brown like hers, too, though not as dark, and both Dylan and I had inherited our parents' considerable height.

"Those people aren't going to let you teach any of their females," Mama said, just as she had the first time I'd told her. "They'll think you're gonna poison their brains. You know they think a Seminole woman educated by a white person is totally immoral."

"Maybe they do," I said. "But who's to stop the girls from *overhearing* what the boys are learning? I'm gonna teach those girls one way or another! And if Papa will let me help with salvaging some more wrecks, teaching those girls will be a much easier thing to accomplish."

"Here she goes," Papa muttered under his breath while winking at my mother.

"The way I figure it," I continued, choosing to ignore my father, "if I can offer the Seminole men a little somethin' or other from a wreck I've salvaged, then maybe they'll be more accommodating about letting me teach their womenfolk."

Dylan laughed. "Somehow, sister, I doubt they can be so easily bribed. Now, that's not to say you won't find a way to get the job done, though. If I had to bet on anyone doin' it, it'd be you, hands down."

"Thank you, Dylan," I said, truly meaning it. I adored my brother for his never-failing confidence in me, among many other reasons, and I knew that the feeling was mutual. He wanted me to be happy even if that meant taking a few chances other young women might not. I'd never been the conventional sort, and in truth, I had the feeling I'd disappoint my family if I ever tried to be. After all, there was nothing very conventional about any of us.

Mama and Papa had helped Mama's twin sister, Ivy, find refuge at a Seminole village in Immokalee, Florida, when Ivy had fallen in love and gotten pregnant by a black man. Ivy and Moses had fled their homes in Silver Springs when my grandfather had found out, but he went after them, intent on killing them. Fortunately, Mama had enlisted Papa's help since he was an experienced tracker, and they'd found the runaways before my grandfather could. Immediately, they'd taken them to the Seminole village, where Ivy, Moses, and their three children still lived now.

Dylan, though more of an introvert than I was, was rather unconventional in his own way. He shared Mama's love of writing, and he studied authors from John Audubon to Plato. Some years back, Mama thought he might be working on a manuscript. Dylan had replied, "That's just it, Mama; I'm working on it, and I haven't quite figured out exactly what it's supposed to be. But you'll be the first to know if and when I do."

While Dylan's life of substituting as a keeper at the lighthouses and houses of refuge suited him for the time being, I knew that he felt something was missing and that he hadn't been able to quite tap into that special calling of his heart. There were times I could see his frustration, especially since he'd turned twenty. At those times, he would wander the beach, or take out the glade skiff or sailboat and be gone for hours exploring the Everglades, sailing around Biscayne Bay, or beyond into the Atlantic.

"So, Pa, you still thinkin' about going back down to see what's left on the *Alicia*?" my brother asked. He was referring to the wreck that had occurred the year before, just off Elliot Key, an island south of the lighthouse where Dylan was going. It was as though my brother was presenting the perfect opportunity to put my plan into effect.

Papa tried to hide a smile, no doubt guessing he was now dealing with a son who was in cahoots with his daughter's harebrained scheme. "Thinkin' about it," Papa said noncommittally as he scooted his chair back from the table and lit a thin black cigar.

"Talk him into it, Dylan!" I urged. "Honestly, I've tried bargaining with him, and even tried to figure out a way of blackmailing him into going, but so far, he hasn't budged."

As Papa had gotten more and more involved in wreck salvaging, I got more and more interested in wreck diving. To my mind, there was nothing more exhilarating than exploring the shattered remains of some unlucky mariner's disastrous voyage. My father employed a couple of young Seminole men to dive the wrecks, for they were the best at it, and through much begging and pleading, my parents had allowed Simon and Turtle to teach me the art of wreck diving. As often as I could, I took part in the salvaging.

My father had a fifty-five-foot, steam-powered fishing trawler, and with the help of a winch and pulley system installed in it, we'd been able to pull up some wonderful treasures from the reef wrecks. Once it was decided that there was cargo of value in a sunken vessel, we would attach nets, ropes and hooks to the cargo and Papa would haul it up. We'd recovered beautiful jewelry, as well as silver and gold coins, but we'd also raised larger cargo including casks of wine and barrels of nails, cotton, and molasses, as well as crockery, glassware, and canned goods. After everything was recovered, Papa took the bounty to the Port of Entry, in Key West, where it was recorded, appraised and sold.

Papa's salvaging work had been lucrative enough to allow us to expand our tongue and groove pine board two-bedroom into a four-bedroom home. We'd also extended the wide veranda so that it ran along three sides of the house instead of just the front, and we'd painted the place white. We'd built a far more substantial dock to accommodate my parents' sailboat as well as Dylan's, and the trawler. To some people's minds, having three boats seemed extravagant, but they were our means of making a living, and they were also an easy way of traveling along the coastline of South Florida. The woods, hammocks, and mangroves were difficult to navigate, and, in some places, virtually impenetrable.

Mama said it reminded her of when she was a young girl in Central Florida, and had to travel down her beloved Ocklawaha River in a small steamboat. Her family had been deeply involved in working and riding on the steamboats, and though she had broken all ties with her parents, who were now long dead, she was still close to her brothers. And the oldest one, Joseph, still made a living as an engineer on the enormous and opulent paddle wheelers running the Mississippi and Ohio Rivers. Being on the water had been a way of life for our family for many years, and it seemed that would continue to be the case.

When we were done with our supper, Papa and Dylan finished up some minor repairs on the refuge house that they'd been working on all afternoon, while Mama and I finished cleaning up the kitchen. Then we settled down in rockers on the veranda with fresh cups of coffee. The storm had finally run its course and the day ended in a spectacular sunset of various shades of orange, pink, and red. I wondered if the next day would dawn in the same vibrant colors, but I hoped not, for any man worth his salt on the seas knew: Red sky at night, sailor's delight. Red sky in morning, sailor's warning.

Chapter 3

An Isolated Heart

The refuge keeper replacing my brother was Art Hennessey, and he was due soon after daybreak. As we waited for him, I stood out on the veranda enjoying the colorful sunrise. The sun crested the horizon like a red ball aflame, and then transformed itself into an intense orange orb. Bad omen or not, the sight was one to behold, and as the family came out of the house to join me, the volume of their conversation dropped as if in respectful reverence to its powerful beauty. No matter how long someone lived in Florida, the sunrises still took one's breath away.

Before long, we spotted Art's sailboat, the *Salty Dog*, curving sharply in the wind and then heading for the dock. Grabbing the last of our gear, we walked out to help him tie up and unload.

"Hello, Harjo clan! Ain't it a purty mornin'?" Art enthusiastically called as he tossed the spring line to Dylan. Art was a transplant from Orangeburg, South Carolina, and his heavy southern accent was both endearing and warm.

"It sure is, Art," Mama agreed. "But what the afternoon might have in store for us has me a little wary." She reached down to take a crate of eggs nestled in a large amount of sawdust that Art handed up to her.

"Pshaw, Eve! That sky is clear as all get out. It looks to be a fine day in the makin'. Lord, but you're lookin' good! Listen," Art continued conspiratorially as he threw the stern line to Papa, "if that no-good husband o' yours don't treat you like the queen bee, then you let me know about it, ya hear?"

"I will, Art," Mama laughed, looking over at my smiling father as she did. Papa thought a lot of Art, and they enjoyed ribbing each other whenever the opportunity arose.

"Now, Art," Papa chided. "You know I'm not about to give her up. It took me a while to get her. Besides," he continued as he reached down to grab a duffle bag from the man, "she cooks the best fried fish and hushpuppies this side of the Mississippi."

"Well, doggone it!" Art said, looking crestfallen. "That was the *one and only* thing you coulda said to keep me from snatchin' Eve away. Seein' as how I'm a man of integrity, I wouldn't think of deprivin' another man of a great fish-fryin' hushpuppy-makin' wife. Anything else, maybe, but not a good fish-fryin' gal!" We all laughed as Dylan gave Art a hand and pulled him up onto the dock.

"Where y'all headed from here?" he asked after shaking Papa's hand and giving both Mama and me a bear hug.

"We're droppin' Dylan off at Fowey Rocks," Papa replied. "The regular keeper, Jim Altman, fell and hurt himself pretty good—mainly ribs 'n such, we hear. They need a third man for the crew right now and Dylan's it."

"Well, son," Art said, turning to address Dylan. "You keep an eye out for any purty mermaids, y' hear?"

"Yes, sir," my brother laughed, as he stepped down into our boat, and then raised his hands to help Mama down. "I will."

"And if she has a sister," Art continued, "you send her up the coast to me."

"Yes, sir, Mr. Hennessey, I sure will," Dylan laughed as he helped me down next. Papa threw our spring line onboard and then jumped in.

"Have a safe journey, folks," Art said as he pushed us away from the dock.

"We'll be seein' ya, Art," Papa replied. Then, turning away, he focused on setting our course, which would run south on the Atlantic ocean, staying well away from the barrier reefs, and on down to Fowey Rocks Light.

The wind was stiff, and Papa and Dylan were constantly adjusting and trimming the sails to allow for it. Everyone's hair whipped like the sails, and salt water sprayed our faces. There would be nothing leisurely about this trip. We rode parallel to the long island of Miami Beach, and noticed there were no sunbathers or picnickers yet. The only way to access the island was by boat, and the ferry hadn't started his daily runs at this early hour. All along the beautiful white-sand beaches, palm trees swayed in the wind, with their fronds slashing around like frenzied dancers.

We sailed past the newly dredged Government Cut, which provided a shortcut for mariners between Biscayne Bay and the Atlantic. While it meant not having to go to the south end of Miami Beach to get in and out of the Atlantic, the cut across the mangroves was an enormous example of how the need for convenience was quickly and permanently changing Florida's landscape—both on land and at sea. The fact that it seemed to change overnight was both frightening and exciting to me, though more of the latter than the former. But I knew there was nothing I could do to slow the changes down, and I doubted many people would want to anyway. The more progress that took place, the higher the returns for those who dared to invest in this land early on.

The northern-most barrier island of Virginia Key came into view, and soon after, the far bigger island of Key Biscayne, where the Cape Florida light was. Key Biscayne had been used as a vantage point for pirates lying in wait to raid ships moving through the shipping lanes. The nautical marauders hid their boats deep within the cover of Key Biscayne's thick mangroves, waiting for their unsuspecting victims. At times, crews on the cargo ships would throw their goods and treasures overboard with the intention of coming back for them later on. They stood a better chance of salvaging some of it from the sea floor than recovering it from the pirates. But once dumped, it was hard to find their cargo again, and even if it was located, much of it was overlooked, or carried off by the strong currents, especially during a storm. Years later, Papa had been able to successfully recover many valuable things simply by combing the seabed in that area.

As we sailed along the island's coastline, an eruption next to our boat startled us. A pair of gray and white porpoises shot out of the water, arcing gracefully before diving back down into the watery depths again to continue racing alongside our boat. Every several yards, they exploded from the water, jumping high above the surface in a beautiful display of strength and agility. It seemed as though they'd been sent to escort us. I looked toward the south and saw our destination about six miles away.

The Fowey Rocks lighthouse looked like a ghostly mirage hovering above the water. In actuality, the structure was anchored firmly into the seafloor, allowing it to withstand every storm that had tried to bring it down for nearly three decades. The cast iron skeletal framework soared a hundred and ten feet high.

Looking off to the west, I could see storm clouds building over the mainland, just as they had the day before. From the direction the wind was blowing, I knew it was just a matter of time before they reached us.

As we neared the lighthouse, Papa was well aware of the reef just to the west of us. The current was especially strong in that area, and with the tide coming in, and the winds building in advance of the storm, our approach was difficult. If the wind shifted even slightly, and we were caught up in one of its powerful gusts, we could easily end up on the rocks. When we finally slipped past the reef, I exhaled and shifted my attention back to the lighthouse. I spotted Striker hurrying down the steps from the keeper's quarters to the first platform. Aside from the tanks and the outhouse on the platform, there were davits which could be used to hoist a boat out of the water.

Striker came to the edge of the platform and shouted down to us. "If y'all want to stay awhile, let me drop this boat so Adam can get out of here, and then I'll hoist yours up. Seas are gettin' too rough to just tie up."

"We're not stayin'," Papa shouted back. "We need to be out of here before that weather hits. We'll unload Dylan and head on."

Striker nodded and waited while Papa maneuvered the boat into place by the ladder, and then climbed down to help us unload supplies.

"Sure wish y'all could come in for a while," he said with a warm smile. "It's not often we get company out here."

"I wish we could, Striker," Mama said. "But Max and I have to work tomorrow, and we can't take the chance of getting caught out here."

My mother had started writing for the local newspaper soon after we arrived in Miami, when I was almost eight. Over supper most nights, she'd entertain us with stories that were born from the daily events of a fast-growing town that was being erected by people from different places, social statuses, and viewpoints.

Striker then focused his attention on me. "Eliza"—he nodded slightly— "You doin' all right?" His voice was an octave lower when he addressed me, and I wondered why.

"Doin' well, thanks," I answered just as the wind flipped his cap off his head, revealing a full head of thick, wavy, golden hair. The cap landed right behind him and he snagged it before it was lost to the sea.

"Already lost two this month," he laughed. "Not sure they'll issue me any more if I lose this one." Then, his broad smile gentled into a softer one. "Well, it's good to see you," he said to me. Almost as an afterthought, he added, "And you, too, Eve. Next time you're out here, we'll do some fishin'."

Papa handed Striker a burlap bag of fresh vegetables and another with a smoked ham, and then Striker climbed the ladder up to the platform while Dylan hugged Mama and me good-bye; then he, too, went up the ladder. At that moment, Adam Wilson came out of the keeper's quarters with a duffle bag over his shoulder. Dropping it, he hurriedly clomped over to the ladder, reached down and grabbed Dylan's duffle bag, then enthusiastically pumped his hand when my brother came bounding up onto the platform. Adam, who was a stocky man in his thirties, was good-natured and jovial, but there was nothing graceful about him. He was the complete opposite of my tall, slender brother, and Striker, who was built much like Dylan, but maybe an inch shorter. Clunky and round though Adam was, he had pulled shipwreck survivors from the sea on more than one occasion. He was a well-respected keeper and rightly so. Adam had been working the Fowey Rocks Light for the last year, and had been about forty miles north at the Hillsboro Inlet Light for several years before that. I always wondered why a man who seemed to enjoy people decided to make a living in such an isolated way, especially at an offshore lighthouse like Fowey. But perhaps he liked people so much because he didn't have to be around them all the time.

"Adam, you want to hitch a ride in with us?" Papa called up to him. "Then you won't have to mess with gettin' your boat in the water, plus they'll have a boat here if it's needed. I'd tell ya we'd bring you back out, but Eve and I have full plates this week, but someone'll be headin' out to do some fishin' and can bring you back."

"I can, Papa! I'll bring him whenever he's ready." It wouldn't be the first time I'd sailed out that far alone, although I hadn't done it but a couple of times. Papa didn't look too sure about my offer, but Mama spoke up.

"She'll be fine, Max. She needs the experience. We won't always be around, you know."

"Yeah, but by then maybe a husband will be," Papa teased.

I could feel the blush spread across my face all the way to the roots of my hair, and quickly bent over, busying myself with coiling a rope that was already coiled.

"No doubt there will be, Max, no doubt at all!" Adam enthusiastically responded, but Striker said nothing. I wondered if there might be something in his eyes that would give away what he might be feeling, but I wouldn't look at him, not for all the Pieces of Eight on the ocean's floor.

"I'll take ya up on that ride in, Max!" Adam said. He descended the ladder to our boat and jumped aboard, causing the boat to dip significantly when he did so. After a quick handshake, Papa and Adam pushed the boat away from the iron structure and then Mama and Adam began raising the sails as Papa manned the tiller. I stood in the stern, out of the way, watching as the lighthouse grew smaller. I saw Dylan climb up to the keeper's quarters and go inside, while Striker worked with something over by the davits. When he was done, he stood at the edge of the platform with his arms folded across his chest and watched us for several minutes before raising his hand in farewell. I lifted mine in response, and then we both turned away.

I would have liked to stay for a little while, but I had to work in the morning, too. I had to be at the trading post early to help stock new inventory, and both of my parents had to be at the Royal Palm Hotel. Papa was taking several of the guests out to the Everglades for a day's hunting trip and they were leaving at first light. And Mama had a breakfast meeting scheduled with the railroad baron, Henry Flagler.

She'd been excited to get the interview. Mama would be talking with Mr. Flagler about the building of the overseas railroad to Key West, which was an enormous undertaking and unlike anything that had ever been attempted before. Once completed, the train would run one hundred and twenty-eight miles, connecting the mainland to the Florida Keys, with the last seven miles of track spanning open water. If successful, it would be the world's longest bridge and considered the "Eighth Wonder of the World." Undoubtedly, it would be Flagler's crowning glory, and Mama was anxious to hear all about it.

Another reason my mother had such an interest in the project was that her brother, James Stewart, had been employed by Flagler's company, the Florida East Coast Railway, to help with the engineering and design of a large hotel in upper Key Largo, which was the gateway to the railroad's massive extension. There was very little doubt in anyone's mind that once the Keys were attached to the mainland via the railroad, investors would swoop in to capitalize on the area, and a building frenzy would ensue. The Florida Keys would join Miami as a tourist destination. Hundreds of workers would be employed, if not thousands, in just the Keys alone, and my family couldn't have been more proud of the role Uncle James was playing in it.

I sat down in the cockpit since the wind was picking up. It was coming in on the port side, so the going would be slower than usual with our bow toward the wind, making us tack all the way home. As Adam trimmed the mainsail, he filled us in on the latest news about the injured keeper, Jim Altman.

"Jonas Lowery stopped by Fowey on his way out to catch some wahoo yesterday and said that Jim had a fit the night before. Said he started shaking like a rag doll and foamin' at the mouth. Then he started tryin' to swallow his tongue, but his brother, Ty, stuck a ruler in his mouth and held his tongue down. Doc Jackson came over right away and said that Jim's concussion was worse than he first figured. Told Ty not to let Jim get out of bed and to shove a pan under him when he needs to take a shi—" Adam caught himself just in time but still turned a bright shade of pink. "Pardon me, ladies. I been around men too long and I'm afraid it shows."

"Never mind that," Mama said. "So what more did Doc say?"

"He said that if Jim ain't no better by tomorrow, he's gonna send him up by rail to St. Luke's in Jacksonville. Doc was disgusted there wasn't a hospital worth two beans any closer, and said he's givin' great consideration to building a small one in town."

"Tacking!" Papa warned loudly and we all ducked to avoid the swinging boom. Then, picking up the subject again, my father said, "Lord knows, we need a hospital in Miami. Besides, if the investors want to lure more folks down here, then a hospital is not only vital for the health of the people, but for the health of the economy, too."

"So, Adam, is there talk of bringin' another lighthouse keeper in?" Mama asked.

"I'd imagine so," he replied. "My guess is the government's lookin' as we're speakin'. They'd be pretty foolish not to. Costs them a lot when there's a wreck, considerin' court costs over salvage rights, not to mention the headache of it. Then there's the cost of lost cargo—especially if it's government-owned cargo. And if the lighthouse is undermanned, and there's a wreck…Woo-wee, there'll be hell to pay! And the government'll be the one reachin' into its pocket. Aye, I'd say they're lookin' for one faster 'n people are askin' for the job. They're gettin' stricter on who can man the lighthouse. They'd rather not have a man and his family out there. It's too risky. They want someone who's willin' to be alone. But sometimes that someone might have reasons for wantin' isolation, and some of those reasons ain't too good. Say if a man is hidin' out from the law, a lighthouse is a pretty good place to do it, while gettin' decent enough pay. Shoot, if I were some Billy the Kid, I'd be in line for the job of a keeper. Then, I'd just sit back, count my money and let things cool off for a time, all while looking out at the purtiest turquoise ocean God ever did make, and catchin' the finest fish, too. Not a bad life for someone wantin' to lay low."

Or someone who wants to run from a broken heart, I thought, w*ithout fear of it ever breaking again.* I changed the subject. "Adam, anyone been pokin' around the *Alicia* lately?"

"Actually, the Byron brothers were on it early in the week," he confirmed. "Said they came up with a few things, too: couple bottles of wine and a man's wedding band."

My head snapped around to look at my father. "See, Papa! I told you it was worth takin' a look."

Adam laughed. "Well, you might come up with a little thing or two, but I'll tell you what, three guys were anchored off of Star Reef, and they were pulling stuff up left and right from that wreck that went down the week before the *Alicia*."

That got my attention, as well as my father's. "I heard about it but was told there were only hams on board and the sharks got both them *and* the crew," Papa said. "Remind me, what kind of rig was it?" he asked before alerting us that he was tacking again so we could duck.

Once we sat back up, Adam said, "It was a nice little trawler; single stack on it, one boiler, if I'm rememberin' correctly. Little smaller than your trawler, I'd guess."

"Papa, let's take a look! Please!" I pleaded.

"Lord, Eliza, we don't even know what the cargo was," my father laughed.

"Well," Mama spoke up, "there's only one way to find out. Take a look, Max. However, if you're not interested in doing it, then maybe Eliza, Simon, Turtle, and I will just ride out there. 'Leave no stone unturned' is my motto."

"And 'curiosity killed the cat' is mine," Papa quipped. "I've not heard a word about this wreck."

"Yes, you have," Mama corrected, "from Adam. And if there're three fellas on it now, there'll be more soon enough." She was right. I knew it, and Papa did, too.

"Adam," Papa said as he shook his head, "right now, living the life of a lighthouse keeper with nothin' but the sky and sea for company sounds a lot like heaven on Earth."

"You suggestin' livin' with two women can be hell on a man, Max?" Adam chuckled.

"No, sir, I'm not suggestin' it. I'm *confirmin'* it." Papa sighed, looking quite defeated.

Chapter 4

Battle Plans

The next day, my folks and I left the house before the sun was up. When it set that evening, only Mama and I were home, though Papa was due in at any moment.

"How'd the interview go with Mr. Flagler?" I asked as I pulled out part of a leftover pork roast and a bowl of collards. Mama was at the stove preparing to make a hoe cake, which was simply a flattened version of cornbread. She was swirling bacon grease around in the bottom of the iron skillet.

"Well, interesting," she said, setting the skillet on the stove and pouring the batter in. "And somewhat disturbing," she added.

I stopped slicing the roast and looked over at her. "How so?" Mama had become a well-seasoned reporter and very little ruffled her feathers anymore, so to say that she found something disturbing was worrisome.

"Well, when I got there, Mr. Flagler wasn't alone. Sitting there with Henry, shoving a giant ham biscuit into his mouth, was none other than our fair state's governor, Mr. Napoleon Bonaparte Broward."

"You're joking!" I exclaimed, amazed that Mama had been able to scoop an interview with two of the most influential men in all of Florida. "What was said that bothered you so?"

"It's this cockamamie plan of draining the Everglades," Mama said, turning away from the stove to look at me. "Broward is going to carve his name into the Florida wilderness by wiping out enormous chunks of it. In order to create more land for the great masses he thinks will come flocking into the area, he's dredging out the Everglades, and those who live in the path of his destruction are going to be out of a home."

I was afraid to ask, but I had to. "Does that include the Seminole village, Mama? Are they going to be forced to move?"

"I asked that very same thing and Governor Broward said he didn't think his plans 'encompassed that particular area.' Then he sniffed that arrogant nose of his, wiped strawberry jam out of that horrendously thick mustache, and said, 'Why, Mrs. Harjo, could I interest you in buying a parcel of that rich land? You hang on to it for no more 'n a year or so and you'll be able to sell it for a handsome profit.' Lord, that man! This is the third time I've had the displeasure of speaking with him, and each time I leave wonderin' what the poor state of Florida did to deserve him." She flipped the hoe cake.

"When are they startin' on the dredging, Mama?" I went to the ice box and got out a jar of peach chutney.

"They already have," she said. "Eliza, you want these greens warmed up a tad, or you want to eat 'em as is?" Mama stirred the large brown bowl of collards I'd left on the counter.

"Let's keep things easy and eat 'em cold," I suggested. She set the bowl on the table and then went back to the stove for the hoe cake, while I poured glasses of iced tea for each of us.

"You know, Mama," I said after we'd both sat down. "It's time to set my plans for the future in motion, and take a good look around while I'm doing so." I ate a large forkful of greens.

"What in the world you talkin' about?" Mama glanced sideways at me as she squeezed a wedge of lemon into her tea.

"I'm goin' over to have a little talk with the chief of the Seminole village, Paroh Monday. I'm gonna see about teaching those children out there, both the boys *and* the girls. And while I'm out there, I'll take a look around to see if there's any sign of that blasted dredging anywhere near the village."

"And if there is?" Mama asked with an amused but skeptical look on her face.

"Then we're going to see if we can do some re-routing of things, and I might just need you to help me with that."

"I'm afraid to ask how," Mama sighed, bemused.

"Oh, that's easy enough." I smiled. "You'll just have to arrange a sit down between me and that uppity Napoleon Bonaparte Broward."

"Heaven help me," Mama said, lifting her eyes to the heavens.

"Heaven help Governor Broward," I corrected, "should he try to force the Seminoles to vacate their land."

"Unfortunately, my darling child, you'll be the one needing Heaven's help. It would take God and an entire army of His angels to get Broward to rethink his plan. One little spit and vinegar gal and a small village of red-skinned people certainly aren't going to have a speck of influence on that man."

"Well, we'll see about that," I said. "But my first order of business is to convince Paroh to let me teach those children. Until I get that accomplished, I can't be focusing on anything else," I added before taking a large bite of hoe cake. A girl had to have sustenance before going into battle.

Chapter 5

Deep Cuts

Papa came in as Mama and I were finishing up slices of key lime pie. After helping himself to a plate of supper, he told us where he'd been.

"After I brought the hunting party back in, I stopped by Duke's Saloon." It went without saying that if you wanted to know something in this town, you went to Duke's. "Ebner Betts was there warmin' the same ol' stool he does most every night. You know him, Eve; he works for Standard Oil, down the river, and has that houseboat docked right off there. We've bought oil from him before. Anyway, he said he sold some lubricating oil to some fellas the other day, and those guys happened to be the ones salvaging that wreck Adam was talking about, off of Star Reef. Said it was a medium-sized cutter that went down named the *Paso Rápido,* out of Cuba, and it was carrying a load of cigars and hams to market in Jacksonville. No one's quite sure what brought her into that reef. Most likely the captain just didn't know the waters off Star, and hit it. When the cutter sank, the scent of the hams brought in a school of tiger sharks, and everything—the crew included—was eaten up by 'em. Men making their livin' from the sea are a superstitious bunch, you know, and that's why salvagers left the wreck alone even once the sharks were gone. Everyone pretty much forgot about it when the *Alicia* went down near Long Reef a week later, carrying a much bigger load of cargo on her. What the salvagers on the *Alicia* didn't know was that along with the hams and cigars on the *Paso Rápido,* was fifty thousand dollars in gold and silver coins, and even some bars, that were going to be used in the illegal acquisition of a large office building in Jacksonville. One of the guys salvaging the *Paso* is a Cuban sponge diver by the name of Herrera, and during a night of heavy drinking at Duke's, he told ol' Ebb what had really gone down on the ship 'cause his uncle was the one captaining it. Said it took a lot of convincing and a nice share of the profit to get Herrera to go on out there, but said that it's been worth it. So far, they've found several thousand in gold and silver, and they're goin' back for more."

"Who's 'they,' Max?" Mama asked. I noticed she was absently playing with the pendant she always wore around her neck, one that my father had made for her many years ago when they'd first fallen in love. It was made from mother of pearl, and Papa had exquisitely carved the face of a tiger into it. My father lovingly called my mother "*kaccv hokte*," which was Creek for "tiger woman," and the pendant was a beautiful symbol of her animal totem. Originally, it had hung from a leather cord, but Papa had gifted Mama with a beautiful gold chain he'd recovered from a Spanish wreck some years before, and the pendant had graced it ever since. She never removed it, and whenever she was troubled, or in deep thought about something, she moved it back and forth on the chain.

"Apparently, there're three guys—including Herrera—working the wreck from a trawler named the *Waylaid*. The captain is a man by the name of Asher—Ezra Asher."

"Papa, you know we have to go out there!" As far as I was concerned, there was no debating the issue.

"Lord, Eliza, don't you have enough to keep you busy right now?" Mama asked, and then looked at Papa. "She's gonna save the world, Max," she laughed.

"Well, at least our part of it," I responded. "Aren't you curious about what-all's down there, Papa? C'mon, let's take a look."

"We'll see, baby girl." Papa smiled. "But it won't be any earlier than a couple of days from now."

"Which means we will, then!" I smiled, satisfied.

"One of these days, Eliza, you're gonna get into a world of trouble." Mama smiled and shook her head as she refilled Papa's glass.

"Oh, I hope so!" I laughed as I put the last forkful of pie in my mouth. "I surely do."

"All right, I'll tell you what I'll do." Papa sighed as if he'd finally resigned himself to the fact that I wouldn't give up until he gave in. He scooted his chair back from the table and lit a thin cigar. "First thing in the morning, let me confirm who's got the rights on salvaging the *Paso*, and who the wreck master is. Sounds like it's probably this guy Asher, but I'll check it out at the courthouse to make sure. Once I do find out, I'll need to talk to the man to see what percentage of the cargo he'd give us for helping with the salvage. If it's too little, then it won't be worth the time and trouble to go out there. Fair enough?" he asked as he blew out a thin stream of smoke.

"Fair enough!" I agreed. "And first thing in the morning, I'm going to tell Mrs. Brickell I'll be going to part-time."

"Isn't that a little premature?" Mama asked as she began to clear the table.

I got up to help her. "Not at all, Mama, because come hell or high water, I'm going to be teaching out at that village, and even if it's just the boys to start, I'll wrangle the girls in at some point."

"Don't take the Seminole traditions too lightly, baby girl," Papa warned. "They're very set in their ways, and can be unbelievably stubborn about changing things, even when it would help them out in the long run. My advice is tread lightly. If there's anything they hate, it's to have an outsider come in telling them they're doin' it all wrong, and especially a white woman. Be careful, Eliza, and I mean it."

"I will, Papa. I promise."

I told Mama I'd finish cleaning up the kitchen, and she and Papa went out to the veranda to have their coffee. As I stood at the sink washing the dinner dishes, I thought about my father's warning. He was right. I needed to go about this slowly and patiently in order to convince Paroh, as well as his people, that an education for both sexes was a good thing. And a little gold or silver might help to convince him.

Suddenly, the glass I was washing slipped from my hand and shattered against the enamel sink. Carefully, I picked up the shattered pieces I could see. Then I felt around in the cloudy, soapy water for any others that might be hidden and felt a sharp prick on the tip of my right index finger. Quickly withdrawing my hand, I began to suck on the drop of blood that oozed from the cut. As I stood there, waiting for the bleeding to stop, I thought about what the future might bring. If all went according to plan, I'd begin a new chapter in my life as a teacher. I was both excited and a little frightened, too, for I had learned that when it was least expected, something sharp and unseen could cut a person deeply, just like broken glass in a sink of soapy water, or a jagged reef beneath the waves.

Chapter 6

In a Clerk, Out a Teacher

Sundae sidestepped a baby alligator that was heading toward the river for a swim. Quickly scanning the area to see where the mama was, I caught a glimpse of her sleeping contentedly beneath a young cabbage palm off to my left. I gave my white and dark brown-spotted horse a gentle kick with my heels, and Sundae picked up the pace slightly, while I reached back to reassure myself that my rifle was still secured behind my saddle. I figured I'd probably have enough to wrestle with at the Seminole village without having a bout with an alligator beforehand.

Refocusing on my task, I rehearsed, for the umpteenth time, what I would say upon my arrival at the village. Hopefully, my satchel of supplies would help convince Paroh, as well as the other elders, that I was "dedicated and committed to helping their people, and that given a little time, they would see there wasn't a blasted thing wrong with allowing the girls to learn alongside the boys." *Leave out the word 'blasted'*, I thought, and then continued with my memorized speech. "Being educated is an honorable thing," I would tell them. "As well as a *necessary* thing in today's society. And, if they wished to be respected in that society, they had to be educated." Period. End of subject. It sounded good to me. I just hoped it would sound good to them. Especially because, as of yesterday, I was otherwise unemployed.

The day before, I had arrived at the trading post a little after seven in the morning and found Mrs. Brickell stocking a shelf with blankets from a large box that hadn't been among the inventory delivered earlier in the week. She'd about pulled her hair out wondering where the blue blazes it was. "Honest to the sweet Lord above," she'd said. "If I were running the United States Postal Service, things would go a whole lot smoother." I had no doubt that they would, but largely because no one would want to mail or ship a thing for fear of having to deal with the White Witch—my name for her.

"Well, better late than never," I said as I hung up my straw hat and then put on the required blue and white-striped canvas apron. "Where'd you find it?"

"By the front door this morning with a note attached from Duke Whitehead," she replied. "He got the box by mistake in a delivery yesterday and left it by the door last night. So, my question is: If he got my blankets, then did someone else end up with a case of bad whiskey? Man ought to be ashamed of himself. Thanks to his immoral trafficking, nearly half the men in this town go gallivanting to his den of iniquity to get a snootful. He'll not get away with it, though. The good Lord is keeping track of all he's doing, and in the end, he'll be accountable for it all," the self-righteous woman sniffed.

"Oh, Miz Brickell, I don't think it's as bad as all that. My father has a drink down at Duke's every once in a while, and he's about as good a man as there ever was."

"There are always exceptions to every rule, Eliza," she said.

I picked up another stack of blankets and began to stock them, and as I did, my eyes caught a selection of books on a shelf down to my right; among them were a number of elementary primers. I knew a sign from Heaven when I saw one, so I dove in.

"Mrs. Brickell, I'm going to have to cut my hours to part-time just as soon as you're able to find someone else to fill in."

She stopped re-folding one of the blankets, and from the look on her face, you'd have thought I'd hauled off and slapped her.

"And pray tell, Miss Harjo, why is that? Have offers you just can't refuse poured in all of a sudden?"

"Actually, Mrs. Brickell, I had two attractive offers some weeks ago, but turned them both down," I answered, thinking about Mr. Burdine, and Mr. Cohen. Because of my unusual looks, I'd caught the eye of the rival merchants, and each had offered me more money than the Brickells ever would if I would sell their fine merchandize in their respective stores while wearing the garments they carried. And both of the enterprising retailers wanted me to model some of their newest New York-inspired fashions at the elegant Royal Palm Hotel, as well. They'd offered me high wages to walk through the beautiful dining room during the dinner hours to give the female guests the chance to be tempted by the latest fashions. But the idea of selling and modeling clothing as my livelihood just didn't appeal to me. Though I was flattered by the enthusiasm and high wages both retailers offered me, I wanted more out of life than that. In truth, I wanted to do something that had more meaning behind it, and was far more challenging.

"Is that so?" she replied, squinting her eyes at me as if trying to decide whether I was trying to pull one over on her or not. "Well, what kept you from taking off for greener pastures until now?" She looked as smug as her answer was intended to be, and I could feel my temper rising.

"Mrs. Brickell, I'm planning on becoming a teacher, and I need part of my day free in order to do that. Now, if you'd rather I just go ahead and quit altogether so that you can find someone to do a two person job on a one person paycheck, then I'll gladly oblige."

The woman looked as though I'd slapped her. The truth of the matter was she was very unaccustomed to being spoken to in that way, especially by one as unimportant as a little shop clerk. "Perhaps it would be for the best, Miss Harjo, if you moved on. There are quite a few folks who would be only too happy to take over your position, and the sooner you're off my payroll, the sooner I can employ one of those *qualified* applicants."

The woman emphasized the word, insinuating that I was unqualified. I'd had enough. I untied the apron from around my waist and hung it back on the peg. Then, grabbing a pad and pencil that were sitting on top of a barrel that we'd been using to record the inventory, I began making some quick calculations.

"What in the world are you doing?" Mrs. Brickell asked, peering over my shoulder as she did so.

"Well, I'm figurin' out what you owe me since you paid me last week." Looking up from the pad, I pointed over to the book shelf with the end of the pencil. "How much are those primers?"

"A dime each," she replied and then a thought seemed to occur to her. "Little Miss Uppity-Britches, what makes you so sure you can teach anyone? You've only just graduated!"

"That's exactly right!" I agreed. "I've been taught and tested, grilled and groomed, and am now ready to pass on what I've learned."

Looking back down at the pad, I circled the final figure I'd come up with and laid it and the pencil back down on the barrel. Then, pulling an old burlap bag from a stack of them hanging from a hook, I walked around the store gathering up everything I'd need, including all ten of the primers presently in stock, plus two story books, one encyclopedia, a dictionary, a small blackboard, twenty pieces of chalk, and a jar of licorice. If Paroh would agree to let me teach, then I'd have Papa help me make blackboards.

It was easy enough to make them from pine boards covered with a mixture of egg whites and the black rubbings from the skins of charred potatoes. If Paroh refused to let me educate the children, I'd donate what I was purchasing to my alma mater.

"You owe me a dollar thirty, Mrs. Brickell. But please put it down as a credit. I'll be back." And with that, I left the woman huffing and puffing as I walked out the door, no longer her employee, but a customer, instead.

Mama and Papa thought I might have been a little rash, leaving a semi-decent paying job, but, as I explained to them, once I knew what my schedule would be at the Seminole village—if there was to be a schedule—then I could go to work for Mr. Burdine, either full-time or part-time. I also added that if we were able to salvage any of the gold from the *Paso Rápido,* I wouldn't need a paid position. "A bird in the hand is worth two in the bush, you know," Mama had said. And I told her that only applied to situations where there weren't gold bars waiting to plucked off a reef in the Atlantic.

I was beyond excited about salvaging the *Paso.* The day before, Papa had confirmed that Ezra Asher was the *Paso's* wreck master, so he had the say over who could work the sunken cutter with him, and what percentage of the cargo each additional salvager would get. After some canny negotiating on Papa's part, they'd settled on 35 percent and decided they would head out to the *Paso* in three days.

As my father was returning from his talk with Ezra Asher, he'd run into Adam Wilson coming out of the trading post. Apparently, a third lighthouse keeper had been hired, and he needed to get the man settled in at Fowey and give Striker his much-needed shore leave. Papa asked him how soon he needed to get out there, thinking that he might drop them off on the way out to the *Paso,* but when Adam told him that he was expected to be on the job in two days, my father had to fall back on my offer to take them out. Papa said he should have just let Adam bring the lighthouse's boat in when we'd dropped off Dylan, but I told Papa I was more than happy to take Adam and the new man out. Mama had been standing there listening, and the smile on her face seemed to say, "I bet you are," though she'd never have said it out loud.

Mama knew me inside and out, and though I hadn't talked about it much when it happened, she knew my heart had been bruised by Striker when he'd abruptly ended the relationship we'd started to build. To my mind, it was the beginning of something long and beautiful; but to Striker, it was something that could be started and finished in one short chapter. Mama had told me that my aching heart would heal in time, and that someone wonderful and special would come along when I least expected it, just as

Papa had for her. But, as far as I was concerned, the only thing that would heal my heart was keeping my distance from the man who had inflicted the damage, and having him out in the Atlantic tending to Fresnel lenses was fine by me. I just wondered if I was a bit of a glutton for punishment, volunteering to go out there when I could have let Adam find another way to get to Fowey. It was like pouring salt water into the wound.

Chapter 7

Far from the Beckoning Shore

I was still several miles from the Seminole village when I came to the fork in the river. Taking the north branch of it, I slowed for a moment to admire the small rapids, and then I continued on. I'd only been to the village once before, when Papa had taken some tourists out fishing and we stopped by to drop off medicine for an ailing newborn. Just as I remembered, there were no signs of civilization as far as the eye could see. Off in the distance and to the right of me was a prairie dotted with marshes. Guiding Sundae away from the water, I rode up to slightly higher ground. There was nothing more interesting for me to see than the usual gnarled cypresses, scrub pines, oaks and palms, and a variety of birds among the water hyacinths, eating their fill of bugs and small fish, so my mind drifted back to Striker. Seeing him when we'd dropped my brother off at Fowey had brought to mind those memories I tried not to think about.

The first time I laid eyes on him was soon after we'd moved to Miami from Lake Weir. Miami was a tiny hamlet then and everyone knew everyone else. Dylan was a couple of years behind Striker in school, but they'd become fast friends over their shared love of boats. There were many times the two of them would go sailing in the bay, and though I begged to go along, the sailboat was a floating boys' club and girls were always left behind. As the years went by, my school girl crush secretly grew as I watched the once lanky boy from Leesburg grow into a ruggedly handsome young man. Soft-spoken and serious, Striker seemed to know exactly where he was going and what he wanted to do in life, so unlike the other boys who couldn't see a future beyond a night of shark fishing or frog gigging. Striker's maturity and good looks caught the eye of most every girl in town, but he was too entranced by boat building to be interested in romance. That seemed to change, however, when he returned home from Jacksonville to open the boatyard.

It had been a year since we'd seen each other and I was working for the Brickells, in my last year of high school. Striker had come into the trading post and was busy reading the label on a bottle of castor oil when he came up to pay for it. He hadn't seen me yet, and I didn't say a word as I waited for him to look up. The surprise on his face when he did made me glad he'd set the bottle on the counter beforehand so that I didn't have to clean up a mess of the thick oil. After he muttered a rather flustered hello, it suddenly seemed to dawn on him that he was purchasing a remedy for irregularity. His face turned a deep red as he stuttered his way through the explanation that it was for his mother not him. I said not a word, but quickly tucked the medicine away in a burlap bag and then put my elbow on the counter, rested my chin in my hand, and waited for him to finish. Suddenly, he stopped mid-sentence, looked at me hard as if he was seeing me for the first time, and said softly, "Damn, you look good."

"It's good to see you, too," I responded. "I know how your mother's doin'," I said, glancing at the bagged bottle of castor oil. "But how're you and your daddy?"

That seemed to set things right and we started to laugh, then laughed some more as we kept talking over each other, trying to catch up. We both stopped talking at the same time, too, and stood there for a few seconds just looking at each other, smiling. Finally, Striker paid me, told me he'd see me around as he was back home to stay, and left the store. Not a minute had passed when the front door bell tinkled again. I stopped mid-stride on my way back to the stock room and turned around to see that Striker had returned.

"Will you go sailing with me after work?" he asked.

"Where to?" I replied.

"Key Biscayne?" he suggested.

"How 'bout I bring a picnic supper?" I offered.

"Meet me at my folks' dock," he said.

And I did.

We sailed up the river into Biscayne Bay, and then headed southeast toward the key. Instead of going all the way down to the south side, where the Cape Florida lighthouse stood, we stopped about mid-way on the island. Tall coconut palms majestically lined the beach and seemed to beckon us ashore with their waving fronds, promising to provide the shade we would need from the sun even as it continued inching lower toward the horizon.

"This ought to do," Striker said, navigating us in toward the beach. Before the bow could touch the shore, he hopped out of the vessel and gently pulled it onto the sand. It was clear that he spent much time and effort on the care of the single-mast sloop, for the native mahogany wood was polished to a high sheen, and the brass hardware was neither pitted nor blemished.

"Did you build this boat, Striker?" I asked, handing him the picnic basket before jumping down from the bow. The name *High Hopes* was painted on the boat's transom, and neither the boat nor its name was familiar to me.

"No," he said as we waded ashore in the shallow water. "I bought it off a guy who needed some cash. It's a good little boat, and very similar to one I'm building for my parents' twenty-fifth wedding anniversary. But I gave my parents' sloop an additional twelve feet so they'll have plenty of room to sleep on it."

We spread a blanket out and anchored it with the picnic basket and rocks. Then I sat on it and rolled down the bottom of my canvas pant legs so that they could dry. They'd gotten wet as I waded in to shore. If it hadn't been getting so late in the day, I would have considered wearing a bathing outfit, but with the wind coming out of the east, it was too chilly.

"Dylan said you've been back for a couple of weeks and plan to open a boatyard down the river from your folks' house," I said, looking up at him as he secured the boat's bow line to a small palm tree.

"Merrill-Stevens Boat Yard will actually own it. They're the ones I worked for in Jacksonville, and they invested the money to open the shipyard down here. I'm just overseein' things."

"Don't make so little of it, Striker." I was truly impressed. "That's a real accomplishment for someone your age—or any age, really."

He was uncomfortable at having a fuss made over him, so, after muttering a humble 'thank you,' he quickly changed the subject and asked me if I wanted to eat, go for a walk, or even cast a fishing line out. I told him I'd like to do some beachcombing, if he had a mind to, and when he said that he did, we headed south in the direction of the lighthouse.

All manner of things washed up on the beach, but one of the things I loved hunting for the most was sea glass. It was formed from bottles or other glass items that had been lost to the sea. After the glass was broken into small pieces, salt water would wear it down to a smooth-textured, frosted finish. Jewelry could be made from it, so I collected it and gave it to a sweet Seminole girl named Rose, who was perhaps a year or so younger than I. Every so often, she spread her blanket out on the lawn at the trading post to sell or trade her lovely handmade jewelry, all of which was made from unusual materials, including a variety of sea shells, shark and alligator teeth, bone and ivory (which she traded for), coconut shells, and sea glass. To thank me for giving her the glass, she'd given me a lovely pair of light green glass earrings and a matching necklace.

I bent over to examine a tiger's eye sea shell, but seeing that it was broken, left it there. "You glad to be home?" I asked.

"Yeah, I am." He skipped a small flat stone across the water.

The breeze blew his golden, shoulder-length hair away from his face, giving me a clear profile of his strong, straight nose and angular features. He'd matured in the year since I'd seen him. He was ruggedly handsome but in a quiet, thoughtful kind of way, and it made him that much more appealing.

He glanced over at me and caught me studying him. We both smiled a little self-consciously before quickly looking away. Ahead on the sand, I spotted a small conch shell and started toward it, but as I did, Striker grabbed my arm. "Watch it!" he warned and I looked down to see what had alarmed him. Bending down and grabbing a piece of sun-bleached driftwood, he poked it into a hole that I had almost stepped into. Suddenly, a giant land crab climbed out to see what had disturbed him. "Want some crabs for supper?" he asked, and when I told him I did, he reached down and snatched up the crustacean from the back, avoiding his painful pinchers. He dropped it into a burlap bag he carried over his shoulder, and then pointed ahead of us with his driftwood. "Look."

Dotted across the sand were dozens of crab holes. I grabbed a stick of driftwood and we both began poking the holes until we filled Striker's bag with six large crabs.

"Do you want to eat them now, or take them home?" Striker asked.

"Let's eat 'em now!" I said without hesitation. The food I'd brought could wait. There was nothing in the world I liked better than freshly caught crab.

We gathered up more driftwood and returned to our blanket. "See about gatherin' up a few green palm fronds while I grab a pot from the boat," he said, withdrawing a knife from a sheath at the waist of his canvas pants and handing it to me.

I cut several fronds, then looked around for rocks about the size of a man's fist. Once we had gathered up all we needed, we laid the driftwood on top of the fronds and got a fire going.

"Too bad we don't have any butter to go with 'em," he said as he squatted down to put another branch on the fire.

"Now, Striker." I smiled. "I brought fried chicken for our supper, and what goes better with fried chicken than bread and butter sandwiches?" I lifted the lid on our picnic basket, removed the sandwiches, which were wrapped in waxed paper, and, using Striker's knife, skimmed off the thick layer of butter that I'd generously slathered onto the white bread and knocked it off into another empty mason jar I'd brought for beach combing. After setting the jar close enough to the fire to melt the butter, I sat back down on the blanket with Striker, and we waited for the required twenty minutes it took to cook the crabs. While we did, he told me more about his plans for the boatyard.

Striker intended on building a line of sleek, small to medium-sized sloops that would cut through the water more efficiently and smoothly than anything else on the seas at the time. But the thing he was most excited about was building his first motor boat.

"I've seen a few of 'em out here in the bay, and some while I was up in Jacksonville. I even worked on a couple. They're going to be the workhorse of the seas; sailing will become nothing more than a leisure activity. Actually, I designed one using the wick carburetor that a fella in England designed. Now I just have to build it."

As he spoke, his dark brown eyes were lit from within. The passion he felt for his trade was obvious. Though he had learned much while working at Merrill-Stevens, he said that he'd learned most of what he wanted to incorporate into his own boat designs through trial and error. Apparently, he'd taken possession of several vessels that were broken beyond repair, including a motor boat, and had worked with a skill and understanding of the craft that went far beyond what the Merrill-Stevens people could teach him. They had realized early on that he was far from simply being a marine repair man; he was a designer—and a re-designer—as well. Which was why Merrill-Stevens invested in his business.

"I'm fortunate," he said. "I've been given permission to run electricity from the Royal Palm Hotel's massive generators over to the large building I'll put up to house the boats I'll be working on. It'll be nice having electric lights rather than kerosene lamps."

"Papa has been talking about running power to our house, too. What a thing that'll be, to turn on a light with the flick of a switch instead of having to light wicks. Good of Flagler to let us use the power from his hotel."

"Don't fool yourself, Eliza," Striker laughed, making the dimple near the right side of his mouth appear. "He'll make nice money by allowin' us that little luxury. At some point, some company's gonna come in and run power to any and all who want it, and become extremely rich because of it. Makes me wish I was more of a Thomas Edison, instead of a John O.

Johnson." Seeing the lack of understanding on my face, Striker laughed and explained that Johnson had designed a beautiful championship sailboat.

"They're ready," he said, nodding toward the pot on the tripod, and our attention immediately turned from boat building to crab eating.

We broke off the legs, and then broke the shells open by hammering them with rocks. The hot white meat was succulent and sweet, and the melted butter we dipped it into added a deliciously rich coating. Once the crabs were thoroughly picked over for the small amount of good meat they offered, Striker ate two pieces of chicken and bread; then we each had a fried apple pie with a chunk of cheddar cheese. When we were done, I stretched my legs out in front of me, leaned back on my elbows and tilted my head toward the late day sun. It was good living on the coast of Florida, and never more so than with a belly full of fresh seafood.

"Much as I hate to do it, we'd better get back," Striker said, standing up and stretching. "We need to get in while there's still some daylight left."

I knew he was right, but I hated for the day to end. I started gathering our things together while Striker doused the fire with the water from the crab pot, and then kicked sand on top of the smoldering mound. As I looked around for anything I might have missed, I spotted my mason jar of sea glass and leaned over to pick it up just as Striker was picking up his burlap sack. Our eyes met and we kept them locked on each other as we stood up. Striker put his left arm around my waist and gently pulled me to him. Whispering that I was beautiful, he ran his hand up through my hair and studied my face as if he was seeing it for the first time, and as he did, I dropped the jar back onto the sand. Then Striker slowly leaned down, still watching my eyes, and kissed me.

The kiss was like liquid heat, and his one hand moved from my hair to the back of my head, while the other remained around my waist, holding me firmly to him. Wanting to be closer still, I wrapped my arms around his neck as if he was a life preserver in a turbulent sea. His lips were both salty and warm, but it was the heat of his tongue, which he hungrily intertwined with mine, that gave away the true depth of his passion. We attempted to end the kiss once or twice, but each time one of us couldn't bear it, and the kiss began again. Finally, Striker pulled back from me, looking into my eyes intensely.

"We have to go now," he said in a low husky voice, the sound of it affecting me nearly as much as his kiss had.

"Yes, I...we do," I answered so softly that I could barely hear my own words. Then he released me and I turned away without saying anything else.

I climbed into the boat while Striker untied the rope from the tree and pushed us off the beach, setting a course for home. As he did, I looked back at the sand where I'd forgotten to retrieve the jar of sea glass. I felt as if I'd left the last vestiges of my childhood behind with it.

Three weeks later, after spending several more glorious afternoons with Striker, sailing the bay, picnicking, and even sharing a candlelight supper at the Royal Palm Hotel one Saturday evening, I began to think that perhaps we were starting to build something as strong and durable as one of his boats. But, just as I was beginning to believe in the potential of our relationship, Striker's parents were killed when they hit that reef in the boat he'd built for them. Something in Striker died along with his parents. Immediately, he distanced himself from everything and everyone he ever cared about, including me. He preferred, instead, to be completely isolated and apart from it all, just like the lighthouse he took care of, standing alone at sea, miles from the nearest shore.

Chapter 8

A Battle Half Won

A mongrel dog's barking drew me out of my thoughts about Striker, and I realized I was no more than a couple hundred yards from the Seminole village. Taking a deep breath, I tried to collect my thoughts so that I was no longer dwelling on the past. As I began to silently recite my speech once again, the dog ran up and took a nip at my left bootie, startling both Sundae and me. My horse pranced away from the dog, and I held the reins a little tighter and spoke softly to her, trying to keep her calm, all while kicking out at the dog to get him away from us. But each time I did, he tried to bite me again. Finally, I took the end of the reins and popped the dog on the top of the head with them. The little dog gave out a sharp cry, more of surprise than hurt, and ran off with his tail between his legs. *Now, if I can only get Paroh to submit as easily*, I thought, though I knew my odds were far better with the dog than with the chief.

As I came to the edge of the village, I realized that all of the people had stopped their activities to see who I was and what I wanted. When I held my hand up in greeting, they seemed to relax a little, especially after they realized that they knew me from the trading post, and that I was Max Harjo's daughter.

"Eliza!" I heard someone calling my name to the left of me and turned to see Rose—the young woman who made the lovely jewelry—coming toward me with a basket full of guava fruit.

"Oh, Rose! I'm glad to see you!" The relief was evident in my voice.

"Why you come to the village?" she asked, not unkindly.

"I've come to see Paroh Monday. I want to talk to him about teaching the children to read and write."

The quizzical smile on her face instantly faded. "You mean the *boys* to read the English," she tried to clarify, so that there would be no misunderstanding.

"Well, maybe at first..." I said, knowing I had to tread softly, even with my friend. "But I'm hoping that maybe he'll allow the girls to join us..."

Before I could finish, she set down her basket, glanced over her shoulder as though she was afraid someone else had heard me, and then closed the distance between us. "No, no, Miss Eliza!" Rose said in a hushed but urgent way. "Girls don't read the English! The elders not like it! They say it bad for us."

"Surely you believe that's pure hogwash, don't you, Rose? You're a smart girl. You know better than that. Y'all deal with the white world on a daily basis, and in order to do so without being taken advantage of, you have to know how to read a sign in a window, or be able to add and subtract numbers."

"Well...yes. I like," she admitted, "but..."

"But what, Rose? There is absolutely no reason for y'all not to read and write in the English language as well as I do. It's just plain ignorant not to!"

With those last words, Rose's eyes squinted slightly and I could see I'd insulted her or hit a nerve. "No go sayin' that to Paroh, Miss Eliza! Following the old ways don't make us stupid. No. We honor them. It's something we still have that the white man hasn't stolen from us."

If the girl had thrown a bucket of cold water in my face, it wouldn't have snapped me out of my one-sided thinking any faster. Her words were plain enough. In truth, I'd never considered the issue from that perspective, but she was right. These proud and intelligent people had had enough stolen away from them by the greedy hands of the white world; those few things they had left in the way of traditions were going to be held on to for as long as they could.

"Rose, I'm sorry. I never meant to insult you or your people, or to tell you that the white people's ways are better than the Seminoles'. But I've seen your people cheated more times than I can count when y'all are on the lawn at the trading post." The Seminoles had a surprisingly good relationship with the Brickells, poling their canoes downriver from the Everglades with loads of goods to trade: egret plumes, alligator steaks, eggs and skins, and coontie starch for thickening soups and stews. "I can hear what's going on outside the window when I'm at the cash register. I can hear y'all negotiating your trades loud n' clear. I've had a mind to walk out there and straighten some of your customers out a time or two when they've tried pulling a fast one on you. But when I'm waiting on folks, I just can't go stompin' out there to tell y'all you're bein' taken advantage of. Besides, Mrs. Brickell would have put up a fit if I had."

The pretty young Seminole woman said nothing for a few seconds but stood there looking at me intently, as though she was debating whether or not it was foolish to take me to see Paroh. "Come, Miss," she concluded with a sigh that seemed to say that the logical side of her had just lost the argument. "We'll see if Paroh is back yet. He was still out burning the grass when I left for the fruit." Looking off in the distance, I could see a blanket of thick gray smoke rising up from the sawgrass, perhaps a mile away from the village. I knew from stories my half-Creek father had told me that the Indians did this so that new grass would grow in the burned areas, which would lure the deer in to eat the sweet young shoots. It was an old but easy way of hunting them.

I dismounted from Sundae and, leading her by the reins, followed Rose into the village. There were fifteen or so open-air dwellings called *chickees* arranged in a circle, with the exception of one which was larger and set back a little from the rest. It was obvious that it was the eating house because women were preparing food over an open fire right next to it. Suddenly, I ran into Rose's back when she stopped unexpectedly while I was watching the women cooking. "Over there," she said, jutting her chin forward to indicate which direction she was referring to. "Paroh comes."

Twenty or so men, some on foot and some on horseback, entered the village to the left of us. A man who looked to be in his mid-thirties, and was of medium height and build, was walking in the middle of the group and speaking Miccosukee. Though I didn't understand a thing he was saying, all the men with him were hanging on to his every word. He was dressed in a long patchwork tunic, well-worn tan buckskin breeches, and a turban that was made from a large, red, plaid cotton scarf. On the side of the turban was a small ostrich feather, which indicated that he was indeed the chief of this village. It was secured in place by a round beaten-silver medallion. Beneath the turban, his hair was a little shorter than the other men's and a little lighter in color, too. His was more of a dusty-brown color. Though he wasn't extremely tall, there was something large about him, something proud and different that set him apart from the others.

One of the men must have said something about me for his head quickly turned in my direction and his forward motion slowed just enough to let me know he was surprised to see a white person—especially a white *female* person—in his camp. Quickly recovering from his momentary surprise, he smiled politely and immediately came toward me. I wasn't sure what to do or say, but Rose quickly stepped in to help me.

She began talking to him in their native language, and gesturing toward me as she did. The man's piercing dark eyes looked me over, assessing me, but I felt as though he was looking right through me. Other than hearing her mention my name, and Papa's, I didn't understand anything they said. The language they spoke was my father's native language; and though he'd tried teaching Dylan and me some basic Muskogee words, I'd never had an ear for it. However, whatever Rose was saying obviously didn't put him off, for his smile remained in place as he responded while still keeping his eyes on me.

"Paroh says he remembers you when you and your good father brought the medicine water to help Liddy Tiger's baby, Emanuel," Rose said.

I honestly couldn't remember having seen Paroh then, but I wouldn't dare say as much. "Please tell him that it's an honor to be in his presence again." I smiled and bowed my head slightly.

The two of them spoke for another moment and she must have explained my reason for being there, for his smile instantly faded. When he spoke again, his tempo increased and his words sounded slightly terse. Rose kept her voice low and in control, and I respected her for it. She was obviously holding her own.

Finally, she turned to me and said, "Paroh wishes for you to join him." When I looked away from Rose and back to the man to tell him I'd be happy to, he was already walking away. Apparently, he assumed there'd be no argument on my part.

As I approached Paroh's chickee, I could see that it was slightly larger than the others, with the floor raised about three feet off the ground. The raised construction was an effective way of keeping deadly swamp critters out of people's homes. Paroh did not offer a hand to help me, but waited as I hiked up my dress and stepped up; then he gestured over to two chairs. The chief walked away from me and removed his turban. Picking a pipe and tobacco pouch up from a small table, he filled the pipe's bowl, then worked at lighting it. While he did, I took the opportunity to look around at the neatly kept home. Canvas curtains had been rolled up and hung from the rafters of the palmetto palm thatched roof, keeping them safe and dry until they were needed again to keep out the rain or cold. There were also 'comfortables' stored up there, which were blankets or hides used for bedding. Clothing hung from the wooden beams as well as fishing nets, and several different sizes of knives, as well as a couple of rifles. This man was quite wealthy compared to other villagers.

Suddenly, Rose appeared at my side, startling me, and offered a tin cup filled with freshly squeezed papaya juice. The cool, rich, orange-red juice soothed my parched throat and I drank it down at once. She told me she would bring more, but I asked her for a drink of water instead, and then wished I hadn't, for I desperately wanted to get this conversation between Paroh and me underway, and I would need Rose to do that. However, Paroh turned toward me, exhaled pipe smoke, and then asked: "Why do you want to teach the red children?"

Hearing him speak English caught me off guard. I'd just assumed he didn't since Rose had translated for him. But I was relieved that we could carry on a conversation ourselves so that nothing could get lost in translation.

"Mr. Paroh…I beg your pardon, Mr. Monday, I feel it's in the best interest of your people to be able to read and work with numbers. As I told Rose—"

He cut me off immediately. "No, no! No 'people'! Boys, maybe, but no girls. No, no, no!" He was adamant.

"But, Mr. Paroh—I mean Monday." Lord, I was flustered already, and we'd been conversing for less than a minute! I took a deep breath and started again in a more measured tone. "Mr. Monday, if you're gonna do business in the white world, then you need to be better prepared to do it. Too often, I've seen y'all taken advantage of down at Mrs. Brickell's—you know, the White Chief." He smiled at my use of his people's name for her. "That's not what I'd call her, but that's a conversation for another time," I said under my breath. But even under my breath, he'd heard me, and he threw his head back and laughed for he clearly understood my meaning. I realized then that this man had a firm grasp on the English language, as well as a good sense of humor.

"Mr. Monday, may I ask you something?" I laughed, relieved that he'd found my small slight against Mrs. Brickell so humorous.

"Somehow, Miss Harjo, I think you will anyway," he quipped.

My smile lessened a little. "Yes…well. Mr. Monday, who taught you how to speak English so well?"

There was a definite twinkle in his black, intense eyes. "My grandmother was from Omaha, Nebraska. She was as white as coconut meat."

Smiling at his comparison, I said, "And I assume you're glad you can speak English—since you trade with white people, 'n all?" It was really more a statement than a question.

"Not always. No," he said, watching me closely.

I was genuinely surprised. "Would you mind telling me why?"

"Because," he began, sitting down in the chair next to me. "If I didn't speak English then I wouldn't understand the ugly things the white man says, calling me as low as a gator, and about as dumb as one, too. I know they're cheating us at times, Miss Harjo. But what the white man doesn't know is that for every deal he cheats a Seminole on, that Seminole is turning around and cheating him twice as badly. Do you think that when we name our price on something we're selling or trading, it's always the same amount for the white man as it is for the red?"

"I...um...well. I always assumed it was." I was quite humbled by my naïveté.

"And every white person between here and the bay Biscayne assumes the same thing," he continued. "We always deal fairly with those who deal fairly with us. But, when it comes to the matter of cheating, as your people are so fond of saying: 'Two can play that game.'

"But getting back to the reason for your visit, I will allow you to give the boys lessons, and there might be a few of the men who would like to learn, too. But, I'll only permit you to do this on one condition."

"I bet I can guess what that is," I said, somewhat sarcastically. "No females allowed."

"You're a fast learner, Miss Harjo," he said, beaming.

"But Mr. Monday!"

"Apparently, I'm faster than you," he said with an amused smile. Regardless of the fact that I wasn't getting my way, I had to admit that his smile was warm, kind.

"Won't you reconsider letting the girls take a few simple lessons, too?" I had to try one last time.

"Can't you be happy with the fact that you won half the battle?" he asked, much like a patient father.

"I guess I'm not used to losing many battles," I answered honestly.

"Well, Miss Harjo, take it from someone who knows all too well about losing battles: Grab that fifty percent while you got the chance and run like hell."

I left the camp, agreeing to return at the beginning of the week, and set a leisurely pace with Sundae. Only halfway content over the outcome of my conversation with Paroh, I was still far from giving up the battle about teaching just the males. But, for now, I'd follow the chief's advice and take what I could get.

As I was enjoying the beauty of the vast marshland, I suddenly remembered that I had specifically wanted to look for the dredging machinery that was rerouting the Glades' natural water flow. Scanning the area, I didn't see any sign of the machines, but I was afraid it was only a matter of time before I would. It frightened me to think of what would become of this beautiful fragile wetland, but I pushed the thought from my mind and decided to enjoy this place.

Out in the shallow water, thick with sawgrass, I saw a large, dark gray-blue anhinga watching the water closely for its next meal. Suddenly, it speared a small fish and then whipped his head upward, which dislodged the blue gill fish from its dagger-like bill and sent it skyward. Then the bird caught it and gulped it down. Almost immediately, another movement caught my eye and I spotted the top of a small rough-skinned, dark gray skull making its way quietly through the water toward the bird. Seconds later, the alligator's eyes and snout arose just above the water line, leaving no doubt that it had been watching the anhinga, too. But the giant bird was aware of it, for just as the gator picked up speed, the anhinga beat the air hard with its mighty wings and flew off before the reptile could grab it.

Looking down, I watched the beautiful white water hyacinths flowing along in the river beside me, gently and quietly ushering me out of their sacred place. It was a water wilderness that was never intended to be owned by anyone, yet the land unselfishly gave what it could to whoever needed to take from it. All it asked in return was to be respected. What the Seminole had always known but the white man was not ready to learn, was that once the land was abused, there could be no turning back to right the wrong, and when that happened, the land would find its own way to strike back.

Chapter 9

A Man of Many Places

I sat at a small table in the living area at Fowey Rocks lighthouse reading the list of the keepers' duties that was framed and hanging from the wall.

Common Lighthouse Keeper Duties and Tasks:
Light the lamp at sunset and put it out at sunrise.
Fill the lamp with kerosene every evening.
Trim the wicks of the lamp so they don't smoke when lit.
Clean and polish the Fresnel lens every morning.
Clean the windows of the lantern room every day.
Shine all the brass in the lighthouse.
Sweep the floors and stairs of the lighthouse every day.
Clean tower windows and sills as needed.
Clean, paint, and repair all buildings on the light station when needed.
Maintain all mechanical equipment at the light station.
Maintain lighthouse log book and record all daily light station activities.
Take weather readings every day and record in log book.
Weed the walkways and maintain the light station grounds.
Take soundings of river and inlet channels. Move channel markers as needed.
Lend assistance to ships and sailors in distress as needed.
Keep an accurate inventory of all light station equipment and fuel.
Maintain light station launch (boat) and keep in good

working order.

Keep boathouse clean, organized, and in good repair at all times.

Provide visitors with tour of light station as needed.

Clean keeper dwelling chimneys as needed to prevent fire.

Do not leave light station at any time without permission.

Clean house on a regular basis and make repairs as needed.

Keep privy (outhouse/bathroom) clean. Apply lime as needed.

Stack wood properly in woodsheds.

Maintain a clean uniform at all times.

Plant and tend personal garden as needed.

Because we were out at sea, many of the standard rules did not apply, including the planting and tending of a garden, and weeding walkways. And while some might have been just as happy to not have to perform those tasks, I wondered if some might have preferred having some solid ground beneath and around them.

One person who seemed quite content to be far from any land was Striker, who was occupied at the moment with packing his duffle bag in preparation for his shore leave. While he was busy with that, Adam Wilson had taken the new keeper, Owen Perry, up the fifty foot spiral staircase for his first look at the lantern room above, and the massive Fresnel lens he'd be tending.

The two men had arrived at my parents' house soon after the sun was high enough to allow us to sail, and after brief introductions, we'd shoved off. Adam had offered to man the tiller, and as he'd navigated us through the bay and then the Atlantic, Owen and I had sat and talked while he helped with the sails.

"So, do you prefer the west coast over the east coast, Mr. Perry?" I said, trying to sound relaxed and unaffected by the incredibly handsome man sitting across from me. My first thought upon meeting him was that if Michelangelo had laid eyes upon the man, he'd have been quite sure that his marble statue of David had come to life in vibrant, strong colors.

Owen's hair beneath his navy blue seaman's cap was thick and curly, and from what I could see of it, it was as black as a raven's wing with a sparse smattering of gray hairs throughout. It gave the lighthouse keeper an air of authority even though he appeared to be only in his late twenties or very early thirties, at most. He was tall and strongly built, and his nose was Romanesque, as was the rest of his angular face. But it was his eyes that deserved the most attention: They were gray—as gray as the sea before an approaching storm—and they were piercing, making me feel a little flustered and shy. I wasn't used to feeling that way, which left me pondering the reason why a set of gray eyes could make me react so.

"There are things I like about both," Owen replied. Though he'd been at the Jupiter Inlet light for the last couple of years, he'd spent most of his time on the west coast of the United States.

"They each have their own kind of beauty and challenges—and their own moods, and dispositions. To my mind, they're much like two beautiful, but complex women." He smiled. There was absolutely no denying that there was a natural sensuality about the man. Even the way he moved as he helped Adam with the boat's rigging held my complete attention. Unlike Adam, Owen moved with a precise fluidity that was usually seen in athletes, which made me all the more curious about his past.

Adam had introduced him as 'the man from many places'. When I'd asked Owen exactly what that meant, he'd laughed and said he'd seen his fair share of the coastal states growing up as the son of a lighthouse keeper, then becoming one nearly ten years ago. However, Washington State was where he was born, and his mother had actually given birth to him in the keeper's quarters at one of the lighthouses there.

"I guess destiny had my life all planned out for me from the get-go," he reasoned. "My poor mother had me out at Destruction Light, and she claimed it was surely prophetic as to what kind of child I'd be. She said there wasn't a thing I picked up that I didn't pull apart. Unfortunately, I could never quite figure out how to put it back together again," he laughed.

His gray eyes had a light of their own, and out in the strengthening sunlight, they were clear, almost translucent, and bright. But, in the darkness of the night, I wondered if they could be dark and smoldering, and—

"Have you lived here all of your life, Miss Harjo?" Owen's question startled me out of my musings and he looked amused, as though he knew exactly what I was wondering.

"Oh…yes…yes," I stammered. "I mean, no." I quickly corrected myself and I could hear Adam chuckling, which made me wonder if it was that obvious this man had unsettled me.

"I was born in Lake Weir—up in central Florida," I explained. "But we moved here after the big freeze. I was about seven."

"How old are you now—if you don't mind my asking?" he asked.

He was certainly forward, but it didn't come across as offensive or inappropriate. Instead, it felt like he was truly interested in the person he was talking to. "Nineteen, next month," I replied. "And you?"

"I'm an old man compared to you." Owen smiled. "I'm twenty-nine." He looked at me as though assessing me, and then asked, "So what do you do to keep busy in this lovely tropical paradise?"

"Last week or next?" I smiled.

"Well, that sounds quite intriguing," he encouraged.

"This time last week, I worked at the trading post on the Miami River, for the Brickells. You'll get to know them all too well if you stay here for any length of time," I explained. "But I'll be teaching the children out at the Seminole village starting next week."

"Which leaves this week," Owen pointed out. Apparently, he didn't miss much.

"I'll be working with my father," I vaguely answered. Salvaging was not something that I openly discussed, especially with someone I didn't know. But Adam, who'd been listening to our conversation, obviously thought I was just being humble about being able to do something very few women would dare, and he proudly announced: "She salvages shipwrecks. And she's damn good at it, I'll have you know!" he beamed.

"Is that so?" Owen looked impressed.

"Well...yes," I confirmed.

"That's really something! How long have you been doing that?" He was obviously very interested in my unusual line of work.

"Long enough to know that I haven't been doin' it long enough to know what I'm doin'!" I laughed. We all did. But when I looked over at Owen a moment later and saw him watching me as though he was assessing me in a whole new light, I sat up a little straighter, tossed my hair in an affected way, and decided that Adam hadn't been out of line after all, but had actually been bragging about me with only the best intentions.

We arrived at Fowey, and because the seas were relatively calm, we tied the sloop to the dock instead of hoisting it up out of the water. I'd visit with Dylan for a short while and then head on back to the mainland with Striker. As it turned out, though, Dylan was leaving, too, because he was being transferred to Alligator Reef Light, and he needed to pack up everything he'd brought with him. Because there was no communications system at the lighthouse, Striker and Dylan hadn't known that we'd be arriving, and when we did, they were in a hurry to get their gear together and be on their way. We had sailed over in Dylan's sloop because Papa's was having some work done on it, so my brother suggested that I ride back to Miami with Striker on the government-issued boat. That way he could take his sloop on down to the Alligator Reef Lighthouse.

"You sure you want to have it out there the whole time?" Striker asked. "I mean, you can hoist it up on the davits out there, but, still, it's safer leaving it in port."

"Nah, I'm takin' her," Dylan confirmed. "It's hard havin' only one boat available for all three keepers. One takes the boat in for shore leave and the others are stranded. Somethin' happens out there and somebody needs to get in fast, that's a real problem."

The other men came down from the lantern room just then. "I'll be back in a week, maybe a little before then," Striker said. "I've got the list for the fresh supplies we need. It'll be good having a full crew out here for a change." Striker turned toward me. "You ready to shove off, Eliza?" I confirmed that I was and all five of us walked outside.

Because we were on the second platform, we stood about forty feet above the water, and the view was beautiful. But it was nothing like the one from the lantern room at the very top. From there, it was possible to see the barrier islands far to the north and to the south, and whenever I gazed out from that vantage point, I could understand how many a man felt the calling of the sea deep within his soul.

As I stood at the railing looking out, Dylan and Adam lowered the lighthouse's boat down from the davits to the water below.

"All right, then," Dylan said before starting down the ladder. "That's it for me. Y'all take care. And Eliza, just let Mama and Pa know I'm at Alligator, and I'll be home whenever I get some shore leave." With that, my brother began to descend to the first platform. From there, another set of steps would take him down to the dock. As soon as Dylan was about halfway down, Striker followed; then once Dylan was off the ladder, I began to descend as well. Suddenly, I heard my name being called and looked up to see Owen grasping the top of the ladder, peering down at me.

"I enjoyed meeting you, Miss Harjo. I hope we can see each other again."

My right foot slipped off the rung. Thankfully, I had a firm grip and caught myself. I wouldn't admit it, but this part of visiting a lighthouse always unnerved me.

"Whoa, there!" Owen cautioned. "Don't want to lose you before I have a chance to get to know you."

Trying to sound composed as my knuckles turned white from holding onto the rung too tightly, I replied, "I'm sure we'll see each other again. Miami's a small place."

"If it's all right with you, I'll call on you when I have shore leave," he said.

"That—that'd be fine," I managed. At the moment, I was all too aware that Striker was just below me, and I could tell that he'd slowed his descent.

There was a very good likelihood that he'd heard every word of our conversation, and I was afraid that if I looked down, I'd see disapproval in his eyes. But what kept mine glued to the rungs in front of me instead of looking down to gauge Striker's reaction was the fear that I'd see something far worse in his eyes than disapproval. I was afraid I'd see nothing there, only indifference.

Chapter 10

Changing Tides

Striker dropped anchor on the bay side of Key Biscayne, and we threw our lines out to do a little yellowtail fishing. I was surprised he'd suggested it for he'd been quiet most of the way home.

Sitting up on the bow, I rolled my pant legs up to the knee, tilted my face toward the sun and lay back against the angled front of the cuddy. There was nothing more to do than to wait for the tell-tale tug on my line letting me know that a fish had taken the bait.

"Had I known we were going to stop, I'd have brought a picnic."

"It's fine," Striker said as he worked in the stern cutting up the remainder of the small fish he'd netted for our bait. "I had a huge breakfast. Are you hungry though?"

"No. I ate big, too. Or 'too big' I should say." I smiled. "Mama made pork tenderloin biscuits and I couldn't resist."

"She makes 'em good," he agreed.

Striker climbed onto the bow and threw his line off the port side, away from mine. "Any bites?" he asked, sitting down and dangling his legs over the side of the boat.

"Nothin'," I replied, but no sooner had the word left my mouth that Striker said he thought he had one. Snapping the tip of his rod back so that he could set the hook, he waited for a couple of seconds to be sure the fish was on, and when the line started to tug madly, he reeled his catch in.

"Honestly, Striker! You beat all! I could sit here all afternoon and not get one bite, and within thirty seconds you've landed a...nice one!" I finished as he swung a good-sized fish up onto the boat. The fat yellowtail snapper flapped around furiously on the deck until Striker strung a stringer through its gills and threw the fish back into the water to stay alive until it was time for us to leave.

Picking up a piece of bait on the board next to him, he casually remarked, "That Owen fella seems like a decent enough guy."

Forcing myself not to smile, I agreed, adding that I'd only just met him, though. "You know anything about him—other than that he's from Washington State?" I asked. It wouldn't hurt Striker to think I was interested in the man, and, in all honesty, I was a little curious as to what Owen's story was.

"No," Striker said as he cast his line out again.

Silence followed, thick and heavy, and I tried to think of something to say. Looking back toward the southern point of the island, I could see the ninety-five-foot Cape Florida lighthouse through the trees.

"Wonder how long Dylan will be down at Alligator Reef Light," I said. "Sure wish he'd get a permanent placement somewhere. I can't imagine that it's much fun being bounced around among different houses of refuge and lighthouses all the time."

"Oh, I don't know," Striker said as he reeled in a little of the slack in his line. "Some men like moving around. It's interesting to them to be in different surroundings, under different circumstances all the time. And there are some fellas who just have a hard time settling down."

I bit my tongue on that last statement.

"Take for instance this new guy, Owen. It sounds like he's made the rounds, himself. And there's nothing wrong with that. Some folks just have a hard time letting the dust settle on the tops of their shoes. Maybe they're running from something, or somebody. Or could be they're just running from themselves."

"Is that what you're doing, Striker?" The words were out of my mouth before I had time to consider editing them.

Striker looked startled at first, and then he let out a soft sigh. "Sometimes… yeah, I guess in a way I am." He seemed tired, physically and mentally. "Honestly though, Eliza, it's more than just trying to outrun the pain of losing my mom and dad. It's…I don't know…I guess I just haven't found enough of a reason to let the dust settle, so to speak." He looked at me as if waiting for me to respond, but I wasn't sure what I wanted to say. Instead, I reeled in my line to check the bait, and seeing that it was still on the hook, I walked toward the stern to cast my line in another direction. I needed a minute to think, to take the pulse on how I was feeling, to see how deeply the pain still ran.

It suddenly occurred to me how lost Striker really was and how young he now seemed to me. The feelings that I'd been hanging on to, and fed through blown up remembrances of what had been, and unrealistic possibilities of what might be, evaporated. I realized that I might have finally outgrown Striker. And I felt all right about it. More than all right, really. I felt wonderfully free, and relieved, as if I'd just shed an overly warm winter coat in the month of May.

"The tide's going out and the wind's shiftin'," Striker said as he stood up and began reeling in his line. "We'd better head in if we want to get there in one piece."

That was fine with me. In fact, everything in the world seemed fine at the moment. My heart had gone through its own changing tides, and I'd made it through the low one. Now I was ready to ride the high.

Chapter 11

Something Fishy

The grouper and I were face to face and frozen in place for several seconds before the massive fish turned and quickly swam away. I had scared it out from the reef when I'd jumped in to explore the *Paso Rápido,* and as I watched it fade away into the turquoise abyss, I regretted not having my three-pronged harpoon with me, for the grouper would have made a wonderful supper. Returning to the task at hand, I focused my attention on the position of the wreck.

The cutter had been badly damaged by the initial impact of the starboard side to the reef, leaving most of the vessel submerged and lying on its right side in about twenty feet of water. Our visibility was good, and the currents weren't too bad at the moment, so our biggest challenge was not getting cut on the razor-sharp coral; blood from the smallest cuts would bring the sharks in.

The plan was for the divers to salvage all that could be brought up manually, or be winched up. Then Papa and Ezra Asher's trawlers would attempt to parbuckle the *Paso* through a rotational leveraging method using chains and winches to pull her off her side and back into an upright position. If successful, there was no telling what we might find buried beneath her, though gold and silver weighed utmost on our minds. Aside from what Ezra's crew had found before we joined the salvage, we'd recovered four bottles of rum (one broken); a ruined Spanish edition of *Macbeth*; and personal belongings of the crew, including a comb, straight razor, shaving cup, a variety of clothing, and a wedding band that was still stuck on a skeletal finger. It was a poignant reminder that far more important things than gold and silver had found a final resting place beneath the waves.

Suddenly, I spotted the edge of something shiny poking up through the sand near the stern of the cutter. It was an 1898 Cuban peso, and had most likely been someone's pocket change. Looking around the immediate area, I found two more, and after sticking them into the canvas bag tied around my waist, I checked the locations and welfare of the other divers as I'd been taught to do, then pushed myself up from the sea bottom and surfaced for air.

Anchored near each other were Papa's trawler, *Deep Secrets*, and Ezra's, the *Waylaid*. Swimming over to my father, I climbed up the rope ladder and then began to dry off with a towel he handed to me. "Anything?" he asked.

"Pesos," I answered as I pulled on a pair of canvas pants and shirt over my buckskin shorts and bandeau-style top. Though my swimming attire was far skimpier than any that proper ladies wore, it was necessary for salvage work. Getting bulky swimwear caught on the wreck was a danger I couldn't afford.

Pulling open the strings which held the top of the canvas bag closed, I reached in for the pesos, then added them to a box Papa was keeping the smaller items in. "Honestly, Papa, we could scrounge around for weeks and keep finding these little things, but I think we need to roll this cutter and start salvaging beneath her. We're not making enough money to pay for our oil."

Papa smiled at my last statement, for I was parroting the complaint I'd heard him make a hundred times. "It won't be long now," he said. "Ezra and I agreed that by mid-morning, we'll start trying to parbuckle her."

Just then, Simon and Turtle climbed back on board, and I saw Ezra's two men, Carlos Herrera, and Tony something-or-other, board the *Waylaid*. I'd never met them before, and Papa was only slightly familiar with Herrera, but we were told they'd served in the military with Ezra, and they all seemed friendly enough.

Ezra Asher stood out from the rest of us with his shock of curly snow-white hair. He also had intense bright blue eyes, and both hair and eyes stood out against his sun-browned skin. I guessed him to be just under six feet tall, with a slender build, but he was strong and sinewy from the salvaging work he'd been doing for the last five years, and from being a navy seaman before that. Even though his hair was white, and his face had more lines than a nautical map, he wasn't old. As a matter of fact, Ezra had told my father that he was born in northern California, in '72, making him just thirty-three or four. He was friendly, but intensely focused, and he had the energy of three men. It looked as though we'd hooked up with a man who worked just as hard as my father did, and the two captains seemed to genuinely like each other. Ezra was quick to ask my father's opinion or preference about salvaging matters, just as my father always did out of respect for any captain he was working with. Because of that, a quick and easy camaraderie had developed between the two.

In the late morning, after two hours of connecting chains, ropes and pulleys to the *Paso*, and then another hour for the two trawlers to roll the sunken vessel into an upright position, the enormous task was accomplished without any unforeseen problems. Afterward, we let the stirred up sand settle back down while we ate our noonday dinner, and then we jumped back onto the wreck site with high hopes that the newly exposed seabed would reveal its hidden treasures. And it quickly became apparent that we wouldn't be disappointed.

Within fifteen minutes of exploring the area, Simon came up with five silver pieces and three gold. But the best find of the afternoon was what Tony brought up: the captain's log. It listed all of the cargo on board, with the exception of the fifty thousand dollars worth of gold and silver to pay for the illegal acquisition of the Jacksonville real estate. However, what *was* listed as being on board was a bag of tourmalines. The stone was native to Cuba, and the quality was high. This particular shipment (over nineteen hundred karats' worth), had been en route to a gem buyer in New York; if found, they would be well worth the trouble of spending many hours on the wreck site.

We worked on the site for three days, and at the end of each day, everything that each diver had found was laid out on the deck of Ezra's boat, logged, and then kept in a safe in his stateroom. Once the salvaging was complete, he and Papa would take all that had been recovered to the Port of Entry, in Key West, to be appraised; once the appraisal was accepted by all parties, items would then be auctioned off and the money would be divided by whatever percentages had been agreed upon. Ezra had decided that just he and Papa would work the wreck, and as wreck master, Ezra had that right. No one argued the point for the fewer people involved, the more each salvager made.

Our fourth day on the wreck was Sunday. It would be the last day for our crew for several days because Papa had a hunting trip with folks staying at the Royal Palm, and I was teaching at the Seminole village. I was a little nervous about my first day there, so I was just as glad to keep my mind off of it by spending the day diving instead of going to church. I figured God was okay with that since He was the one who made gold and silver in the first place.

Thus far, the grouper and the tourmalines had eluded me, as well as all but one gold bar, which I'd found beneath the outcropping of a medium-size coral rock the day before. Papa and Ezra estimated the worth at about nine thousand dollars, and I was thrilled. Combined with the other treasures we'd found, we figured we'd brought up about nineteen thousand in gold and silver, as well as some of the *Paso* crew's more valuable personal items, including the gold wedding band, a finely crafted cameo brooch, and five pewter mugs. And though there was much more to be found, I was content with what we'd found thus far and, in all honesty, I was exhausted. My fingers were shriveled like prunes from the long hours spent in the water, and I'd had enough for a while.

I had just finished checking around another coral rock and was starting to surface when I spotted the grouper coming back into the vicinity. He was probably hoping to reclaim his home in the reef. But before I could do a thing about it, I saw Carlos spear him. He'd left the three-pronged harpoon lying near the reef just in case, and I was kicking myself for not having done the same. Leaving the victor to his spoils, I pushed up from the sandy bottom and then climbed on board our boat.

Several minutes later, as I finished drying off and getting dressed, I heard the commotion going on over at the *Waylaid* as Carlos surfaced with the grouper, and Tony and Ezra leaned over the side and hauled the fish on board. As they did, Simon and Turtle climbed onto our boat, and then Simon handed my father some small thing he'd found. As they talked, I began to straighten up the deck in preparation to leave, and then I heard my father talking to Carlos.

"Nice catch, Herrera," Papa acknowledged. Then, "You know, that's a mighty big fish. How 'bout we cut her up and I'll take a couple of filets home to Eve. There's nothin' she likes better."

Herrera wasn't so quick to agree, and mumbled something to Ezra. The captain said something in response and then turned to us. "Carlos is proud of that damn grouper," he laughed. "But since little Eliza there has been itching to wrangle that fish in all week, he'll share. I'll tell you what, I'll even do the dirty work and cut it up for you all." But just as he picked up a knife, my father stopped him.

"No, no. That wouldn't be right." Papa stiffly smiled. "If we're takin' some, we'll do the work." Even though Papa didn't say as much, the expression on his face told me something was wrong.

"I pleased to cut fish up, Mr. Harjo," Carlos assured my father. "It's happy for me," he said in his broken English.

But Papa pinned both him and Ezra with a look that I'd never seen him give anyone. "No. Simon'll do it," Papa said more forcefully than I thought was necessary, and apparently everyone else thought so, too, for no one said a word. The tension in the air was getting heavier by the second.

"Pull the anchor line in some, Turtle," Papa instructed. "Edge our bow closer to theirs." Once Turtle had pulled us within a couple of feet of the *Waylaid*, Papa told Simon to board it.

As Simon did, Ezra reacted. "I don't know what's bit your ass, Harjo, but you're way out of line here. The fact of the matter is that it's Herrera's catch, and he has the right to keep the entire fish for himself. We were tryin' to be generous, but forget it. Carlos'll keep the whole damn thing. Get back on your boat, Simon. We're leaving."

"No, you're not," Papa said and before anyone could object or even begin to move, Papa leapt onto Ezra's trawler, and stood nearly nose to nose with the man, though Papa had the advantage in height. "Slice the grouper open, Simon—all the way up through the throat," Papa instructed while not taking his eyes off of Ezra.

As the two men glared at each other, Simon withdrew his knife from a sheath at the top of his breeches, and slit the grouper from its belly up to its boney mouth. Then Simon inserted his hand into the fish's throat and withdrew a good-sized leather pouch.

"Open it," Papa told him. Pulling apart the strings that held the pouch closed, Simon shook out some of its contents into the palm of his hand. There, glinting in the sun, were exquisite multi-colored stones of all shapes and sizes in beautiful shades of green, pink, purple, and yellow. The tourmalines had been found. "Now, toss them over to Eliza," Papa said.

"Here's how this is gonna play out now." My father remained within inches of Ezra's face, which was beet-red at the moment, though I wasn't sure if it was from embarrassment or anger, or both. "You're gonna give us that gold bar Eliza found, and we're gonna consider this matter settled and go our separate ways. However, if you have a problem with that, then I'll leave you, your gold bar, and the tourmalines right here, and go straight to the courthouse and let them know how our salvaging operation is goin'. I have a feeling they'd be mighty interested knowin' how you do business in South Florida waters. You have a problem with that?"

The silence was heavier than a one hundred pound grouper. Finally, after what seemed like an hour but was no more than several seconds, Ezra turned away from my father, spat on the floor of the boat, and then instructed Carlos to open the safe and give us the bar. Once he handed it to Papa, my father tossed it over to Turtle, and then instructed Simon to get back on our boat. Once he was on board, Papa stepped back from Ezra, and quickly re-boarded our boat as well.

"That's the end of this, Asher. Nothing more will be said or done about it, but I'm telling you now, you leave these waters and don't come back. If I see you around, the whole town will know you're a damn thief, and you may not have the opportunity again to get out so easily. People around here are funny. They don't take too kindly to folks who want to steal their hard-earned money, and they have a way of takin' the law into their own hands dealin' with 'em. Don't let me see you or your crew again, you understand?"

Ezra angrily muttered to Tony to pull up anchor and for Carlos to fire up the boiler. Within minutes, they'd built up enough steam to pull away, and they did so without saying another word to us. As we watched them pick up speed and head north, I quietly asked my father, "Do you think that's the last we'll see of them?"

"Probably not," my father said, not taking his eyes off the retreating trawler. "They have gold fever, and that's the worst kind of fever to cure."

Suddenly, a thought occurred to me and I turned toward Papa. "How'd you know about the tourmalines?"

"Simon was checking for salvage behind a large coral rock when Carlos shot that grouper, but Carlos didn't know he was there. Simon saw him take a pouch out of the canvas sack he carries for salvage, and then shove it down the fish's throat. Simon figured it had to be somethin' pretty valuable and somethin' Carlos didn't want their crew to share with ours. If Simon had had to come up for air, he might not have seen it happen. Luckily, the boy can hold his breath for a long time."

"Lucky for us," I agreed. "Not so much for the *Waylaid*." I grinned.

Chapter 12

A Bald Peacock

The afternoon sun beat down relentlessly on Sundae and me as we rode away from the Seminole village. It was early June, the sun was brutal, and there was very little in the way of shade at this point on our regular route. It was the one we'd been taking for the last month and we knew the path well enough to travel it blindfolded.

We came to our usual spot on the river where the bank dipped down so my horse could get a much-needed drink. As she eagerly drank, I splashed handful after handful of water over my head and face, and then hiked up my skirt, removed my booties and dipped my legs in.

Off in the distance to the north, I could faintly make out the dredging equipment that had appeared there just the week before. Seeing it while riding to the village one morning alarmed me. When I told Paroh about it, I learned he'd seen it, too, and had actually ridden north to confront the men digging the canals that would carry the Glades' water out to the sea. They had assured him that the Seminole village would not be included in the many thousands of acres that would be dredged, but neither of us was quite willing to believe that. However, there was nothing we could do but wait and see.

I remounted Sundae and pulled my heavy navy cotton skirt up to the middle of my thighs to allow the sun and wind to dry my skin, and then we settled into a leisurely pace for home. As I rode along, I thought about how far along the Seminole boys and young men had come in just a month's time with their reading and arithmetic skills. While that pleased me greatly, I was also frustrated by the fact that too many times I'd caught the girls watching us longingly from the distance they were required to keep. I was hoping that as Paroh and his council got used to my being there, they might reconsider letting me teach at least a few of the girls the basics in both subjects. But I figured I stood a better chance of sprouting wings and flying.

Just the week before, while the men were out hunting, Rose's younger sister, Rae, had nonchalantly wandered over to within hearing distance of the chickee where I was teaching a lesson on the different uses of the words "to", "two", and "too". Rae sat down beneath a palm with knitting needles and several balls of yarn and began working away, but every time I looked in her direction, I caught her looking in mine. I knew that she was attempting to listen in, so I raised my voice and talked a little louder. As I glanced over at her, I realized that in her lap, along with the knitting paraphernalia, were paper and a pencil, and she was doing her best to take down notes. I wasn't the only one to catch her eavesdropping. Suddenly Rae's grandmother appeared at her side and began hitting her with a thin oak switch. I could hear the soft whistle of it as she brought it down through the air again and again, and the cries of the poor girl each time it stung her skin. I started to go over to them, to intercede on Rae's behalf, but when I rose from my stool and took several steps in their direction, one of my young male students grabbed my wrist, stopping me.

"No, no, Miss Eliza," Jimmy said, looking stricken and shaking his head vigorously. He obviously realized what my intention was. "If you go over there, you make it worse for Rae. She'll get three times as many strikes after you leave."

Knowing he was right, but terribly frustrated about the whole situation, I remained where I was as tears filled my eyes. Finally, the grandmother allowed Rae to run off into the hammock, and I had to wonder if the girl would suffer longer from the sting of being caught and the embarrassment of her public whipping, or from being denied the right to learn. I knew that a salve would ease the girl's welts, but there was no cure for her frustration at being denied the right to learn. I wasn't sure who was more frustrated, the girls or me.

Letting out a loud sigh as Sundae and I continued on toward home, I was suddenly startled by a flock of crows that rose up from the marsh to my left. Something had spooked them, causing them to take to the sky, *caw-cawing* in complaint. Immediately, I spotted a lone horseman coming from the north. Though the man was about a hundred yards from me, I could see that he sat tall in the saddle, and wore a light-colored shirt, dark pants, and had a dark cap on, or perhaps his hair was dark. I slowed Sundae down even more so that our paths wouldn't cross until I had a better chance to figure out who he was, and what he might be doing there. But as the distance closed between us, I suddenly realized who the rider was. It was the new lighthouse keeper out at Fowey, Owen Perry. I smiled when I recognized him and watched the same reaction from him as recognition lit up his face. Picking up his pace, he quickly closed the remaining space between us.

"Why, Miss Harjo!" he said, respectfully tipping his navy blue cap. "Whatever brings you out to this untamable land?" he added dramatically.

"Mr. Perry, I believe that's simply an outsider's way of thinking," I said with a smile. "While some may prefer to tame it, others like it just as is." I was quite pleased with my smooth retort.

"Well said, Miss Harjo! Well said!" He smiled broadly, clearly impressed...or was there a touch of patronizing amusement in there, too? I wasn't quite sure what I was seeing in his startling slate gray eyes. Had they been that color gray when I first met him, or did they change according to his surroundings or mood? Suddenly, I wasn't feeling quite as confident as I had just a moment before. This man was older than me, more experienced, and I suddenly felt a little less tall in my own saddle.

"What brings you out this way, Mr. Perry, if you don't mind my asking?" I said, trying to settle myself.

"I've never been to the Glades before, even during my time up in Jupiter. It's something I always wanted to see," he replied.

"And what do you think of it?" For some odd reason, I wanted him to think it was as special as I did.

"It's beautiful, like many things in South Florida are." He smiled, looking intently at me. "Are you riding alone? If so, may I escort you to wherever it is you're going?"

Lord, he was smooth...and handsome...and apparently kind. "Oh, that's not necessary, Mr. Perry," I replied, trying to sound independent and sophisticated. "I take this route all the time, and I came prepared," I said, turning in my saddle and laying my hand lightly on my rifle. I also wanted him to know I was brave. Somehow, that was important to me.

"I'm impressed, Miss Harjo," he said, satisfying that part of my ego. I pulled my shoulders back slightly and stuck my chin out rather jauntily. But just as I was starting to feel like the proudest peacock in the pack, he added, "Before you get back to town, though, you might want to readjust yourself and perhaps throw a shawl around you, as well. We don't want all of Miami thinking you're up to no good out in the badlands, do we?" He grinned.

Mortified, I followed his gaze downward to see what in the world he could be talking about, and when I did, I realized that my skirt was still hiked up to mid-thigh, and the water that I'd splashed all over me just minutes before had turned my crisp cotton blouse and chemise beneath it absolutely transparent, leaving nothing to the imagination. I immediately understood why he'd looked so amused from the moment he rode up, and I couldn't jump off Sundae fast enough to allow my skirt to fall back into place and grab a shawl from my saddle bag. Suddenly, I felt like the peacock had just lost every one of its feathers, leaving it quite naked and foolish-looking.

Chapter 13

Deeply and Thoroughly

Owen Perry and I sat by the open window, enjoying the light breeze that blew in off the bay while people-watching as fellow diners came and went at the Captain's Table Restaurant in Coconut Grove. It was the second time we'd eaten there, and the second time Owen had ordered steak for dinner.

"I think you're better suited to be a rancher than a light keeper," I laughed, as I watched him take his last spoonful of beef barley soup while I ate my lobster bisque more slowly. "You hungry tonight?" I asked, though there wasn't a real need to. He'd hurried through his first course as if he'd been fasting for a week.

"Guess it's more about being able to eat some good cooking for a change," he smiled. "Eating Adam and Striker's meals—if they really qualify as such—takes some real getting used to, although, in all fairness, my concoctions aren't much better. We could use a woman's touch out there."

"I couldn't help you much, I'm afraid," I laughed. "I cook a lot of seafood." It was easy being around him, and even though this was only our second date, I was completely at ease.

Looking around at the décor of the new restaurant, one knew immediately what the menu would offer up. The walls were adorned with all kinds of nautical items, including a ship's wheel, fishing nets and lobster traps. Proudly displayed on a large shelf in the room was a variety of model ships that had been meticulously put together. But it wasn't just the nautical items that let every patron know what culinary treats awaited them. It was the unmistakable aroma of fried seafood, as well. My mouth watered at the wonderful smells wafting through the dining room and I realized I was quite hungry.

"You look very pretty tonight," Owen said, drawing my attention back to him.

"Oh, thank you," I said, pleased that he'd noticed the new dress I'd bought just that afternoon. It was cream-colored with tiny light blue roses covering it, and though the light blue eyelet lace came up my neck and was tight at the wrists, the dress was made from the new lighter weight cotton, making it much more comfortable than the suffocating wool dresses and heavier cotton we'd always worn. One thing I refused to wear, though, much to the chagrin of the proper ladies in our community, was a bustle. I figured if the good Lord had wanted me to have a good-sized rump, He'd have put one on me Himself. I wasn't about to add a bulky mess of material to my backside to increase the weight and the heat of my dress, especially during a brutal Miami summer.

"I bought this dress off the rack at Burdine's," I said. "I'm glad he's carrying such a nice variety of ready-made clothing. Folks love having so many choices available to them. I particularly appreciate it since I don't have the knack with a needle that my mother does."

"Have you worked at the store much lately?" he asked.

"Some. Just two afternoons a week, and on Saturdays. It's nice having that money since I'm not getting paid at the village."

"If you ask me, those Seminoles are taking advantage of you," he said, shaking his head in disapproval.

"Can't bleed blood from a turnip, Owen," I replied. I could see why folks didn't understand why I spent so much time teaching the Seminoles without getting a penny for it. But, sometimes, a person just had to do what she felt was right, even if she didn't have much to show for it at the end of the day. However, I'd made an excellent paycheck from the sale of the *Paso's* tourmalines, as well as the gold bar. Between that and the money I made working for Mr. Burdine, I was feeling flush.

We fell into a comfortable silence while the waiter filled our water glasses and then set a wicker basket of yeast rolls in front of us. Owen began to butter one, but deciding I'd rather save my appetite for fried shrimp, I settled back comfortably in my chair and enjoyed looking out the window. To the east, I could see heat lighting flashing off in the distance over the bay, and to the north, I could see another new building going up, changing Miami's young skyline yet again. It seemed to be a weekly occurrence. Right before our eyes, a wild land was being wiped away, and in its place was the rising of a new city.

I felt there should be limitations as to how much of this land could be destroyed. But, Owen made the argument that it was all a matter of supply and demand, and with more and more people willing to invest in our community, we needed to accommodate them. And that meant making land available for the building of their homes and business.

"But, Owen," I countered, "while some people are building a place here, others are being displaced, and that's not fair."

"But what if those people occupy valuable land and are doing nothing more useful with it than just sitting on it?" he asked.

"Like who?" I asked. "Who's just sitting on land, standing in the way of progress?" I had a feeling I knew what his answer would be.

"Well, the Seminoles, for example," Owen replied. "I know there's dredging going on in the Glades. I saw it for myself the day I ran into you—and your three miles of long, tan legs," he teased.

I couldn't help but smile, and I could feel the color rise to my cheeks. He wasn't going to let me forget that afternoon he'd caught me in a most awkward state. I knew he was trying to lighten our dinner conversation by bringing that up, but I wasn't so easily diverted.

"Owen, surely you don't view the native people as being nuisances, do you? I mean, after all, they were here long before you and I were. If they want to do nothing but sit back and make sofkee stew all day and tan alligator hides, then who has the right to tell them to do otherwise?"

"The one who owns the land, Eliza, and that's the government. Like it or not, if the government sees dollar bills in that land, then it'll remove anyone standing in the way of capitalizing on it. And, pretty lady, if that's the case with the land the Seminoles are occupying, then I'm afraid there wouldn't be a thing you could do to stop it. But didn't you tell me that Paroh fellow said the government isn't interested in the land he and his people are on? The government might feel that keeping the Seminoles happy and quiet and out of the way is worth the price of the land. I'm sure they want to avoid another squabble with the Seminoles. Two wars are enough," Owen finished.

"I hope you're right." I said, smiling weakly and feeling a little more reassured. It seemed as though Owen knew just what to say to make me feel better about the world. Even at this early stage in our friendship, I felt safe with him. He had a way of making me feel as if every problem had an answer. He was a strong man, both physically and mentally, and he made me feel like a woman.

I realized I was staring at him, and he did, too. I quickly recovered and launched into another subject. "So, you and Striker are down to a two man crew again now that they moved Adam to Carysfort, right?" But before Owen could answer, a thought occurred to me. "Hey, with Dylan at Alligator Reef, Adam at Carysfort, and you and Striker out at Fowey, y'all are in a line along those reefs! One, two, three!"

"Yes, I guess that's true," he laughed.

"Will they bring a third man in to Fowey to help you and Striker?" I asked.

"We were told that Jim Altman is about fully healed from his fall, and they'll bring him back out as soon as he gets the okay from the doctor. The government felt that Carysfort needed an experienced keeper since they've got a couple of new men there now, so that's why they sent Adam down. Hopefully, everyone's in place now, and we won't have to keep moving from light to light. It's just hard keeping fellows out at those offshore lights. They're very isolated and that gets old."

Just then the waiter arrived with my shrimp and Owen's filet mignon. After refilling our iced tea and asking us if we needed anything else, the waiter left us to our dinner.

"Owen, did you know that a vessel named the *Esmeralda* went down north of Carysfort about a week or so ago?"

Owen nodded. Then, "Yeah, I heard about it; a medium size sloop out of Trinidad, no survivors. Why? You and your father going to see about salvaging it?"

"We are!" I excitedly confirmed. "With the lights out on the reefs now, fewer wrecks are occurring, so Papa and I are really hoping we can get in on this one. Lord, listen to me! I sound like I'm happy that ship went down."

"Oh, I think a tiny part of you is." He smiled conspiratorially.

"I am not!" I objected. "That's a terrible thing to say! You make me sound like a vulture!"

"You're no vulture," he observed. "You're a kid in a candy store." He laughed, which made me laugh, too. But the truth of the matter was that there wasn't a wreck I worked on that I didn't feel terribly sad for the crew who'd gone down, especially when I came across their personal items like lockets or shoes. It brought home the fact that people had perished there, but to allow the cargo to fall victim to the sea as well did no one any good. Sometimes, the captain and crew were rescued, and when that happened, the captain was grateful for the assistance in recovering his cargo.

"Do you know who the wreck master is yet, or what kind of cargo went down?" Owen asked.

"Not yet," I replied. "Papa was looking into it today, but I didn't see him when I got back from the village. And speaking of the village: I'm thinking positively and assuming we will be salvaging next week, so I told my students that they're having a week's break. I have to say, when I was a pupil in school, I was never disappointed to be going on vacation, but these students are."

"Well, that says a lot about you as a teacher." Owen smiled.

"Either that, or they're thinkin' about all the candy they'll be missin'," I laughed.

"You mean you bring them candy all the time?" He looked amazed.

"How else am I gonna get those little boys to sit still instead of chasin' down a gator or a moccasin?" I asked.

"That, m' dear, is a world in and of itself," he said, shaking his head.

"And one that's fast disappearing," I quietly added.

Both of us were too full for dessert, so we decided to take a walk along the bay. But just as we began to make our way down Main Street, a light rain started to fall. Grabbing my hand, Owen hurried me back to the buggy parked alongside the restaurant. The conveyance was one that Owen had borrowed from Mrs. Brickell. It surprised me that she'd been so generous, but as I watched my handsome escort climb up onto the seat next to me, I realized that even she would have trouble saying no to a man as charming as he was.

"I'm sorry you're wet," he said, watching as I pulled a handkerchief from my small yellow-and-blue-beaded reticule and began wiping the dampness from my face.

"In this heat, I'm not sure if it's raindrops or perspiration," I laughed. He wasn't smiling, however. Instead, he was looking at me intensely, seriously. Then, he took my chin between his thumb and forefinger and gently brought his face within inches of mine.

"I'm about to kiss you thoroughly and deeply, Eliza Harjo. So if you'd rather I didn't, tell me now."

I didn't say a word, and then Owen made good on his words...very, very good.

Chapter 14

Falling Bridges

"Mornin'," Papa said to me over the top of the *Miami Metropolis*, the paper Mama worked for. "How was your evening with Owen?"

"Lovely," I said, taking a plate of scrambled eggs from Mama and joining him at the table. "Owen took me to that new restaurant again in Coconut Grove, the *Captain's Chair*...or is it *'Table'*? Anyway, it's lovely—not fancy, but the atmosphere is cozy, and the food is exquisite."

"Oh, exquisite, is it?" Mama asked over her shoulder as she stood at the stove flipping Papa's fried eggs. There was no mistaking the amusement in her voice. After I'd had my first date with Owen and described it as being "divine," she'd teased me by saying that my vocabulary had become just as sophisticated as my dates were. When she'd said that, I knew she was talking about the old schoolgirl crush I'd had on Striker. Just as she'd predicted, I'd found someone who made me feel special and made that heartbreak seem childish now.

"Well, he seems like a very nice man, Eliza," Mama said as she put Papa's plate in front of him and refilled his coffee.

"He is," I sighed, and even I could hear the dreaminess in my voice.

"Papa, did you find out anything about the *Esmeralda*? What was she carrying, and when can we start salvaging her?"

Folding his newspaper, he set it aside and looked at me. "Yes. Cocoa and copper, among other things. And we're not."

"What?" I said, confused by his answer.

Resting his forearms on the table and leaning in slightly, he explained: "The *Esmeralda* was carrying cocoa, copper and, according to the manifest, "assorted things," which could be anything, but it's a pretty sure bet there'd be some items of real value. But we're not salvaging her." He looked rather grim.

"Why not?" I cried. "What's stopping us?"

"It's not a matter of what's stopping us, Eliza, it's *who*," Papa said.

"Who is, Papa? I don't understand."

"Ezra Asher, that's who. He's the master wrecker, and he's not about to let us have a piece of that salvage," Papa said.

"But you told him to stay away from Miami waters," I reminded him.

"I did and he has—at least for now. The *Esmeralda* isn't sitting anywhere near Miami. She's northwest of Carysfort, on Anniversary Reef, and that's part of the Keys."

"Why don't you just tell the other salvagers what a thief he is?" I urged.

"Because, baby girl, at this point, he doesn't have anyone else working that wreck with him, except for his own crew. It's all his. And I have a feeling he's going to do everything he can to keep it that way. If the ship should need to be parbuckled, instead of getting someone to help him roll it, he'll just have his crew tear her apart, board by board. Then he'll salvage as much as he can. Even if that means leaving some valuable cargo behind, he won't have to split any of what he does bring up, and that could make him a pretty good chunk of money."

"Where did this man come from?" I angrily asked.

"Other than being born in California, I don't know," Papa said. "But wherever he's been, I'd be willing to bet he's burned a few bridges there, too. And just like the good ol' London Bridge, one of these days, one of those bridges is gonna come falling down—and right on top of Ezra Asher."

Chapter 15

T for Trouble

I helped Mr. Burdine set up his storefront window with the newest selection of fall clothing. Then, after cleaning out the stock room, rearranging inventory to display it more effectively, and painting the women's dressing room a lovely shade of lavender, I decided I'd had enough of retail to last me for a while. Since there was no salvaging to be done, I returned to the village two days early with a saddlebag full of candy, and quite a few fun new lessons planned. Even though they weren't expecting me, I figured the temptation of a lemon drop or peppermint stick might entice the boys into the little chickee I used. I missed the children even more than I'd thought I would, so I was glad to be on Sundae again, heading down our usual trail to the Glades.

It was just after nine in the morning when I rode into camp, and it was unusually quiet. I saw only girls and women going about their chores, while a few of the mostly elderly men sat near the central fire pit conversing and smoking their pipes.

The mongrel dog who'd accosted me on my first visit ran up to me, but not because he was attempting to protect his people from a stranger. Now he was accustomed to my bringing him a treat of some sort.

"Mornin', *Fotcho*," I said as I pulled a half-eaten biscuit from breakfast out of my gaucho pants' pocket and threw it to him. His name, *Fotcho*, was the Seminole word for "duck," and when I asked Rose how he'd gotten that name, she said it was because one of the elders thought all of the fur between the little dog's toes made them look webbed.

Running alongside in case any more treats might be forthcoming, he arrived at Rose's chickee with me, and then politely waited outside while

I went in to speak to her. At the moment, she was thoroughly engrossed in making something bright and beautiful on her manual sewing machine.

"Knock, knock," I said softly as I rapped my knuckles on one of the chickee's vertical poles. Though I tried not to startle her, I did, and she nearly fell off the little stool she was sitting on.

Rose made some exclamation in her native language, then, smiling, said in English, "Miss Eliza! You about gave me a heart attack!" She set her sewing aside and waved me in. "Come in, come in! Why you here?" she asked but not unkindly so. "You supposed to come Monday. You have no thing to do?"

"That's 'nothing', not 'no thing'," I gently corrected her. I knew she wanted to learn, that she was as thirsty for knowledge as a man is for water in the desert, but there'd been no persuading Paroh. Pushing that thought from my mind, I asked her where the boys were.

"They learn how to make a *pithlo*...How you say?...A canoe! Yes, canoe! Little Mac teach them. They find good cypress trees this morning." Little Mac was a man in his thirties, and there was nothing little about him. He was gigantic in height and width, and just as big in kindness, though the alligators didn't think so. He was the tribe's best wrestler, and he was legendary for subduing one that weighed half a ton.

"What time will they return, Rose?"

"Late day," she replied. "They stay long today."

"Ah, well then, that's that." I was disappointed, but there was nothing more I could do in the village. "I'll see y'all next week," I said, but just as I turned to leave, Rose knocked a magazine off her little sewing table and I went over to retrieve it for her. It was *Vogue Magazine*. I was curious now. "What are you working on?"

"I show you," she said, holding her hand out to take the magazine. She flipped through the pages until she found what she was looking for and then handed it back to me. It was a clothing pattern, which was a regular feature in the popular magazine, and this one happened to be for a woman's skirt and shirtwaist. Though the skirt was fairly simple, the shirtwaist was more complicated. Its waistline was tailored like a man's shirt before becoming more generous up the torso to accommodate the bosom and then it was finished off with a high neckline. Instructions were provided, as well as specific measurements, and they needed to be followed explicitly or one would have a mess on one's hands.

"Are you making this for yourself, Rose?" The outfit was quite different from the way the Seminoles dressed.

"No, no. I make it for white lady in town. You know Miz Brubaker? She very big one." Rose smiled mischievously. "She no can find her size in store."

"It's not 'no can find...'" I started to correct her grammar. "Oh, never mind that right now. How are you able to make this, Rose? It's a complicated piece, even for someone who is able to read the directions." I was amazed she was even trying. "Is she paying you to do this?" I asked, squinting my eyes.

"Yes, she pay!" Rose looked and sounded indignant. "She pay good, too!"

"But how are you able to follow these directions since you can't read?"

"I follow pictures best I can," she replied, looking rather deflated.

"Oh, that's ridiculous! There's absolutely no reason you shouldn't be able to read this every bit as well as I can. You wait right here," I ordered. I jumped down from the chickee, retrieved a few items from my saddlebag, went back inside, pulled a chair next to Rose, twisted my ponytail into a bun, opened the *ABC* primer, and went to work.

"This letter is *A*, Rose. *A* as in apple and alligator. This next one is *B*. *B* as in boy and boat. This next one is *C*." And so we continued through the morning and into the afternoon, until we got to the letter *T*. Then capital *T* trouble arrived.

"Rose!" Paroh shouted, startling both the young woman and me as we sat hunched together over the primer. The chief had returned early, and we'd not seen him coming.

Paroh spewed out a string of words in their native language, and even though I didn't understand any of it, I knew it wasn't good. The poor girl was ashen-faced, and tears flooded her eyes. Paroh added a last word to his sentence, pointing away from us as he did, and I knew that word must have been "Go!" And she did—fast. Rose ran off through the palmettos and as she fled, Paroh turned his controlled wrath on me.

"We had a deal, Miss Eliza. We had a deal which you didn't keep!" His dark eyes flashed and his mouth was hard. Paroh stepped up into the chickee and came to within a few feet from me. Then he studied my face as if trying to figure out my thinking, or perhaps wondering how he could have misjudged me so.

"I was only..." I began but was immediately cut off.

"I know what you were only trying to do! Did we not agree that you would just teach the boys, Miss Eliza? Did we not? I hesitated to let you do even that, but I gave in. And, as is always the case every time our people do, your people take advantage of us! Why is that? Please tell me! Why are the white people so set on breaking every bit of trust and every treaty they've had with the red people? Explain it to me!" He was absolutely furious, and I was stunned into silence...until. "You're evil people! Every one of you! You—"

"Now you just wait one minute, Mr. Monday. I highly resent you clumping all of us together. We're not all evil, and we don't all break the trust that—"

"Then what would you say you just did?" he interrupted. "I set limitations with you, ones that we both agreed to."

"Yes, but—"

"No, 'buts', Miss Eliza! There are no 'buts'!" Paroh said loudly.

"Mr. Monday, please hear me out. Rose is trying to earn some money by making clothes for a woman in town, and, in order to make those clothes, she must be able to read the directions on the patterns she's using. She has to know arithmetic in order to follow proper measurements."

"Rose won't be making clothes for the white lady. Rose will not be going to town anymore. She stays here now!" he adamantly declared.

"Well, that's the most ridiculous thing I ever heard!" I said. It was the wrong thing to say.

Paroh's eyes narrowed at the insult, and then he lifted his left hand and pointed off to the east, toward Miami. "Go. Go now!"

I was frozen to the spot and my mind raced as I tried to figure out a way to calm him, to appease him. Then I remembered my earnings from the wreck! "Listen, Mr. Monday, I would actually be willing to pay you if—"

The look on his face stopped me mid-sentence. If I'd thought that telling him he was ridiculous was the wrong thing to say, this was even worse. Paroh's narrowed eyes flashed like glowing coals of fire. In a dangerously low, flat voice, he said, "Never come back to this place again. You are no longer welcome here."

Grabbing my books from the sewing table, I rushed past him and out of the chickee. Before mounting Sundae, I turned around and faced him, unable to stop myself from adding one last thing.

"You know, Mr. Monday, following time-honored traditions is fine when it helps your people. But when it comes from stubbornness and resentment toward a world you can't stop from changing, then you're only hurting the ones you claim to love. You're oppressing your own people, Mr. Monday, and you're causing them to suffer. They deserve far better than that."

Paroh said nothing more to me. Instead, he just stood there and watched me. I jammed my books into my saddlebag, got up on my horse and rode out of the camp. Tears blurred my vision so that I could hardly see, but I caught a glimpse of Rose turning her back on me as she disappeared within a hammock of gumbo limbo trees.

Chapter 16

Growing Pains

It was a good thing Sundae knew our route because she found her own way home. I cried the entire time, but not entirely out of frustration with the tribe's chief. Some of my tears were because of the way I'd handled everything. As soon as the words had come out of my mouth about paying him, I'd realized how offensive they sounded, but there was no taking them back. And now there was no going back.

We made our way along the Miami River slowly because I needed time to collect myself. Finally, we came upon the Stricklands' old home, not far from mine. It was a white two-story home, with a large porch that ran across the front and down both sides, just as ours did. And just like every home on the river, it faced the water to take advantage of the cooling breezes. Though Striker still lived there when he was on shore leave, the house had taken on a forlorn, faded look. In truth, there was nothing wrong with the structure. It was as solid and strong-looking as when Mr. and Mrs. Strickland had lived there. The paint still looked fresh, the steps didn't sag and the railing wasn't broken, but the home's spirit was. It was as though the house had withered and died when the family it had sheltered and protected had been stolen away by the sea. Where once there had been lamps brightly glowing in the windows of every room, now the windows remained dark, save for one or two if Striker was home. And, in some ways, the weak illumination of one light struggling to break the darkness was even more heartbreaking than no light at all.

From where I stood on the trail, looking at the back of the house, I could see the separate oversized shed that stood to the side and rear of the home. It had been used for the construction of the Stricklands' glade skiffs and small sail boats, but it, too, had been dark and locked up since their deaths. Today, however, both front and back doors of the building were open wide to allow a nice cross breeze to blow through. Shielding my eyes from the sun, I could just make out Striker standing at a workbench with his head and shoulders bent over something he was working on.

I nudged Sundae over to the river's edge and dismounted. While she drank, I splashed water over my tear-stained face, dried it with the back of my shirt sleeve and then released the bun of my hair and retied it into a ponytail. I didn't want my outside to reflect the way I felt on the inside. When Sundae was finished drinking, I took her reins and walked her over to Striker's shed.

"Knock, knock," I called softly, which painfully reminded me of saying the same thing as I stood at Rose's chickee. Striker turned toward me, peering out over the top of a pair of wire-rimmed glasses, and his expression went from surprise to a dimpled smile. "You don't need to knock," he said.

"When did you get glasses?" I smiled.

"When I couldn't think of any more excuses not to," he quipped. "C'mon in. Just give me a minute here. I'm about done." He turned back to his workbench and some small piece of metal he was working on.

"Don't hurry," I said as I looked around at the shelves, and the large variety of boat parts and pieces filling them. "This place has a lot more stored in it than last time I was here." What I didn't say was, *"when your parents were alive."*

"When I came home after working for Merrill-Stevens up in Jacksonville, I brought a lot of this with me," he said, glancing up toward one of the shelves. "It was pieces I'd bought over time to play around with—to test some new things."

There was a comfortable silence for a couple of minutes as he concentrated on his work, and I browsed around the large shed. Finally, he broke the silence. "So what's wrong?"

The question caught me off guard, so much so that I wasn't ready with some clever answer, or one that would downplay what had actually happened. Instead, I blurted out the truth: "I opened my big mouth at the Seminole village and the chief, Paroh Monday, told me I was never to come back. Ever!"

The tool in Striker's hand stilled and he threw his blond head back and laughed, which really irritated me. "Ah, Eliza," he finally said, turning around to face me. "Only you and the white generals from the Seminole wars could get those kind and patient people so blasted angry they'd ban you for the reminder of your days. Lord, woman, what did you go and do?"

His amusement at my expense did not make me want to cry my heart out to him. On the contrary. "Never mind," I said. I turned and walked out of the building and over to Sundae, who was busy nibbling the grass. Grabbing her reins, I got one foot in the stirrup, and started to pull myself up, but suddenly a firm grip on my forearm stopped me.

"Hold on, hold on," he said, trying to smother a laugh. "Just calm down. Why are you gettin' so mad at me? I didn't ban you from my shed. C'mon, let's go inside and have somethin' to drink and you can tell me all about it. I promise not to laugh…well, I promise to try not to." He smiled. "This is one story worth putting a carburetor on hold for." I had no idea what he was talking about, but I followed him up the back steps of his house and into the spacious kitchen. It was exactly as I remembered it.

Sitting down at the farmer's table, I looked around, both enjoying the familiarity of the room and feeling saddened by it as well. Light blue beadboard lined the bottom half of the walls, while the top half was still painted in the same pretty shade of cream. Curtains, adorned with tiny birds of all kinds and colors, and painstakingly made by Mae Strickland, still framed the window on the backdoor we'd just come through, as well as the large window above the deep enamel sink. Because the kitchen was at the back of the house, there was only a partial view of the river, but the enormous avocado tree that grew right outside the window helped keep the kitchen a little cooler during the day.

To the left of the back door was a large Boynton cast iron cook stove. Once, when my family had come over for dinner and my mother was admiring it, Jerry Strickland laughingly told us that when Mae insisted on bringing it down during their move from Leesburg, they'd had to leave a whole other room of furniture behind. He said that the poor horses pulling their wagon had known hell on Earth when they'd been tasked with hauling that enormously heavy stove all those miles.

I sighed as my mind moved on from that memory to others. How quickly things had changed, I thought, and how quickly a house of lightness and laugher had become one of darkness and pain.

"Warm tea or hot coffee?" Striker asked.

"Huh?" I replied, still shaking off the past.

"You want hot coffee—though it'll have to be black 'cuz I'm out of both milk and cream. Or warm tea since I don't have any ice."

"Oh, the tea'll be fine," I assured him.

He poured each of us a glass from an ironstone pitcher he kept in the iceless ice box, then pulled a chair back from the table, turned it around and straddled it. "Okay, so tell me," he said. "What happened with Paroh Monday?"

I started at the beginning and Striker rested his arms on top of the oval back of the chair. Then, as I got deeper into the story, he rested his chin on his arms, making me wonder if he was totally bored, or totally engrossed.

"Am I dragging this story out too long?" I asked, cringing slightly.

"Oh, no, Eliza. Remember, I've been out at sea with not much more to amuse me than Jim Altman's stupid jokes, or Owen's tales about where-all he's been. Although, I have to admit, some of those are pretty interesting."

At the mention of Owen's name, something immediately shifted in the room and between us. Silence hung heavy in the air for several seconds as we looked at each other. It was as though we each wanted to say to the other, "*So...what do* you *think of him?*" Suddenly, I felt I needed to be going.

"Anyway, that's about all that happened, which is quite enough, don't you think?" I forced a laugh, hoping to switch us back to that easiness we'd shared up until that moment.

"I think," Striker said as he rose up off the chair and then turned it around so that it was back in place at the table again, "you still haven't learned what the word 'patience' means." There was no laugher or lightness in his statement. He was being very serious with me.

"Eliza, many things in this world that are really worth waiting for take time. But you get your heart set on something, and there's no stopping you. You decide what's going to be, how and when. And that, pretty lady, is the fastest way of pushing something away—or someone. You've got to hear what people are saying to you. No, let me rephrase that: You need to *listen* to what people are saying to you. You need to listen to what it is *they* want and need. Instead, all you hear are your own wants and wishes. And because of that, in the end, you'll be hard put to get exactly what it is you're after—if you even know what it is."

I'd been glued to my chair as he'd lectured me, but I finally stood up and moved away from the table. "I never realized you saw me as such a shallow person, Striker," I said in a calm, controlled voice, though inside I felt anything but calm. I knew my hands were shaking in anger so I shoved them down into the pockets of my gauchos. He started to object to my statement but I held my hand up to stop him. "I'm glad we've cleared the air. I have to go now."

"Eliza, I'm sorry...If I—"

"It's fine," I said as I brushed past him. He reached out and grabbed my arm, but I flung it off. "Really, I have to go," I said one last time, before throwing open the kitchen door and running down the back steps.

I mounted Sundae, then pulled her reins around to turn her in the right direction while Striker stood at the door watching me go. When I hit my horse's rump with the ends of the reins, she took off for home. And as she did, I realized that I hadn't outgrown Striker; he had outgrown me.

Chapter 17

To Taste, Touch, and Smell

"I will *not* jump from this height!" I laughed. Owen was forty feet below but I instinctively took a couple of steps back from the edge of the platform, as if afraid that some phantom hands might shove me off.

"Then come on down to the lower platform and jump from there," he shouted, as he treaded water beneath Fowey Rocks lighthouse.

I climbed down the ladder, walked to the edge of the platform, and gracefully dove in—as gracefully as I could, anyway. I was wearing a navy-blue sailor-inspired bathing costume that was the fashion of the day. It was heavy and awkward with its ballooning skirt, but the costume covered me more modestly than my wreck diving outfit did, so I grudgingly wore it.

My dive cut through the water perfectly. I entered the underwater world, immediately aware of how quiet everything was even though the ocean was teeming with life. All manner of aquatic creatures had darted away from me when I startled them with my explosive entrance, but they quickly resumed their constant hunt for food. Off to my left was the reef that had caused so many casualties, but it was a safe haven for natives of the sea, so I swam over to it to see if I could spot any lobsters. Sure enough, just as I peeked into an opening between two sea fans, I saw a pair of lobsters looking back. Carefully reaching in, I grabbed one by the back, but before I could grab the other, it ducked further into the coral, so I surfaced with just the one. As I broke the water, I saw Owen swimming toward me, and even from a distance away, I could see relief replace the concern on his face.

"I thought you were drowning!" he said sharply. "You were under a long time."

I was surprised by the intensity in his voice. He looked and sounded so angry, though I figured it was because I'd frightened him. Still, it was a quickness to anger I'd not seen before. It was quite obvious he didn't like losing control of a situation.

"I'm sorry," I laughed uncomfortably. "You forget I can hold my breath for a good three minutes or so. It's all the wreck diving. Look!" I said, holding the lobster up high out of the water. "Your birthday dinner!"

"Perfect!" Owen laughed, delight replacing the anger on his face. "And what will you be eating?" He carefully took the lobster from me.

"Its mate," I replied, relieved that his good humor had returned. Then I dove under the water again to try to catch the other one.

An hour later, we had a large pot of water boiling on the stove, and three lobsters turning bright red within. Corn steamed on top of them, and as they cooked, I made coleslaw. Sitting on top of the ice box, waiting to officially celebrate Owen's thirtieth birthday, was an orange cake I'd baked back home. One side was slightly flattened from sailing out to Fowey, but no one would mind.

Jim Altman was joining us for dinner, though he'd been up in the tower all morning cleaning the Fresnel lens. Given the time he'd stayed up there, the powerful lens was probably cleaner than it'd ever been, but he'd worked on it far longer than necessary in order to afford us some privacy. I liked Jim, and never minded his being there when I came out for a visit; however, I tried to plan my trips during the time Striker was on shore leave. Owen had asked me if I was avoiding him, and I simply explained that Striker and I bumped heads at times and that I didn't enjoy being around him any more than I had to. As vague an answer as it was, it seemed to satisfy Owen's curiosity and he never asked again. I never mentioned the fact that Striker and I had courted, and I doubted Striker had ever said a word about it either. Owen never mentioned it, anyway. That was fine with me. It wasn't something I felt I needed to discuss with him. That chapter was over.

After dinner, Owen and I sat outside the quarters. It was the middle of the afternoon, and the sun was high and hot, so we sat in the shade of the building and enjoyed the cool breeze off the water.

"Nice, isn't it?" I said, closing my eyes to the brightness of the sea and relaxing in one of several Adirondack chairs.

"It is," Owen replied. He was sitting on my left, and I felt him reach for my hand, but instead of simply holding it, he gently pulled. "Come here," he said. "I want to talk to you."

I could hear the seriousness in his voice, and thinking something was wrong, I quickly moved over to his chair. "You look so serious. Has something happened?"

"Not yet" —he smiled— "though I'm hoping it will." He placed his large hand behind my head and drew my mouth down to his. Owen tasted of the sea, and smelled like the wind and the sun. If I could have absorbed him fully into me, I would have.

Finally, he drew back from me, and his steel-gray eyes locked on mine. "I love you." The three words, spilled forth in his deep, sensual voice, made chills run through my body. On a day when the temperature was well into the eighties, my body's response echoed what my heart and mind already knew: I wanted this man, in every way.

"Marry me, Eliza. Marry me and I'll love you deeply and thoroughly, always."

I smiled at his choice of words for they reminded me of the first time we'd kissed.

Then a thought suddenly occurred to me. "I'm not allowed to live out here, Owen," I reminded him. "The government doesn't want a keeper's family living at an offshore light. You know that."

"I know." He smiled. "But I'm way ahead of you. I put in a request to be transferred to the light down in Key West. It's on land, and when a light is on land, the government has no objection to the family living there, too."

"Key West?" I asked, startled. Not only had this man been thinking about marrying me, but he was also assuming my answer would be 'yes' and preparing for it. "But what if the transfer doesn't come through? We could wait forever."

"True. But I'm not willing to wait for *you* forever. If I don't get an appointment to the Key West light within a certain amount of time, or even one of the other onshore lights, then I'll figure something else out. I've made investments over the years."

"Investments?" I asked. This was the first time he'd mentioned such. "Like what?"

"Eliza, when a man is out to sea for a long while, he doesn't have much to spend money on," he explained. "I've been able to put quite a bit away. We'd have more than enough to live on until I figure out what else I'd want to do, but the way Miami is growing—and the Keys, too, once the railroad connects them all—I might just go ahead and invest in more land. But, did I hear you right when you said *we* could wait forever? Are you—"

I stopped him before he could finish his question. "Yes, I'm going to marry you, Owen." I smiled. "I'll marry you," I repeated in a breathy whisper as I laid my head down on his chest.

"Ah, Eliza, you've made me one very happy man." I could hear the smile in his voice. "Very happy," he repeated softly as he began stroking my hair. Lying against him, I could hear his heart beating rapidly, and I knew that its rhythm matched mine. *Soon enough*, I thought, *our bodies will be matching each other's rhythm, as well, and I have no doubt that we'll be perfectly in sync in that way, too.* Smiling, I inhaled the smell of Owen's skin once again before he slid over on the chair and pulled me up next to him so that I was lying beside him. He turned onto his side and then rose up enough so that his weight was resting on his right elbow. Gazing down at me, he lifted his left hand to my face and gently followed the lines of it with his fingertips, then lightly ran them over my lips. "God, you're beautiful," he whispered. Then nothing more was said for our mouths were far too busy to talk.

Chapter 18

The Bounty of Land and Sea

Owen came into town two days after asking me for my hand in marriage, and did the gentlemanly thing by properly asking my father for it, as well. When Papa gave us his blessing, Owen asked my mother and me to join them on the veranda, and then he took a small wine-colored velvet box out of his trousers' pocket and lifted the lid, revealing an exquisite emerald-cut ruby ring nestled within. Surrounding the large bright red stone were tiny round diamonds. The gold band was a deep bronzy yellow, indicating the piece was as old as it was valuable. Taking it from the box, Owen slid it on my finger. It was a little large, but not knowing what size ring I wore, he'd had no adjustments made on it. "We'll take it to the jewelers tomorrow," he said. "I want the world to know you're taken."

"With a ring like that," Papa teased, "people will see that she's spoken for from a mile away." Seeing how happy Owen made me brought my parents happiness, too, though I could detect a certain sadness they were undoubtedly feeling now that their youngest was about to fly the nest.

Owen's week in town happened to coincide with a visit from Uncle James. We rarely saw Mama's brother these days for he was busy building Flagler's hotel on Key Largo, but Uncle James was also in the midst of drawing up the architectural blueprints for a large home he wanted to build for himself there. It never failed to amaze me how much he and Mama looked alike, especially with their red hair and brown eyes. But they didn't just share the same looks. They also shared a special bond. Over the years, he and Papa had grown very close, too, so every visit from my uncle was highly anticipated and greatly enjoyed by everyone.

Uncle James had traveled up to Miami via steamboat, and though he enjoyed the beautiful scenery as he traveled along the chain of islands, the trip took far longer than traveling by rail would.

"I'll tell y'all," my uncle said after he swallowed another bite from his second helping of Mama's good country fried steak. "Leisurely travel on the great American steamboat is all well 'n good if time isn't an issue, or if one just wants to sightsee. But for the business man, or for anyone who simply wants a more efficient way of getting from point A to point B, the railroad is the only way to go.

Owen had joined us for dinner, and he and my uncle seemed to hit if off immediately. "How do you think the railroad will fare once the automobile picks up in popularity and becomes affordable for everyone?" Owen asked.

"Frankly, I think automobiles will become the most popular way to travel," my uncle replied. "But it'll take a while for that to happen. Can you imagine the number of roads that'll have to be put in, in order to make purchasing an automobile worthwhile? It's mind boggling!"

"Maybe I should invest in concrete," Owen laughed.

"Not such a bad idea," my uncle said with a smile. "However, buying stock in the Florida East Coast Railway, or land along the train's route in South Florida is pretty much guaranteed to bring about a nice return on one's investment. Just the number of folks who are down here working on the railroad alone is in the thousands. And I'd be willing to bet most of them will find other work down here once the line's been laid, but that's gonna take a long while to finish. Those folks need places to live, which means land is becoming a valuable commodity. And it's not just workers who are putting money into our economy and our pockets. There's a lot more folks coming down for vacation, and because of the trains, the tourists aren't limited to just the well-to-do anymore. Land along the tracks is gold."

"Actually, I did—invest, I mean," Owen clarified. "Some months back."

I remembered he'd told me he'd made investments the day he'd asked me to marry him, but I'd been far too distracted by the proposal to be interested in what those investments were. Now I was more than curious to hear more. My future would be affected by any investments he made.

"I knew I'd heard your name somewhere!" Uncle James exclaimed, snapping his fingers as he did. "Did you invest in the Florida East Coast Railway, specifically the hotel I'm involved in?"

"No, no," Owen laughed. "Though I should have. I invested through a small company out of New York. As far as the Keys go, we have just a small amount of property on Marathon."

Uncle James let out a long, low whistle. "That's about halfway down the chain of Keys. It's a mighty nice spot to own some land." He was obviously impressed.

"Eliza," my uncle said, turning his attention to me. "You have found yourself a very foresighted man. He knows a good thing when he sees it."

"That I do," Owen softly agreed as his intense gray eyes met mine. "That I do."

"Once your investments start paying off, I guess you'll give up life as a light keeper," my uncle said.

"Oh, I don't know. Maybe not," Owen replied, turning away from me to answer him.

"Why in heaven's name not?" My uncle looked completely baffled.

"Someone's gotta be up in that tower watching over the sea, as well as the land. And since I own a small percentage of the latter, who better?" He smiled.

"Who better, indeed," my father said quietly, lifting his glass to toast the man.

Chapter 19

Wise Words

Owen received an appointment to become the keeper at the land-based Key West light a week after having dinner with my parents and Uncle James. I was amazed it happened so fast, but as my ambitious fiancé explained, the present keeper was a single man, and since Owen wouldn't be able to take me to an offshore light like Fowey, the Key West keeper had graciously agreed to switch with him. Suddenly, our plans for the future had to be undertaken immediately, and the first order of business was planning a wedding.

We decided on the date of October 27th, which was only six weeks away. During that time, Mama and I worked on my wedding trousseau, including a beautiful cream-colored satin wedding gown. There wasn't much frill to it, which I preferred; it had a streamlined fit instead, with an elegant draping neckline. The veil I would wear was shorter in length than most veils, only reaching the middle of my back. I would wear my hair in a low bun, and the veil would be attached to it by a small comb. Preparing my trousseau took less time than it otherwise would have because I already owned plenty of clothes, and what I didn't already have, I could easily buy off the rack at Burdine's. The kind retailer was happy for me and my new life ahead, though I knew he hated to lose me as an employee. With the little time I had left at home, I spent a good portion of it working at the store, giving Mr. Burdine ample time to find the right individual to take my place.

The small wedding ceremony would take place at the Presbyterian Church, followed by an equally small reception at the Royal Palm Hotel. Afterward, Owen and I would stay the night there, then take a steamboat down to Key West the following morning. After settling in for a time and learning what was required of a keeper's wife, I hoped to teach at one of the two schools on the large island.

One morning, about four weeks before the wedding, I was standing in front of Burdine's, inspecting the window display, when I heard a familiar voice call my name from behind me. Turning around, I found Paroh Monday standing there. Seeing the dignified man in the plaid scarf turban, long red and black tunic, and buckskin breeches warmed my heart for a second before I remembered that I was mad at him.

"Mr. Monday," I said, giving him a curt nod.

"Miss Harjo," he said, returning the nod, as well. "You making sure that window's clean enough so that everyone can get a good look at the many temptations?" He smiled a mischievous little grin, and his dark eyes twinkled.

"I guess that's one way of looking at it." I grudgingly smiled in response.

"Clean as you make those windows, people will be looking at it all real good." His smile broadened.

I laughed in spite of myself, and then waited, unsure where this was going.

Paroh's smile softened, and he suddenly looked quite humble, almost contrite. "Miss Eliza, sometimes a man can be very foolish when he's told he's wrong about something, especially when the one doing the telling is a woman."

I started to say something to the effect that it shouldn't matter who does the telling, but he held his hand up to stop me. "Sometimes, you need to wait to hear a full sentence instead of a half," he said gently.

As much as I hated to admit it, he was right.

"Sometimes," he continued, "I try to honor the old ones and their ways so much that it dishonors the young ones. Things are changing; new ways are required now. In the end, it causes much division among a people whose greatest defense is their unity. Would you consider coming back again to teach my people?"

"I'm going to be married in a few weeks and then I'm leaving for Key West, Mr. Monday," I said. A couple of seconds of silence passed with neither of us saying anything. He looked as though he was turning to leave, but before he could, I blurted out, "But, I could come out until then." Unable to stop myself, I asked, "Can the girls learn the lessons, too?"

"While I see that the world changes, I also see that not everything or *everyone* in it does." He shook his head, but he smiled as he did so. "Yes, Eliza, the girls can learn, too," he acquiesced.

I was absolutely shocked that he'd agreed to my request, and my first response was to throw my arms around him and hug him, but I held myself in check. However, I had to know why he was relenting. "Was it my offer of money that changed your mind, Mr. Monday?"

"No, woman with spirit like fire," he said softly. "It was your words." With that, he turned and mounted his magnificent dark gray stallion, then set off down the dirt street, walking slowly and sitting ramrod-straight in his saddle, looking to all the world like the chief that he was.

Chapter 20

An End to More than a Day

I was making my way back home along the river after finishing up a long day. I'd worked for Mr. Burdine in the morning, followed by an afternoon of lessons at the village. Now, as Sundae and I ambled along, I was thinking about my upcoming wedding in less than three weeks, and the fact that Dylan was able to come home for it.

Mama and Papa had gone down to the Keys on their trawler, the *Deep Secrets*, and their first stop was at the Port of Entry in Key West. Papa needed to have some things appraised and sold from a small wreck that he'd been working off Fowey. The wind had caught the ship and slammed it against the reef. Fortunately, the crew had all made it ashore and was able to recover most of their cargo of hides, ginger and brandy after Papa helped parbuckle the ship. In payment, he was given a barrel of brandy, seven hides, and half-dozen chamber pots. We'd laughed about the latter, but, as my mother was quick to point out, they'd bring in money that was just as good and green as any other cargo. After my parents cashed in on their salvage, they'd pick up my brother at Alligator Reef lighthouse. Dylan had worked plenty of overtime while at Fowey, due to the shortage of keepers, and was finally able to take a much-needed vacation. From Alligator, they would return home for the wedding.

I was sailing down to Fowey in the morning, which was Saturday, to spend the day with Owen, and I was bringing plenty of cleaning supplies with me. Though part of a lighthouse keeper's daily chores was cleaning and maintaining the entire facility, the men's housekeeping left much to be desired. The new keeper from Key West would be coming in within the next couple of weeks, and, as a way of thanking him for switching places with Owen, I decided to give the quarters a good scrub down. Besides, I needed something to keep me busy since Mr. Burdine had started my replacement the day before, and I didn't teach at the village on the weekend.

The late afternoon was giving way to dusk and as I got closer to home, I could see the lights beginning to shine out of the windows of the few homes along the way, as well as in the massive Royal Palm Hotel down at the river's mouth. Just a ways down from me was the Strickland home, and I could see light emanating from the open shed door. Striker was in.

I hadn't seen him since we'd talked in his kitchen, and that was intentional. Our relationship was strained, at best. Somewhere along the line, we seemed to have lost the ability to be friends. I'd been busy with wedding plans, and preparing for my new life with Owen, while wrapping up my old life in Miami, which didn't leave me much time for socializing. But, as I rode closer to Striker's shed, I knew I needed to say something to him, to neatly tie up and put away that part of my life. So, I pulled Sundae's reins to the right and rode up to the door.

Striker was hunched over his workbench, working on something that his body blocked from my view. But what wasn't blocked from my view was the sleek, unusual boat sitting on a trailer in the middle of his shed. The boat had no masts or sails. Instead, there was a motor with a three-pronged propeller positioned in the center of the craft.

"Striker," I said almost reverently. "You've built a motor boat."

My sudden intrusion startled him, and he dropped whatever was in his hand; the loud bang as it hit the workbench startled me.

"Hell, woman, you scared the bejeezus outta me!" he laughed, holding his hand to his rapidly beating heart.

"And you did me," I laughingly countered.

Then the room grew quiet as we stopped laughing and just looked at each other.

"It's good to see you," Striker said, not moving from his stool.

"It's good to see you, too," I said before turning my attention back to the boat. "It's beautiful, Striker," I marveled. "How long have you been working on it? I'm...well...I'm just amazed."

"Don't be. It's far from perfect." He pushed himself off the stool and walked over to the boat as he wiped his hands on a rag. "I've been doing some experimenting, and a lot of reading." He nodded toward a stack of magazines and manuals spread across a small table in the corner nearest to me. "The French are way ahead of everyone else in the field of motor boats right now, and I'm learning from their successes, and everyone else's mistakes, including my own."

"How long before she's ready?" I asked, running my hand along the smooth lines of her starboard side.

"Probably never," he laughed. Then, "Honestly, Eliza, I've just been tinkering around with it. It's something to do when I'm home. Anyway, enough about that," he said, obviously wanting to change the subject. His days of boat building—at least from a serious standpoint—were over as far as he was concerned.

"So, how many days to the big event?" He smiled, though it didn't quite reach his eyes—eyes that couldn't seem to meet mine.

"Just a little over two weeks," I replied, finding something else in the room to look at. "Striker...I'm sorry I didn't invite you to the wedding." I turned to face him. "We just invited immediate family. Owen's mother is the only one of his parents still living, but she's ill and unable to travel from Washington State. So, that just leaves my family."

"It's fine, Eliza," Striker interrupted, smiling softly. "I have to be at Fowey, anyway. And even if I didn't, I...well...it's just better the way you planned it. So you're going to Key West right after, I hear," he said, moving on to another subject, though this one didn't feel any more comfortable than the last.

"Yeah, we'll go right after our wedding night..." This was definitely not the conversation I wanted to have. "Striker, I have to get going. Sundae needs to be fed and—"

"And you have a new life to start," he finished. Striker walked up to me, looked me directly in the eye and asked me if I was sure this was going to make me happy. When I assured him that it would, he gently cupped my shoulders, leaned in and kissed me softly on my forehead. "May the wind be always at your back," he said, quoting part of an old Irish blessing, one that was particularly significant to anyone who sailed the seas.

Without another word, I turned and walked away.

Chapter 21

More than Enough

The small sailboat I'd borrowed from our neighbor, Gus Mueller, struggled to make any headway in the light breeze. Papa and Mama had taken the trawler to the Keys a couple of days before, and our larger sailboat, the *Eve of Salvation,* was too much to handle by myself. When I finally got close to Fowey, I saw Owen hurry down the steps to the dock, ready to catch the boat lines to tie the craft to the pilings.

"Lack of wind held you up, didn't it?" He smiled knowingly.

"One of these days, I'll be zipping around these waters in a motor boat," I replied as I handed him a bucket filled with cleaning supplies, and then a basket of food for our dinner.

"The engines are too unpredictable," he said as he reached a hand down to pull me up from the boat.

"You look ready to work," he laughed, assessing my outfit from head to toe. I had on an old pair of canvas trousers that had paint spattered all over them from the numerous times we'd painted our boats, and the denim shirt I wore wasn't much better.

"Well," I laughed, looking down at my clothing. "I could have worn a lovely little dress, complete with bustle and parasol, which would have allowed me to do nothing more than sit and look pretty for you. Or wear this and leave you with fresh, clean living quarters at the day's end—quarters you'll be proud to turn over to Lincoln Nodd." I'd learned the new keeper's name just this past week. "With a name like that, I envision a tall, stately watcher of the seas, complete with well-manicured goatee and a full-bent mahogany pipe."

Owen laughed. "I hate to disappoint you, but I've met the man before and he's not much bigger than you are, and is missing a couple of teeth and a finger or two from his left hand."

"How in the world did he lose his fingers? Please tell me it was something as heroic as pulling a shipwreck survivor from the jaws of a shark."

"Again, I hate to ruin that Jane Eyre-worthy picture you've created, but he lost his fingers in a wood chipper when he was just a kid on a farm in Oklahoma."

"Ah, well, a girl has a right to dream," I said in a breathy voice. "But, enough dreaming," I said firmly. "I have a meeting with dirt and grime."

"Ladies first," he said, bowing slightly and sweeping his arm out in front of him to allow me to go first up the steps.

Jim Altman was up in the lantern room cleaning the lens and windows, and Owen needed to get back to work on his log book. But before he could retreat to the quiet of his bedroom to work on the daily entries, I asked him to get a large pot of water going on the stove. While I waited for the water to boil, I started on the outhouse, but other than scrubbing the floor with a stiff brush and soapy water, along with the board that acted as a seat, there was nothing more to be done. Going back into the quarters, I stripped all of the beds, and stuck the first set of sheets into the pot of water. After stirring them with a paddle, I let them boil for a few minutes before using the paddle to carefully lift them out and drop them into a basket by the stove. Then I hung them on the clothesline to dry in the fresh air and sunshine. When I returned to the kitchen to wash the rest of the sheets, I found Jim sitting at the table with a folder of papers spread out before him.

"Ah, Eliza, I bet I'm in your way here. Just give me a minute to move my mess."

"Don't be silly, Jim. Stay where you are," I assured him. "Let me get these sheets on to boil, then I'll grab a cup of coffee and join you—unless I'll be in your way, of course."

"Gal as pretty as you are could never be in my way," the good-natured keeper replied.

After putting the rest of the sheets in the pot, I grabbed a cup and the coffee pot, then sat down at the table. As I topped off Jim's coffee, I glanced at the papers he'd been reading. The documents were very official looking, but they looked different from the usual ones the keepers were required to regularly fill out.

"Whatcha workin' on?" I asked before carefully taking a sip of the scalding hot liquid.

"Oh, just this F.L.E.A.C. stuff," Jim said, as though that would explain it all. "Owen finally convinced me to invest in the company. Lord, God, but that man o' yours won't take no for an answer," he laughed, shaking his head. "Anyway, looks like you and I are gonna be partners—that is if I can ever figure out what all of this legal mumbo jumbo means." He shook his head again before taking a sip of his own coffee.

I was at a complete loss as to what he was talking about. "The F.L.—what, Jim?"

"You know; the Florida Land Expansion and Acquisition Corporation," Jim replied. "Bless the Dawes Act," he beamed. "Though I'm sure the Seminoles would replace the word 'bless' with 'damn.'" Jim laughed at his small attempt at a joke.

"May I?" I asked, reaching over and pulling the folder to me before Jim could object.

Inside were about a half dozen bills of sale, as well as additional legal paperwork pertaining to them. Every purchase was for a large parcel of land in Florida, and each bill of sale contained the same identical sentence in legal description: "*...as authorized under the amended Dawes Act of 1905.*" Rifling through the documents, I found what I was looking for, a copy of the amended Dawes Act itself. Quickly scanning what that was, I saw that the original act gave individual Indians the right to own one hundred and sixty acres. However, the amendment declared that any land left unclaimed could be purchased by others—whites included. My stomach dropped. Included was a map of each parcel of land that the F.L.E.A.C. had purchased, and one of them was for the land that Paroh's tribe lived on but in all likelihood had never legally claimed. All together, over ten thousand acres of Everglades land had been purchased by this group, and, according to the purchasing agreement's description:*...for the primary purpose of bettering the land through large monetary investments, as well as large-scale projects of development that can only occur through an aggressive rerouting (or draining) of the overabundance of water presently contained within the property.*

At the bottom of every legal document was a set of signatures, and when I saw them, I knew that I'd be sick. Quickly going back to a page I'd seen moments before with the F.L.E.A.C. letterhead on it, I saw that the company's address was in New York. Below the address were the names of the company's officers and board members and they matched the names signed on every bill of sale. Among them were: Owen Perry, Vice President; Ezra Asher, Treasurer; and Adam Wilson, Board Member.

Ezra Asher and Adam Wilson? I thought. *Owen is involved with Ezra? And Adam is involved with them both?* My mind was reeling.

I glanced up at Jim and saw that he was watching me. He said nothing, but looked very ill at ease. If the look on my face mirrored the anger building inside of me, Jim was starting to realize that he'd somehow opened Pandora's box.

"Eliza, what are you doing?" Owen was standing at the kitchen door, and though his voice was calm, it was flat and somehow chilling. Neither Jim nor I moved. We were frozen in place by the anger that was clearly etched into Owen's face.

"I—I was just saying to Eliza here that we're gonna be partners 'n all," Jim said, finally finding his voice and the legs to get up out of his chair. "But you can do a better job of explaining than I can." He laughed nervously. "'Sides, I gotta get back to that lens. Damn smudges and…" His voice trailed off as he quickly rushed past Owen and out of the room.

Owen's eyes had remained glued on me since he'd appeared at the door, and as soon as Jim was gone, I rose up from my chair, holding the map of the Seminole village land out to him with a shaking hand.

"What have you done?" I whispered hoarsely. My mouth was so dry I could barely speak.

Owen crossed the room in two strides and snatched the paper from my hand. "This has absolutely nothing to do with—"

"It has *everything* to do with me!" I countered. "I care deeply for these people you're running off."

"I'm not running them off, Eliza! They've made their own beds. What you don't pay for you lose. It's as simple as that." Owen's voice grew louder.

"I'm not gonna let you do it, Owen!" My voice nearly matched his in volume. I was angrier than I'd ever been in my life. "I swear on a stack of Bibles that I'll do whatever I need to do to stop this—to stop you! How dare—."

Before I could finish, he viciously backhanded me across the left side of my face. Immediately, there was a ringing in my ears from the blow. I staggered sideways and stumbled against the table, which kept me from falling to the floor. Owen grabbed my arm and pulled me back to him so that we were face to face, just inches from each other's nose. "Don't you *ever* try to interfere—"

Before he could finish, I yanked my arm free from his painful grasp and ran through the kitchen door, and out of the keeper's quarters. Making my way down both sets of ladders, I fearfully watched for Owen to pursue me, but he didn't. I reached the dock and struggled to untie the lines holding my sailboat to the pilings for my hands were shaking badly. As I worked at the knots, I kept looking back at the ladders to confirm that I wasn't being pursued. With no sign of Owen there, I looked up and saw that he was watching me from the railing on the second platform. The sun was in my eyes so I wasn't able to see his face clearly, but the image of him so full of rage just moments before was enough to last a lifetime.

Chapter 22

The Smell of the Wind

The breeze had picked up substantially. So much so that I made it home in a third of the time it'd taken me to get to Fowey. After returning the boat to Gus's dock, I ran back down to ours, saddled up Sundae, and headed to the village to see Paroh. I felt sure he didn't know about the sale of his land or he would have said something to me about it. What I didn't know was how long the tribe had before they'd have to vacate it.

As we hurried along the river, I kept thinking about the fact that Owen, Ezra, and Adam were in business together. After what I'd experienced with Ezra, and now Owen, that didn't surprise me. But *Adam*? He'd always seemed so good and sweet! Now I knew there was a whole other side of him. As I rode along, trying to connect the dots, to figure out when and under what circumstances they'd joined forces, I realized there were just too many things I didn't know to be able to make all of the connections.

I stopped at our usual low spot on the bank of the river to let Sundae get a drink, and to wash some of the tears and grit off my face. Looking at my reflection in the water, I saw the swollen, bruised area at the corner of my left eye and upper cheekbone, but there was nothing that could be done for it now. Remounting Sundae, I hurried on to the village.

When I got there, people were busy working on projects or chores, and though most of them stopped for a moment to greet me, they returned to their work immediately. Dismounting, I saw Rose coming toward me, smiling as usual but also looking a little surprised to see me. She knew my schedule well, and I was never there on the weekend.

"Eliza, you come on extra day!"

"Yes," I said, smiling, "but no lessons today. Is Paroh here?" I asked, looking toward his chickee but not seeing him. Rose could undoubtedly hear the tension in my voice.

"Yes," she said quietly and I saw her look at my bruised face. "He just over at creek fishing for mud fish. I get him. Wait in his house, Eliza. He want you to. I bring you cool drink…and salve," she said, tapping her face in the same area I was injured.

After tying Sundae to a cabbage palm, I stepped up into Paroh's chickee, glad to be out of the sun, and away from the others. I hadn't been there for more than several minutes when Paroh came in with Rose directly behind him. He looked at me hard and immediately his eyes went to my injury; then he patiently waited while Rose applied the salve. As soon as she was done, she left.

"Who did that?" Paroh said, lifting his chin slightly toward the battered side of my face.

"Owen. Owen Perry. The man I was going to marry," I answered without hesitation.

"Why?"

"Because I found out about something he didn't want me to—something concerning this village, Paroh." My mouth was bone dry. The chief waited as I took a long drink of the cool coconut milk Rose had left for me. I continued. "A company he's a part of has bought this land. Y'all are going to be forced to leave it—and probably very soon. They're going to dredge it. I'm sorry. So sorry," I repeated softly.

Rather than looking surprised or upset, Paroh just seemed resigned. "It's not the first time," he said, shaking his head. "We're good at moving," he added, smiling a small smile. "Don't look so surprised." He correctly read the look on my face. "I figured it was just a matter of time.

"The white man's greed is like a cancer, Eliza. It takes and destroys, and then goes after more. I know your mama's white, but understand that my hard words are not about her. Your mother's heart is nothing like the others. She has the heart of a warrior, and I can see that her daughter has one, too. You have the heart of both your mother *and* your father. You're strong like the Seminole," he said. "And just like the Seminole," Paroh went on, walking over to me. "you'll survive this time in your life, too." He lifted my chin with his thumb and index finger, and turned my face toward the right so that he could see the left side more clearly. "You know this, yes?"

"Yes," I whispered. "I do. But, what about you?" I turned my face back to look him in the eye. "Where will you take your people?"

"Don't know yet, but as far away from those Earth-eating machines as we can go."

A strong wind blew through the chickee, causing the various items hanging from the roof beams to clank and clack against each other as though in protest at being disturbed. There was something different about this wind, though, something wild and foreboding. Turning toward the front of the chickee, I walked over to the edge of it and inhaled deeply. Then again. "Do you smell it?" I asked the chief as he walked up beside me, inhaling deeply, as well. "Oh, my God," I whispered. "Do you smell that?"

"Big wind comes. Smells like fish," Paroh confirmed.

A massive storm was approaching from the east, off the Atlantic, and it was pushing the smell of the sea ahead of its arrival like some kind of macabre calling card. On such short notice, we had little time to properly prepare, or brace ourselves for the chaos that was about to ensue.

"Stay here with us, Eliza," Paroh urged. "It's far safer than your home by the water."

Staying with the Seminoles meant riding out the storm in the mangroves, lashed to one of the trees. It was the Seminoles' best line of defense because the *chickees* offered nothing in the way of protection and would be carried off with the first squall. The mangrove trees were rooted deeply, though, so if a person could stay attached to one, and do so without being drowned, then they stood a good chance of surviving the storm. But I just wanted to be home, even if it was on the water.

"I have to go," I said, panic starting to edge its way into my voice. "I need to get home."

"Stay safe, little warrior," Paroh said as I jumped from the chickee.

Running over to Sundae, I quickly mounted her and could feel her quivering beneath me. She knew that a storm was approaching. And we both knew we didn't have much time.

Chapter 23

Landfall

Sundae and I made our way home along the river, but riding into the wind made the going slower. The sawgrass and smaller vegetation was flattened by the force, making it look as though the plants were bowing down in servitude, while trees all around us thrashed wildly. When a stronger gust would come, the crowns of the palm trees would be pushed over as if by a mighty hand. Warily eyeing the coconuts swinging in the fronds, I knew it was just a matter of time before they became as deadly as cannon balls.

When I finally rode into my yard, I saw that the windows of the house were wide open, and nothing had been secured or brought inside. There'd been no one home to do it. We passed the shed, which was where I would put Sundae, but it hadn't been cleaned out to make room for her. I would do that as soon as I secured the house. After tying her to an avocado tree on the west side of the house, out of the wind, I ran up the porch steps and pulled open the screen door, but the wind caught it and ripped it away from me, smashing it against the porch wall. Bracing it open with a doorstop, I dragged the rocking chairs and small table off the porch and into the living room, and then I ran from room to room lowering the windows. As I did, I removed things that were breakable or could become projectiles from the tops of tables, dressers and such, and placed them on the floor against the wall, or in closets or drawers. All the while, I listened to the wind rising outside, and the creaking and breaking of things fighting to resist it. After securing what I could, I ran back outside and began closing the colonial shutters on every window, saying a silent word of thanks that our home was only a single-story, as opposed to Striker's, which was…

Striker! If he was home, I could ride the storm out with him! The last thing I wanted to do was sit by myself through the night, watching the ceiling for the spreading of water stains, or, worse still, watching as the roof peeled back like the top of a sardine can.

After working my way around the house, I hurried back to Sundae, and as I did, the first real rain squall hit. The poor horse was very agitated and when I mounted her, she instinctively took off toward the west, away from the storm, which also happened to be in the direction of Striker's house. We ran through the backyards of several homes, and once we got to his, I saw that the shutters on the windows had already been closed. Pulling the reins to the left, I guided Sundae over to his shed, lifted the heavy wooden latch that kept the doors firmly shut, and then led her inside. When I closed the door behind me, I heard another horse whinny. Peering into the darkness, I was thankful to see Striker's horse, Odie, standing in the back. He'd be company for Sundae, and was quite a bit calmer than she was. The solidly constructed slash pine and cement building greatly muffled the noise outside, and I hoped that would help calm Sundae as well. Pulling carrots from my pocket that I'd grabbed on my way out of the house, I fed them to both horses and said a quick prayer asking God to take care of them.

Pushing the shed door open took some effort. The wind was determined to keep me contained in the building. Once outside, I made my way to Striker's kitchen door, but it was locked. Pounding and shouting as loudly as I could to be heard above the wind, I got no answer, so I started to move around to the front of the house. Suddenly, the kitchen door was pulled open and Striker was standing there.

"Eliza? What the hell...?" I saw his mouth form the words, but the wind swept the sound away. Grabbing me by my forearm, he quickly pulled me inside and then locked the door securely behind me.

The sudden quiet of the kitchen was in stark contrast to the roar outside, and it was a safe and welcoming oasis. Oil lamps had been lit, casting a warm golden glow over the room, and the smell of coffee on the stove was a comfort and a reminder of calmer times in a calmer world. It felt good to be with someone.

"Thank God you're home," I said as I sat down at the kitchen table and accepted a dish towel Striker handed me so that I could dry my face. He poured us each a cup of coffee, then grabbed a lamp and joined me at the table.

"Where are your folks? I saw the trawler was gone, but I figured they'd be back and you'd be with 'em, so I—"

He stopped mid-sentence, softly grabbed my chin and turned my face so that he could see the left side of it. Holding the lamp up, he inspected my bruises.

"Who did it?" he asked in a flat voice, setting the lamp down on the table. "Who?" he repeated a little more forcefully.

"Owen," I whispered.

"When?"

"This morning. I found out he's involved in a company that's dredging the land out there. And so is Adam Wilson, and that wrecker, Ezra Asher. Did you know they were involved in a company acquiring land?"

"It's the first I've heard of it," Striker replied tightly. It was obvious he was trying to keep his anger under control. "Adam and Owen never talked to me about any business that didn't involve the lighthouse. And as far as this Ezra guy is concerned, I don't know him. I've heard that he's done some salvaging around here, but other than that, I don't know anything about him. Who is he?"

"I don't know much about him either," I said, looking down at the damp dish towel I held in my hands. Without realizing it, I'd been wringing it. Folding it, I set it aside and looked up at Striker. "I don't want to talk about this right now, okay? I just need to be quiet for a little while, so would it be all right if we dropped the subject for the time being?"

"Just for now," he replied.

As we sat there looking at each other, I heard something bang sharply against the front of the house. It startled me, making me jump slightly. Even though we were as closed off from the storm as we could possibly be, I could hear the hurricane building in intensity outside. At times, the shrieking wind sounded like a group of wailing women as all manner of things were hurled around, slamming against the house's walls and roof as though demanding entry.

"How hard you figure it's blowin'?" I asked, looking up at the ceiling, willing it to stay intact. Fortunately, there was another floor above us, offering that much more protection between us and the deadly force outside.

"I'd guess about ninety or so. This thing really came in fast." A bang against the side of the house was followed by a tremendous burst of rain that pounded out a cadence on the tin roof.

"My folks took the trawler to the Keys day before yesterday," I said, taking my eyes off the ceiling and glancing over at Striker. I was hoping he'd make me feel better by assuring me they were fine.

"Damn," Striker whispered.

"What?" I cried. "*What?*"

"They're getting the brunt of the storm down there. We're just gettin' a glancing blow. The barometer kept falling this morning so I went over to the trading post to get any news that was coming in. They'd gotten wires saying that warnings had gone up in Miami, as well as in the Keys. I called Lincoln Nodd, down at the Key West light, and he said they're going to get hit hard."

Seeing how panic-stricken I must have looked, he added, "But your parents aren't stupid, and they'll get in before this thing hits."

"You know as well as I do that there's hardly any place to 'get in' to down there, Striker! There's nothin' but mangroves, low islands, and open water. They couldn't be in a worse place! And then there's Dylan at Alligator Reef light, and Uncle James is in Key Largo."

"Listen, Eliza—they'll all know what to do. As far as your parents go, they're probably in Key West, or at the light with Dylan. They know how to survive these storms."

"And I'm supposed to sit here and hold the fort down 'til I see which ones are lucky enough to make it home?" I cried.

"That's about all you—"

I cut him off. "Now you listen to me, Striker! When this storm is all said 'n done, we're gonna get that fine motorboat of yours out of that shed and into the water, and we're gonna go find 'em!"

Striker looked as though I'd slapped him. Then his face became angry and fixed. "I'm not takin' you out on that boat," he flatly stated.

I leaned in slightly, meeting his eyes, daring him to defy me. "Oh, yes, you are. Now you listen to me; come tomorrow, I'm gonna go down to the Keys to find out what's what—to see if they're dead or alive, and you're gonna be the one takin' me!"

He suddenly got up from the table and went to stand at the sink. Placing his hands on the edge of it, he leaned forward slightly, looking down into the enamel basin as if it held the answers he sought. Then he lifted his face and stared at the shuttered window. I knew that certain terrible scenes were playing out in his mind's eye, ones that he had created for himself, and I knew exactly what those scenes were.

Striker finally turned around but couldn't meet my eyes. "Why don't you try to get some sleep," he said, putting an end to our conversation. "It's safer down here on the first floor, so take the small bedroom back there," he said, nodding toward a tiny bedroom off the kitchen. "I'll be on the couch in the living room. I want to keep an eye on things." Striker had completely shut down. He walked out of the kitchen, and back into his haunted world.

Chapter 24

Anger vs. Fear

"Eliza." I woke up to someone calling my name in an unfamiliar room, softly lit by an oil lamp on a strange dresser. Striker was gently shaking my shoulder, and I was disoriented and drenched in sweat. "Eliza," he repeated softly. "It's time to go."

He'd awakened me from a restless, nightmare-filled sleep, and at first I was confused as to where I was and why I was there. Unlike my own bedroom at home, with its large open windows allowing even the smallest breeze into the room, this boarded up bedroom was like an oven; my hair and clothing were soaked.

I swung my legs over the side of the bed and sat up. "Where're we goin'?" I asked, in a thick, sleepy voice.

"To the Keys," he said. "To get your family. We gotta go."

Everything came rushing back to me. Jumping up, I immediately started looking for my shoes before Striker amusedly pointed out that they were still on my feet. Then I remembered that I'd slept in them in case the roof went and we had to make a run for it in the middle of the night.

"Is it over?" I asked, straining to hear the angry wind or the banging of flying debris.

"Yeah," Striker confirmed. "The wind died down a couple of hours ago, but I had to give the water a chance to calm down a little before we tried to get out there." He picked up the lamp from the table and led the way into the kitchen, with me right on his heels. "It's still gonna be plenty rough, but with the motorboat, we ought to be able to get through. Here," he said, pouring me a cup of badly burned coffee. "There's a plate of not-so-fresh biscuits on the table. Sorry, but it's the best I can do in a hurry.

As soon as you're ready, we'll get goin'. I'm gonna go stick a few more things in the boat."

He started out the back door but I stopped him. "Striker, what changed your mind?"

"About what?" he asked.

"About taking your boat out."

"Anger conquered fear," he cryptically stated.

"I don't understand."

"Finish up and let's get out of here," he replied, and said no more.

Ten minutes later, after letting the horses out of the shed so that they could freely graze, we walked down to the river, and, there, tied to his dock's pilings, was Striker's newly built motorboat. I waited on the dock to untie the lines as Striker jumped into the bow, walked over to the inboard motor positioned in the center of the vessel, and gave the rope that was attached to the engine several hard tugs. Suddenly, the motor roared to life as the smell of gasoline filled the air. Striker revved the engine by turning the end of a handle that extended out from the motor, and the power of it amazed me. I had seen motorboats before, but they had belonged to a couple of very wealthy visitors from the north. Striker's boat was an amazing feat of talent and skill, and a testament to the fact that he was a true master of his craft.

I untied the lines and boarded the boat, and we headed east on the river, towards the trading post to get the latest information on the storm. As we moved down the river, I sat on the bow, guiding Striker around debris in the water and looking out at the damage inflicted on the homes and vegetation along the banks.

I held my breath as my home came into view, then let out a sigh of relief when I saw that it looked as though it had survived the storm unscathed. The roof was still intact, the windows remained boarded up, and the veranda seemed to be in one piece. Our sailboat, the *Eve of Salvation,* was a different story, however. It had been smashed to smithereens against the seawall. Parts of it were submerged, while those still above the water were impossibly twisted or broken. It looked as though some giant sea monster had taken the vessel in its mouth, chomped down on it for a while, and, finding it inedible, spit it out. And ours wasn't the only boat destroyed. There were several more that had been mangled, including the small sailboat Gus Mueller had loaned me just the day before.

Suddenly, it dawned on me that we could be gone for a while. Searching the Keys after a major storm wasn't going to be easy, but I wasn't going to leave until I knew where everyone in my family was, and the condition they were in.

"Let me grab a few things from the house, Striker."

Carefully, he navigated his boat up to the dock, away from our shattered sailboat.

"I'm not gonna tie up," he said. "I'll sit here in idle while you get what you need, but try to hurry. There's a lot of debris floatin' in the river. If we get banged up, we're not goin' anywhere."

"I'll hurry," I said as I stepped off the boat and onto the dock. Other than the corner where our boat had violently slammed into it, the dock was intact. I hurried up to the house and found that it had fared all right, too. Other than a couple of leaks in the roof, everything else was just as I'd left it. Relieved, I hurried to my room and quickly changed into a fresh pair of canvas pants and shirt. I stuffed a few more clothes into a burlap bag, grabbed some money from my desk drawer, and then moved on to the kitchen where I bagged up some food. Finally, I had all that I needed and hurried back to the boat.

As we continued down the river, we came upon the home of the Parkers, a newly transplanted young family from Lexington, Kentucky. Though the house was still standing, the entire roof was gone. Looking around, I saw that it had landed in a vacant plot of land on the other side of the river! As we drove right in front of the house, I could see that the windows had been blown out and the inside was a chaotic mess. Standing in the yard were the Parkers, all six of them, including Mrs. Parker's elderly mother. Striker pulled the boat closer to their seawall and asked if everyone was accounted for and all right. Grim-faced, Mr. Parker confirmed that everyone was, so we moved on, but not before I saw Mrs. Parker holding her youngest child, who was perhaps two, and trying to calm her cries, while Mrs. Parker's mother stood next to them sobbing into her cupped hands. Everyone was traumatized.

There was a crowd of people at the trading post when we arrived at the dock. Some of the pilings were broken off, while others had two and three boats tied up to them. Rather than trying to maneuver his boat in among them, Striker called out to several people milling around talking, one of whom was my employer, William Burdine.

"William, what's the latest?" Striker called out.

Mr. Burdine walked to the edge of the dock. "Striker! Eliza! I'm glad to see you both in one piece. Your folks okay?" he kindly asked me.

"I don't know. They left for the Keys a couple of days ago. We're on our way down there now."

The relief on Burdine's face at seeing us abruptly shifted to one of deep concern. "Storm hit hard down there," he honestly stated. "Took out the railroad tracks they'd already laid. We're hearing there're lots of casualties, though they've only been able to give us a list with a few names so far."

I could feel my heart increasing in tempo. "Were any of my family's names on that list? Dylan and Uncle James are down there, too," I reminded him.

He offered me a small, encouraging smile. "Didn't see their names, and didn't hear mention of them either. Y'all be careful goin' down there. The *St. Lucie* wrecked off Elliot Key. It was bringin' a bunch of railroad workers up from the Keys—more 'n a hundred of 'em. A couple of folks from here took their boats down there and they're pullin' bodies out of the water—both dead and alive. Heard another boat sank around Elkhorn Reef, northeast of Key Largo. God only knows how many casualties there are from this storm," he said, shaking his head.

I asked Mr. Burdine to let my family know that Striker and I had gone down to look for them if he should happen to see them. After he assured me that he would, we thanked him for the information, then Striker threw his engine in reverse, and we pulled away from the dock. A moment later, we drove out of the mouth of the river, and into Biscayne Bay.

All along the coastline and the barrier islands beyond, debris floated and bobbed atop and below the water. Striker drove out into deeper water to avoid what he could while still staying close enough to shore so that we could keep an eye out for any shipwrecked survivors. But we saw nothing as we passed Virginia Key and Key Biscayne. Then Fowey Rocks Light loomed up in the distance.

Neither Striker nor I said anything as we got closer to the lighthouse. All along, we'd been discussing what we might come across as we made our way down through the Keys, but, as we drew nearer to Fowey a thick, uncomfortable silence replaced all conversation. Suddenly, instead of steering clear of the lighthouse, as I'd assumed we would, Striker made a beeline straight for the dock.

"Striker?" I said, turning to look at him from where I sat on the ship's bow. "We don't need to stop. Please, let's just keep—" But before I could even finish my sentence, he pulled up to a piling with far more speed than necessary, shut the boat off, threw a cork bumper over the side to keep us from slamming against the dock, and snatched up the bow line that was coiled next to me. Before stepping up onto the dock, he turned to me and said in a low voice that left no room for argument, "Don't move." Anger flashed in his dark brown eyes. I'd never seen him look that way before, and it scared me.

Striker quickly tied up the boat, and then started up the ladder. As he did, I saw Owen come out of the keeper's quarters, looking both confused and perhaps a little apprehensive. When Striker bounded up onto the second platform, Owen forced a small smile and started to say something, but he never got the chance. Striker grabbed him by the front of his shirt and pushed him back against the platform's railing, knocking Owen's cap off in the process, and forcing him to lean precariously over the rail.

"You like hittin' women, Owen?" Striker asked, pulling him off the railing and then slamming him back against it again. "Is that how it works for you?" He shouted loudly enough that I could hear every word.

"Get off me!" Owen shouted back, trying to push Striker away from him.

Striker pulled Owen to within inches of his face. "Hear me when I tell you this, you disgusting son of a bitch: You ever hurt Eliza again, I'm comin' for you. You'll be dealin' with me, and there won't be another time after that. *You understand me?* Even if you just step on her toe…" Striker didn't finish, though he added an exclamation mark by slamming Owen back against the railing again. Then Striker released him with a look of contempt on his face, as if Owen was something he just couldn't stomach touching for another second. Owen didn't move. Instead, he stood there watching Striker descend the ladder to the platform below. Once Owen lost sight of Striker, he turned away without even glancing in my direction and retrieved his cap from the deck. Dusting it off, he calmly placed it back on his head and adjusted it so that it was sitting just right. Then, walking perfectly erect, Owen went into the keeper's quarters without ever looking back.

I was absolutely stunned. It amazed me that Owen had walked away without even trying to explain his actions or apologizing for them, though there was nothing he could have said that would have justified his hitting me. I knew it was over the minute he'd struck me. Before that, really. I knew it when I read the bill of sale for the Seminoles' land. But I would have thought Owen would at least try to offer up some lame excuse, or ask for forgiveness. The fact that he didn't was terribly disturbing. I realized that I knew absolutely nothing about this man—a man I'd come very close to committing my life to.

Striker walked onto the dock, untied the line and jumped back into the boat. His anger was almost palpable. Without saying a word or even looking at me, he walked over to the motor, pulled the rope that cranked the engine to life, and then turned us to the south.

As we motored along without speaking, I suddenly remembered what Striker had said that morning when I'd asked him what had changed his mind about taking one of his boats out again. He'd responded, "Anger conquered fear." At the time, I'd had no idea what he meant by that. But now I did.

Chapter 25

A Cool Blue Hell

The scene that we came upon at Elliot Key could have been the inspiration for Dante's *Inferno*. The difference, however, was that this version of hell was not red hot, but a cool blue instead. And the fact that the day had turned into one of calm winds and clear skies added a surreal horror to it.

We passed the remains of the *St. Lucie* sticking up and saw many survivors bobbing around in the water like corks. Those who were unable to swim clung to debris from the ship and some moaned in agony from their injuries. Many had already been pulled onboard several boats that were working as fast as they could to assist them, but Striker's streamlined motorboat was able to reach them with greater speed and agility than the trawlers could. We pulled five of the injured from the water and delivered them to the larger vessels that would take them back to Miami. Then we began the horrific task of recovering the bloated bodies of the dead. We retrieved three of them, and transferred the battered bodies to the largest trawler, which was storing dozens of them below deck to keep them out of view of the living. As we went from one victim to the next, both the living and the dead, I continued to watch for floating debris, but I was also watching for quick-moving fins hunting down those flailing around in the water.

"Stay as still as you can," Striker shouted. "The blood in the water will bring the sharks in. If you're flailing around, you'll get their attention. Just raise your arm and we'll see you."

The captain on board another recovery boat, the *Little Pearl*, asked Striker to search along the beach on Elliot Key, since he could get his boat in there more easily. As we slowly made our way along the debris-strewn beach, we spotted a body horribly twisted up in the mangrove trees, and then another. All in all, we found five. The noonday sun was quickly starting to decompose the bodies, and the sickly-sweet smell became overpowering. There was so much death around us that rescuers and survivors alike had to hang their heads over the sides of their boats.

By mid-afternoon, we'd done all we could. Those passengers on the *St. Lucie* who couldn't be accounted for were left to the care of the sea. As we pulled away, I looked back and said a silent prayer. I prayed that those who were lost had made it to a heavenly shore, with calm seas and a gentle wind blowing forever at their backs. Then I faced forward and tried to ready myself for what might be waiting ahead.

Striker set a course for Carysfort Light, where Adam Wilson was the keeper, on the off chance that my parents and Dylan might be there. If they'd already left Alligator Reef Light, but the seas had gotten too rough for sailing, they might have pulled in there. If they weren't there, we'd continue on down to Alligator. I prayed that my family was in one of those two places, for they'd have been far safer in a strongly anchored screw-pile lighthouse during the storm than in one of the slipshod structures on land.

As we made our way along the coastline, we stayed vigilant in case we saw other wrecked survivors in the water or along the shore. We were quiet much of the time, only speaking when necessary, for the morning's grisly task had marked us, leaving us both stunned and saddened, as well as terribly worried that my family had suffered a similar fate as the men aboard the *St. Lucie.*

Thinking about seeing Adam brought to mind his involvement with F.L.E.A.C., and the acquisition of the Seminoles' land. I knew this wasn't really the time to talk to him about it, but I also knew that I might not have another chance since he was now stationed on Carysfort, and I'd rarely see him. As much as I wanted to talk to him about the land deal, I also wanted to talk to him about Owen and Ezra Asher. Specifically, I wanted to know how Adam knew them, for how long, and how they'd come to be involved in business dealings together.

From my seat on the bow, I looked back at Striker. He was scanning the shore, looking for more victims, and didn't notice me watching him. I studied his strong profile, and how the wind caught his thick golden hair and blew it against the side of his face as he looked off to the right. This was a good man, I thought. But then, I'd always known that. How I'd missed his friendship, the ease and enjoyment of it. Though I had girlfriends from school that I saw every now and then, Striker had been my best friend, and I missed him. Terribly. I could no longer talk to him about the things that worried me, frightened me, or delighted me. I'd always felt as though I could tell him anything, and he wouldn't judge me for it, no matter how wrong I might be, or how small the problem might have been. Now that I really needed to talk to him about the questionable business dealings of Owen, Ezra, and Adam, I couldn't. It was just too complicated.

Up until a couple of days ago, I'd been engaged to Owen, and Striker would ask how I could have committed myself to spending a lifetime with someone I obviously didn't know very well—at least not well enough to agree to marry. And he would be right to ask that. But I had too much pride to admit that I now realized Owen had just been a replacement for the man I couldn't have, and a salve that I'd prayed would finally heal an open wound.

"Let's pull in here," Striker said, navigating the boat in toward the shore. "From what I can tell, it looks pretty clean. I need to refuel, and we need food, too. I know you're probably not hungry after this morning, but we've got to eat something. The afternoon is likely to be a long one, and we'll be no good to anyone if we run out of energy. Besides, I've got to try washing some of this stink off of me. It's bad."

We both needed a good dunking in the ocean. The smell of death clung to us like leaches. Striker tossed the anchor about ten yards from shore, then handed me a sack that he'd brought from his kitchen, and told me he'd meet me on the beach after filling the tank. As he pulled a gas can from a compartment built into the boat's port side, I climbed overboard into the shallow water and waded to shore.

A line of red mangrove trees were set back from the water, offering us a dry place to eat. After quickly scanning the mangroves to make sure there were no victims hung up in them, I set the food down within the trees' shady coolness, then walked back into the water. Startled angelfish scattered, as well as the tiny bait fish that had lured them in. But they weren't the only fish to feed on the tiny ones, and I needed to keep an eye out for larger predators, especially sharks, since I had the *St. Lucie's* survivors' blood on me.

As I swam around below the surface, trying to wash both the stench and nausea away, I heard a splash. Quickly looking in that direction, I saw that it was Striker. He had removed the dark brown short-sleeved pull-over shirt he'd been wearing, and had changed out of his canvas pants and into a pair of old denim trousers that had been cut to about mid-thigh. His bare skin was a much deeper shade of gold than his hair was, and his body was slender but muscular. Looking over at me, and seeing that I was fine, he grabbed a handful of sand from the seabed, then stood up and began scrubbing his skin with the natural exfoliant. Though my skin wasn't exposed like Striker's was, I scrubbed the filth off my clothes using the same method. After we felt as though we could stand the smell of ourselves again, we left the water and sank down on the sand next to our food. Light blue waves gently lapped onto the shore in a lazy low-tide rhythm, and it seemed like an absurd contradiction to the horrors we'd witnessed just an hour before.

"It's so peaceful here," I said softly. "It seems strange after this morning."

"I was thinking the same thing," Striker said while looking out at the sea.

I would have loved to have spent the afternoon in the shade, being lulled into semi-sleep by the breeze and the sound of the waves, but I knew time wasn't necessarily on our side. We needed to eat and be on our way.

I spread the contents of the bag out, and Striker began cutting pieces of cheese from a block of cheddar. There were crackers, as well, and apples.

"We're not far from Carysfort, are we?" I asked before taking a large bite out of an apple.

"No. It's just southeast of here. Look to the right, way off in the distance. That's Carysfort, just off of Key Largo," he said, before shoving a cracker and piece of cheese in his mouth. "From Carysfort, it's about another hour or so to Alligator. It's just off Islamorada.

"They're gonna be okay, Eliza," Striker said, correctly guessing what I was thinking. "If anyone can survive a storm, your folks can. From what you've told me, they've survived much worse." He smiled. "And Dylan is in a lighthouse that can survive most anything Mother Nature can throw at it. These old lighthouses have been survivin' storms for decades—bad ones, too. As soon as you're done, we'll get goin'."

I reached over and covered his hand with mine. "Striker, thank you for helping me today. I know it was hard taking your boat out."

"It wasn't hard taking the boat out, Eliza," Striker replied, looking a little surprised that I had thought such a thing. "It was hard taking *you* out in it," he softly clarified.

"Let's eat up," he said, abruptly changing the subject before I could ask him exactly what he'd meant by that. "We need to get going."

I stuffed a cracker in my mouth before I could ask him about a subject that he obviously had no desire to talk about...at least with me.

Chapter 26

Talking to God

Carysfort rose out of the water directly in front of us. At one hundred and twelve feet tall, it was the oldest of the six screw-pile lighthouses along Florida's southern coastline, and just like Fowey Rocks, it seemed untouched by the hurricane.

A group of men were milling around the second platform, outside of the keeper's quarters, and I anxiously searched for my family among them, but didn't see them.

After tying the boat to the dock, we climbed the ladders to the second platform and were immediately greeted by Adam, who'd seen us approach.

"Good God in the evening!" Adam jubilantly exclaimed. "You're the last folks I expected to see out here, and in a fancy motorboat, no less!" He slapped Striker on the back and then pulled me into a bear hug. I felt myself stiffen in his arms, but Adam didn't seem to notice. "Let's get us some coffee," he said, then turned and started for his quarters. Striker and I followed him.

"We're not stayin' long," Striker said to Adam's back. "Just long enough to get the latest news, if you have any, and fill our water jug."

A few of the men standing around the platform greeted us in barely audible one-syllable words, with an almost lifeless look in their eyes. Others stood somberly silent as we walked by them. From the looks of things, it seemed as though they had little energy to do anything else. Much of their clothing was torn, while some had had entire sleeves and pant legs ripped away, and many wore bandages made from a variety of odd materials. They spoke quietly among themselves, almost whispering, as if to avoid alerting Mother Nature that they had survived her wrath.

"Where'd they come from, Adam?" I asked, closing the door softly behind me after entering the kitchen. There were several people asleep on the floor in the living area, and Adam told us that there were more in the bedrooms, two to a bed.

"Houseboat number eleven went down off of Long Reef," Adam replied softly. "It was one of the houseboats the men building the railroad were living in. Didn't offer shit protection—'scuse me, Eliza—from the storm. Hell, those piles of junk were put together with spit 'n a prayer. They weren't much good in a li'l ol' rainstorm, much less a blasted hurricane!"

"How many were on it?" Striker asked.

"Over a hundred. That steamboat, *Jenny*, rescued some of them. Those that were hurt the worst were taken to Miami. A couple other smaller fishin' boats plucked these folks up" —he glanced toward the living room— "and brought 'em here. And they'll be here until a passin' ship can take 'em on to Miami. There just wasn't enough room on the *Jenny*. Lord, what a scene that must 'a been. Heard a shark got two poor sons of bitches—'scuse me, Eliza. Thankfully, the *Jenny* was already there, pullin' folks out, and one of the deckhands shot the shark before it could take anyone else."

Shoving thoughts of the gruesome scene aside, I said, "Adam, you haven't seen my folks or Dylan, have you?" I knew if he had, he would have told me immediately, but I still had to ask.

"No," he replied, the worry in his eyes evident. "Didn't know they were all down here."

"Yes, they—they had business in Key West," I said, stopping myself from mentioning my wedding. "Then they were stopping at Alligator."

Striker cut in, sparing me from having to explain any more. "We need to get to Alligator now, Adam. Hopefully, Dylan's okay, and Max and Eve are with him. You ready, Eliza?"

"Yes," I confirmed. I wanted to question Adam about his involvement with Owen and F.L.E.A.C., but it wasn't the time. I was far more concerned about the wellbeing of my family. Seeing the casualties was increasing my anxiety level to near panic.

"I'm sorry to be cutting this so short, Adam," Striker whispered as he ushered me out of the kitchen and through the living room. "But if the Harjos aren't at Alligator, then we'll need to start looking along the barrier islands, and in the Keys," he finished more loudly as we stepped outside. "We're gonna fill up our water jug at your tank before headin' out, if that's okay." Adam assured him it was. "Good luck here," Striker said, looking around at the people on the floor.

"And good luck to y'all, too," Adam replied. "They're no fools, Eliza— them folks of yours. They'll be okay."

"I pray you're right, Adam. I truly do." I said, trying to force a smile and failing.

We left Carysfort within fifteen minutes of our arrival, and as we made our way toward Alligator Reef lighthouse, I carried on a silent one-way conversation with God. I just hoped He was listening.

Chapter 27

A Light in the Storm

We arrived at Alligator Reef lighthouse, and the one-hundred-and-fifty-foot screw-pile structure looked as though it had fared as well as Fowey and Carysfort had. Just as they had at Carysfort, people milled around on the second platform looking as though they, too, had ridden out the storm in the most catastrophic way. But, unlike Carysfort, there were women and children among this group. Standing at the railing with some of them was Dylan. He was looking toward the shore of Islamorada through a pair of binoculars, and then writing something down.

"He's taking tidal readings." Striker smiled, looking very relieved. No sooner had he said it than Dylan turned toward us, the sound of the motorboat's engine alerting him to the fact that he had more company. Recognition dawned on his face, followed by a broad smile that left no question as to the joy he felt in seeing us alive and well. And I was certain my smile mirrored his.

Hurrying down to the dock, Dylan tied our lines to the pilings and then reached his hand down to help me off the boat. Once I was on the dock my brother caught me up in a hug that lasted a long time. When he pulled away from me, he searched my face as if to reassure himself that I was truly there and in one piece. Then Dylan turned his attention to Striker and hugged him, too. I'd never known my brother to be so outwardly affectionate, especially with another man.

"Are Mama and Papa here?" I immediately asked.

"No," Dylan said, and worry instantly replaced the joy on his face. "But, Eliza, you know Pa wasn't going to take any chances with Ma. They probably stayed in Key West. They've got telegraph machines down there, so it's likely they received early enough warnings about the storm to just stay in port. Listen, I'm worried about 'em, too," he admitted, as though he realized that I could see through his false bravado. "But y'all come on up to the house and at least have some coffee before you go lookin' for them."

We followed Dylan to the keeper's quarters, and as we walked through the crowd of folks sitting outside, I greeted them quietly, almost cautiously. Though they didn't look as beat up as the survivors from the *Jenny* had, many looked as though they'd seen a ghost. Some stood off by themselves staring out at the ocean, while others chatted nervously away.

"Where'd they come from, Dylan?" I asked once it looked like we were alone in the quarters.

"We've gotta keep our voices down," Dylan said softly. "I've got two sleeping in John Stack's room. He's the other keeper that's usually here. I'll grab the coffee. Y'all go sit down."

"You said 'usually here,'" I said, sliding onto one of the four chairs at the small kitchen table. "You mean he isn't now? Were you alone through all this?"

"Yeah," Dylan confirmed, setting a pot of coffee on the table, and then retrieving three mugs from a cupboard. "Usually, there's at least another guy with me, but John was taking shore leave before I was due to head for Miami. And when the barometer started dropping, and we knew we had a bad one headin' in, Murph O'Brien was so worried about his wife and kid bein' alone over in Tavernier that I told him to get out of here before it got any worse. He didn't wait for me to tell him a second time, either. Things went downhill real fast after that."

"How bad did it blow?" Striker asked as he spooned sugar into his coffee.

"We had sustained winds at a hundred," Dylan replied. "But the anemometer read gusts up to one thirty. About seven last night, that paddlewheeler, the *Livingston,* went down right off of here. These poor folks were just tourists on it. They were on their way to Key West when they hit Tennessee Reef, about a half mile south of here. They said they didn't get hung up on it so the *Livingston* was able to limp back this way. They got about a quarter mile from here before the ship went down, taking some of the passengers with her, including their captain, Jonah White.

"All night long, the waves kept buildin' and then they started washing over the second platform here," Dylan continued, "one right after the other, like it was nothin'. That's forty-five feet high! I was afraid windows would be blown in, so I got everyone moved into the tower. People sat on the winding staircase, hangin' on for dear life to the railing, peerin' through it like they were in jail. I guess, in a strange way, they were. They were scared to death listening to the storm outside, tryin' its best to get in. Grown men were sobbing like the ladies and little ones, and I can't say as I blame 'em. It took my best not to join 'em. Lord, the sound in the tower was eerie. Bein' that it's a cylinder, it sounded like a weird hollow roar. It was terrifying. We had one oil lamp, but I didn't dare bring any more in there with us. If one fell over, and a fire started…That 'a been the end. It was hotter 'n hell, too," he added. "But it was the safest place for everyone to be, so that's where we rode it out." He looked across to the window. "I can still hear that roar," he said softly.

"Dylan, how'd all these people get from the wreck to here?" Striker asked. "There must be at least twenty of 'em."

"I took—"

Before Dylan had the chance to finish, a boat's fog horn sounded at the same time people on the deck started shouting about a ship coming. We hurried outside and saw a large steam-powered trawler named the *Port o' Call* approaching from the south. Hurrying over to the railing, Dylan rang a large ship's bell mounted to a pole. It was just another way to alert a ship that help was needed. Much earlier, he'd hung the flag upside down as a distress signal, and it had been spotted by the ship's crew.

"Yo, lighthouse!" a man shouted up to us after stepping out of the pilothouse. "You got folks wanna ride in to Miami?"

"We do!" Dylan confirmed. "Got about seventeen here. How many you got room for?"

"We can take 'em all. We were helpin' with the folks that went down on houseboat number nine just south of here, but most of 'em already got picked up. We got plenty of room. I'll pull alongside." The pilot ducked back into the pilot house and maneuvered the boat parallel to the dock.

"Eliza, would you go wake those two in John's bedroom, please?" Dylan asked. "They're two sisters and…well, you better go in and get 'em. Striker, can you help me get the rest of these folks on board?"

I went back into the quarters and softly knocked on the bedroom door. "Who is it?" a young, frightened-sounding voice asked softly.

"It's Eliza. I'm Dylan's sister—you know, the lighthouse keeper."

"Oh, come in," the girl said.

In the bedroom were two young women. One appeared to be about my age, while the other looked a little younger. The older one had light brown hair that had obviously been arranged in a pretty bun on the back of her head at the start of their trip, but was now hanging in disarray around her face. The younger woman had dark brown hair, and it, too, hung loosely around her face. Both had bright blue eyes that had been reddened by crying.

"I'm Eliza," I said again.

"I'm Kathy Baker," the older one said. "And this is Clara, my sister," she added.

"A ship's here. It's gonna take y'all back to Miami," I explained. "It's at the dock, so you'll need to hurry." I started to leave the room but turned back to them. "Are y'all here with anyone?"

"Mother and Father went down..." Clara said, but couldn't finish.

"Do you have anyone else here?" I asked softly, hating the thought that these young women would be alone in Miami. It was obvious from the way they spoke that they were from the north, and they'd been through enough without having to navigate an unfamiliar place by themselves.

"An aunt and uncle," Kathy replied. "Aunt Halcyon gets seasick, so she didn't want to come on the trip." She tried to smile, but it looked more like a grimace. Her grief was too fresh and heavy.

"Okay, good," I said, relieved. "Y'all need to hurry now. Can I help you do anything?" When they assured me they didn't need anything, I turned to leave.

"Eliza?" Kathy stopped me.

"Yes?"

"Your brother...well, he's a hero, really," she said softly.

"What do you mean?" I asked.

"Your brother saved every one of us who's here. Even while the weather was still terrible, he got that sailboat in the water and made four trips to where the ship went down. We'd have drowned, otherwise. He's...well... We're all very grateful."

The young woman had confirmed what I'd guessed. I knew there was no way these people swam to the lighthouse in that rough water. I was extremely proud of him.

"He's a pretty special person." I smiled. "Okay, y'all better hurry," I urged as I left the room.

I walked out of the quarters and over to the railing. Most of the survivors were either on board the trawler, or on the lower platform waiting to board, and Dylan and Striker were assisting them.

"Dylan," I shouted down to him. "Kathy and Clara Baker are comin' down. Don't let 'em leave without 'em."

Dylan nodded, and as I stood there watching my brother and Striker, I knew that I was looking at two of the finest men I'd ever met. They'd put the lives of others ahead of their own, and because of that, people had survived. I just prayed that three more of the four I'd set out to find could be counted among the living.

Chapter 28

A Darkened Light

As soon as the *Port o' Call* departed, Striker said that he wanted to talk to Dylan and me. I was anxious to get underway, especially since it was getting later in the day, but from the seriousness of his tone, and the look on his face, I knew there was something weighing heavily on his mind. We made our way back up to the keeper's quarters and returned to the kitchen table.

"What's goin' on?" my brother asked.

"I was on shore leave last week," Striker began. "Two nights before the hurricane came in, it was lookin' like we might get a bad storm—you know, the typical summer stuff. So I went down to the southern end of Key Biscayne."

"Why would you do that?" I interrupted.

"Just bear with me," he said. "I'm gettin' to that. Anyway, that storm moved on south. It never amounted to anything. It was perfectly quiet. I didn't have to be back at the lighthouse for a few days yet, so I decided to stick around down there. The next night, another storm blew in, but this one was a real gully washer. I stood there on that shore watchin' Fowey Light, and I swear on a stack of Bibles, I saw the light go out for about a minute."

"You mean like it was turned out, or covered, or somethin'?" I asked, incredulously.

"Yeah, somethin' like that," Striker confirmed.

I looked over at Dylan and saw that he had actually gone pale. He looked as though he'd seen a ghost. "Did anything go down that night—any wrecks?" he asked in a low voice.

"Don't know," Striker said. "I wanted to look around the next day but the weather was startin' to pick up. We started getting the outer bands of the hurricane. But I'd be willin' to bet something did. I never got the chance to do any askin' though, and now so many vessels have gone down because of the storm that it's hard to tell what sank before or during it."

"Are you sure the oil didn't just run out, or there wasn't some kind of problem?" I asked, still stunned.

"That's highly doubtful," Striker said. "Those lenses are fairly foolproof. Besides, even a novice light keeper would know that the day's first order of business is to make sure the fuel is filled to the top."

"Maybe it was just an oversight," I said weakly, looking at both of them. And both of them had the same reaction: They smiled at me as if I knew better. And I did.

"After we're done lookin' for your folks, I'm gonna check with the Department of Commerce and Labor to see which ships have gone down around here in the recent past, and cross-check it against who the lighthouse keepers were during those times. Don't know that Miami has that information since the Port of Entry is in Key West, so I'll check down there.

"I wish I'd spent more time at the light with Owen," Striker continued, "but I was usually on shore leave when he was there with Jim Altman and Adam. The little time I did spend with him seemed like business as usual, and there weren't any wrecks. And, Dylan, I know you didn't spend any time with him at all, so there's no way you'd have been able to tell if something wasn't quite right."

"Eliza! Oh, damn!" Dylan exclaimed as he ran his right hand through his long, chestnut hair. "Here we are questioning Owen's part in something that may or may not be so, and you're engaged to the man! I'm sorry. I—"

"I'm not," I interrupted firmly. "I mean, I'm not engaged to him—not any longer," I added. "Let me just say that I think you have all the reason in the world to take a hard look at him. I found out he's buying up the Everglades land that belonged to the Seminole tribe," I explained, but I didn't mention that Owen had struck me when I'd found out. Striker didn't mention it either. No doubt he figured that was something only I had the right to bring up. My bruises had faded enough that unless I pointed them out, Dylan wouldn't notice them on my tan skin, and because I had no desire to revisit that violent moment again, I moved on.

"Dylan, you know who partnered with Owen in those land purchases? Adam!" I said, before my brother could offer up an answer.

"*Adam's* in cahoots with Owen?" my brother asked, almost in disbelief.

"Apparently so, at least in some things," Striker said. "We've just got to get to the bottom of what all those 'some things' might be."

"What do you need us to do, Striker?" I asked. We needed to wrap up the conversation so that we could resume the search for my parents.

"Nothing, really," he answered. "I just wanted you to know what I believe is going on, and what I'm plannin' to do about it. That's all."

"Lord, I wish I could go with y'all," Dylan said.

"You're right where you need to be," I told him as I stood up. "C'mon. Walk us down to the boat."

Once down on the dock, Dylan finally had a chance to take a good look at Striker's motorboat. "She's a real beauty!" he exclaimed. "Is that the one you told me about building some time back?"

"It is," Striker confirmed. "It still needs work, but it's runnin' pretty good."

"It's gotta be!" Dylan replied. "You've made it here in waters that are still plenty choppy. What a fine thing you've accomplished! Really fine!" He was clearly impressed.

"We'll let you know what we find out—about your parents, as well as Owen," Striker said as he shook Dylan's hand before climbing down into the bow.

"Say a prayer we find Mama and Papa," I said as I hugged my brother. "Say plenty of 'em, ya hear?" I let him go and started to climb into the boat, but I turned back to him for a moment.

"Dylan, one of the girls taking a nap in John's room—Kathy Baker, I think she said her name was. She was the one with the light brown hair."

"Yes, I know which one you're talking about," he confirmed. "She was the older of the two."

"Yes!" I said. "Kathy told me how you saved all those people on the *Livingston*—going back several times in your boat to get 'em." I brought my hand up to his face, cupping it. "I couldn't be any prouder of you, Dylan. I honestly couldn't."

My brother's face turned slightly red under his tan. "I didn't do anything any other keeper wouldn't have done."

"That's hogwash!" I exclaimed. "Don't you dare downplay what you did. You put your own neck on the line to save a lot of lives, and because of that, they'll be around to tell their children about it, and their grandchildren…"

"Okay, okay," he laughed. "I get it." Suddenly, he lost his smile and the expression on his face grew very serious. "Y'all go find Ma and Pa."

"We're going to," I assured him. "We're going to," I repeated, though I wasn't sure if I was trying to convince Dylan or myself. Going up on my tiptoes, I kissed his cheek and then joined Striker down in the boat. Watching my brother as we pulled away, I was too choked up to say anything else so I simply lifted my hand in farewell. He waved back from the dock, and then started up the ladder to resume his duties as keeper, while Striker turned the bow toward the south and we resumed our journey into the unknown.

Chapter 29

Long Gone

We stayed as close as we could to the barrier islands, while keeping an eye off the port side for any sign of Papa's trawler. Bits and pieces of boats could be seen throughout the shallows and on the shorelines, and we guessed that some of the crews had sought refuge on the islands. But if Mama and Papa had done that, where were they now? Had they been picked up by rescue boats, or had they succumbed to the storm?

As we passed Grassy Key, we saw a man's body lying in the mangroves at the shoreline. The victim's legs were stretched out toward the beach, and each wave that rolled up onto the sand washed his feet in a macabre ritual.

"I gotta see if he's still alive," Striker said as he edged his boat closer to the shoreline. "From the looks of it, I seriously doubt it, but I've got to check. You wait here."

Striker threw the anchor and waded ashore, carefully approaching the body. Suddenly, he swatted his hands vigorously at something near the man's face, and two large black birds immediately flew up, *caw-cawing* their resentment. Bending over the body, Striker took a quick assessment of it, then, after quickly scanning the area, he returned to the boat.

"He's long gone and there's no one else with him. He was probably washed in from a wreck further out. I wish I could bury him, but we've got to keep going. We're losin' daylight fast."

As we neared Marathon, we saw the back of a sailboat sticking up from a sandbar. Carefully avoiding both it and the end of the sandbar, we had nearly passed it when I saw the last few letters of the boat's name: *DOG*.

"Wait!" I shouted. "Striker, hold up!"

He threw the gear into neutral. "What is it? You know that boat?"

Lying flat on my stomach, with my top half hanging over the end of the bow, I peered into the darkening turquoise water. The boat was the *Salty Dog,* and it belonged to Art Hennessey, our family friend and part-time keeper at the Biscayne Bay House of Refuge. He was the one who had relieved Dylan there.

"It's Art Hennessey's boat, the *Salty Dog.* Do you know him?"

"Yeah," Striker replied, looking grim. "He's a good man. I think we should take a look over there." He nodded toward the mangroves. "His sailboat is pretty close to shore, so he might be up there somewhere."

"I know," I sighed. "I was thinking the same thing. If we don't check for him and he's never seen again, I'll always think that we should have looked. That maybe…"

"I know," Striker agreed. "But, if we do that, then we're not going to have enough daylight left to get over to Sombrero Light today. It's over five miles out."

My heart told me to do one thing, but my conscience told me to do another. "We've gotta look."

"Alright," he said, throwing out the anchor. "We'll camp here tonight and then make a beeline for Sombrero at first light. Okay?"

"Not really, but yes."

We waded through the water and began to search among Marathon's mangroves. And though we saw an enormous amount of debris hung up in the vegetation; including a perfectly preserved small porcelain angel adorned with a Christmas wreath upon her head, we didn't find Art, or anyone else—alive or otherwise.

We searched until it was nearly dark, and as our first day of searching came to an end, my spirits seesawed back and forth between high and low. On the one hand, not seeing evidence of my family or any sign of their wreckage was good, and I was still able to hope that they were safe somewhere. On the other hand, not seeing any sign of them was extremely frightening. There was the very real possibility that they'd gone down between Miami and Key West, and that they would never be found. To me, that would be the worst outcome of all. I'd spend the rest of my life standing on the shore, staring out at the sea, watching for a ship that I knew, in my heart, would never return to port again.

Striker went back to the boat for supplies, including a large tarp to make a lean-to. Since there were so many downed trees, making a shelter took no time at all. Using a palm tree that had blown over but whose crown had gotten wedged between two red mangrove trees, leaving the trunk about five feet off the ground, Striker threw the tarp over it and we instantly had a tent. Using some railroad spikes, he secured each corner to the ground. While he set it up, I went in search of driftwood to get a fire going. Without a doubt, the mosquitoes would eat us alive if we didn't have the smoke to chase them off. Striker said if it got too bad we could sleep in the boat. There was a place built into the bow that had room enough for two people, but it'd be tight and like an oven in there, so we opted to sleep on the beach.

Off in the distance, thunder sounded. Thick cumulus clouds were backlit by lightning, giving them an eerie orange glow. We sat between the tent and the fire, eating biscuits and smoked kingfish. Both of us were tired, as well as worried, so we talked quietly about where we would go after Sombrero Light. Our plan was to scan the shorelines of the islands en route to Key West, as well as to stop at American Shoal lighthouse, by Sugarloaf Key. The lighthouse was at the very north end of Key West, and my parents wouldn't have gone any further south than that.

"It's starting to sprinkle," Striker said, holding his hand out and catching a few tiny drops. At the same time, the fire sizzled as a few of the drops landed on the embers. We moved further back into the tent, taking the remains of our meal with us and silently watching the fire sputter.

"Mosquitoes will come out in droves once it stops," Striker said, as though he felt the need to fill the silence in the tent. From the pensive look on his face, I could tell there was something on his mind that was far more serious than mosquito bites.

"Are you thinking about my folks, Striker? Are you thinking that they didn't make it and that I'm leading us on a wild goose chase?"

"No, no," he quickly assured me. "Not at all. But, if you're asking me whether I think they survived the storm or not, I'd say they had a better chance than most people. Your father knows how to read the weather, the smell of a storm when one's coming, how it's moving, and how intense it's gonna be. He's lived off the land a lot in his life. He knows how to read it, and he knows how to read the sea now, too. And so does your mother. Between the two of them, I think there's a real good chance they're holed up somewhere. We're gonna keep believing that, too, until we're out of places to look. Okay?" He searched my face as if gauging whether I believed him or not. I did believe him, because I needed to. I *had* to. Otherwise, I had no hope to hold on to.

A sharp crack of thunder made me jump, and I scooted further back into the tent.

Striker stayed where he was, looking at the approaching storm as lightning slashed the sky.

"You know, Eliza, sitting under a tree is one of the worst places we could be right now," he said with a mischievous smile.

"So, what's our other option? Wait it out in the boat?" I asked sarcastically.

"No," he laughed. "That's *the* worst place to be!"

In the dying firelight, I watched the smile on Striker's face evaporate as he turned away from the storm to look at me.

"I've been asked to take the job at St. Augustine Light," he simply stated.

I felt as if the wind had been knocked out of me. "Did you take it?" I asked, forcing the words out.

"Yes," he replied firmly. "I leave in three weeks."

Thunder boomed loudly. But I felt as though I'd been hit with a bolt of lightning. It felt hard to breathe. I needed to be out of the tent. I needed fresh air and the feel of the cool rain on my face. But, most of all, I needed to be away from Striker.

"Where're you going?" he asked, startled, as I pushed my way past him.

"I just...I need some air. I just need..." I couldn't finish. Tears were starting to take the place of words. Not caring what dangers might be concealed in the darkness, I ran, stumbling over small obstacles in the sand as I did so. Trying to put some distance between myself and Striker, I moved higher up onto the island, away from the beach and the mangroves, until I found a stand of palm trees that had survived the storm. Stopping there to catch my breath, I didn't hear Striker come up behind me. Grabbing me by the arm, he spun me around to face him.

"Why the hell did you run like that, Eliza?" Striker cried, sounding both bewildered and frightened. He held my upper arms firmly so that I couldn't run again. "Why would you do that?" he repeated.

"Every time you and I start to get closer, you find a way to pull away from me!" I shouted as tears began to run down my cheeks, blending with the rain. "*Every time!*" I sobbed.

My eyes had adjusted to the darkness enough so that I could see conflicting emotions play across Striker's face.

"*Stop it, Eliza!*" Striker shouted, still gripping me by the upper arms and shaking me once to emphasize his words.

"Stop *what*?" I cried, totally at a loss.

"*Stop trying to make me love you!*" he shouted. "Stop it!"

For several seconds, he seemed frozen in place as though he was involved in some inner battle. I heard him swear under his breath before he pushed me back against the palm tree and covered my mouth with his, powerfully forcing his tongue inside, drinking me in, possessing me. He pressed himself fully against me so that I felt all of him, and as my body pressed back against his, and our tongues intertwined, it felt as though we were trying to fuse ourselves together. It was urgent and passionate, and far more intense than anything I'd ever felt with anyone before.

Suddenly, he pulled away from me. As quickly as the kiss had started, it stopped. Completely at a loss, I stood there watching him as he stepped back, putting a couple of yards between us. He held his face up to the rain as if he was trying to wash something away; then he turned to me and said, "I can't go back to what we started. I've changed too much to do that, Eliza. I've just changed too much." He sounded defeated.

"You didn't change," I said, my voice seething. "You broke." Turning on my heel, I walked away from Paul Strickland, for the Striker I knew and loved so well was long gone.

Chapter 30

Planned Coincidences

We resumed searching for my parents at first light, after I'd spent a sleepless night in the boat, while Striker stayed onshore in the tent. We said very little to each other, only speaking when we needed to and keeping the conversation focused on the task at hand.

We crisscrossed back and forth between the remaining lighthouses we needed to check, the shorelines of the barrier islands, and the Keys. Over and over again, we were told that my parents hadn't been seen. But as the keeper at the American Shoal lighthouse was quick to point out, my mother and father could be among the corpses still being collected on the barrier islands, or perhaps buried beneath one of the collapsed buildings in the Keys. Afraid of what might come out if I responded to his insensitive statement, I said nothing at all. Instead, Striker thanked him for his information, and quickly drove away from the dock.

When we finally entered the waters of Key West, there was no rhyme or reason to the destruction. It was as if Mother Nature had decided she liked one building but was offended by another.

After looking for a dock where we could tie up, and only finding either badly damaged ones, or docks that were completely full, we settled for a tree, then walked to town. Every street was bedlam as people searched for missing loved ones, or looked for help, or tried to find fresh water and supplies.

Tents had been set up as makeshift hospitals along Duval and Eaton Streets. The wounded rested on long tables or pallets, while anyone with any sort of medical knowledge participated in caring for them. Blood-curdling screams rang out every now and then as people lost ruined appendages to the hacksaw, while moaning filled the air like some dreadful hum. We went from tent to tent, checking one pain-racked face after another, but my parents weren't among them. And those we asked either hadn't seen them, or wouldn't know who they were if they had.

Nearing the end of the day, I sat down beneath a palm tree on one of the side streets, while Striker went over to talk to a group of men. They were standing around a fire burning in a metal barrel, and every minute or so, they'd drop something else into the flames. From the greasy stench, I assumed they were burning human flesh, and from the size of the pieces being disposed of, I figured they were most likely the limbs that had been amputated throughout the day. Striker spoke with the men for only a moment, and then walked back to me. From the look on his face, I could tell the news wasn't good, or at least not the news I so wanted to hear.

"One man knew—knows—your father, but hasn't seen him." Striker quickly corrected himself, but not before I heard the slip. Just like me, he was losing hope that my folks would be found alive.

"We're gonna keep looking until we can't go anymore tonight. Then we'll sleep on the boat and start again at first light. We're not gonna give up yet, Eliza," he said determinedly.

"Thank you, Striker," I said softly. I was beyond grateful for his tireless efforts to find my family. And though a part of me was still intensely angry with him, as well as with myself, I knew that my anger was helping no one. I needed to put it aside for my parents' sake, if for no other reason.

The night was nearly as hot and humid as the day had been. Little air stirred, so we decided to sleep on top of the bow, instead of inside of it. The terrible noises in the town continued throughout the night, but because we were anchored some distance away, I was finally able to fall into an exhausted, but restless, sleep.

At first light, we ate the reminder of our biscuits and then resumed our search. We checked the hospital tents again in the event that my parents had been brought in overnight, but they had not. We also checked with a couple of private homes that had been opened up to the wounded, but we had no luck there, either. Finally, in the late morning, Striker said aloud what we'd both been thinking for the last hour or so: "Eliza, I think we've done all we can here. What do you think? You about ready to go?"

"Yes," I said in a whispered voice. I felt tears rush to my eyes, and I looked away from Striker, not wanting him to see me start to break.

"Listen, we're not giving up yet," Striker said, obviously seeing me start to crumple. "We'll run up the Gulf side of the islands and check every one of 'em if we have to. But I've got to try to find some fuel first. And I also want to take a quick look at the log books over at the Port of Entry. You okay with that?" I told him I was, and we headed away from the frenzy of people on Duval Street.

The Port of Entry was several blocks over on Simonton Street, and it was still standing, much to our relief. But the large two-storey stucco building was crammed full of people trying to find out the names of the ships that had gone down in the storm, and whether their loved ones were on them. Lists of the doomed ships and their passengers had been posted on the walls inside, and crowds gathered in front of them, reading aloud the ships' names, and the passengers they carried. Cries of grief echoed through the building, completely drowning out the much softer sighs of relief coming from those who didn't find their loved ones' ship on the list.

Standing on my tiptoes next to Striker at the back of the crowd, I strained my eyes to see if I could make out the name *Deep Secrets* on the list. From where we stood, it was impossible to see, but as people moved on, we pushed our way to the front.

"It's not on it," Striker said, turning to me with a smile of relief. But both he and I knew that just because the boat's name was not there, that didn't necessarily mean it hadn't gone down. Because their trawler was a small, privately owned boat, rather than a large passenger ship, merchant vessel, or government-owned military ship, my parents were not required to file a report about who they were, where they were going, or what they were carrying when they left any port. The Department of Commerce did its best to report all lost vessels, but at times like these, it was an impossible task.

Striker guided me over to a counter that was being manned by an agent of the Department of Commerce. Before Striker could even ask a question, the agent pointed to the list on the wall where we'd just been. "You'll find all the names there."

"Mr..." Striker began, but had to lean down slightly in order to read the badge on the shorter man's vest. "Conway," he continued. "My name is Paul Strickland, and I'm one of several keepers at the Fowey Rocks light. I need to see your log book, if you don't mind."

The man might have argued the point if the situation wasn't what it was. Or he might have offered to look up the information Striker was requesting, but at the moment, the man had his hands full. Just then, a rather large woman, close to hysterics, came up to the counter and demanded that Mr. Conway review the information that was listed on the lost ships, saying she was quite sure he must be mistaken about some ship named the *Franny Bee*, that had her beloved son Cyril on board.

"May I?" Striker said, reaching across the counter and pulling the log book to him.

Mr. Conway never had a chance to respond, for the woman grabbed the poor man by the lapels of his vest and pulled him halfway across the counter, screaming her demands that he double-check the reported information. In all honesty, I couldn't say I blamed her. I understood her despair.

Grabbing the log book, Striker headed to the far end of the counter and began riffling through the pages until he found the year he was looking for: 1904.

Below the year, the page was divided into columns. In the first, the date of the wreck was written. In the second, the ship's name was logged. In the third was a list of the cargo carried. And in the fourth column was listed a landmark near the site of the wreck, such as an island, or a lighthouse.

Striker scanned down the page with his right index finger and then stopped at two different wrecks listed on two different days in 1904. One took place on January 24th. It was a merchant ship, and its cargo was listed as "assorted," which usually meant there was plenty of value on board, sometimes in the form of gold or silver. The landmark nearest it was the Hillsboro Inlet Light. The second wreck took place later in the year, on October 3rd. This one was a merchant ship as well, though it was carrying some passengers. Again, the cargo was listed as "assorted," and the landmark closest to it was Jupiter Inlet Light. Striker flipped the page to 1905. Running his index finger down the column listing the landmarks, he found another listing with Jupiter Light being the closest to the wreck.

"There are a lot wrecks," Striker explained as he continued to gaze down at the pages. "And some of the same landmarks are listed over and over again. But those landmarks are the ones closest to the most dangerous reefs to navigate, so it only makes sense that they would be listed more frequently than some of the others.

"For example, there're a whole lot of wrecks off the Keys' reefs, and the Dry Tortugas," he continued. "But those reefs are in areas that are notoriously hard to navigate. There's little room for error. But that's not what I'm looking for."

"Then what *are* you looking for?" I asked. But instead of answering me, he flipped the page to 1906, and quickly ran his finger down the columns. Near the bottom of the page his finger stopped, and I heard him mutter, "Son of a bitch!"

"*What*? What did you find?" I asked, peering over his arm, straining to see what he was reading.

"Look," he said, angling the book toward me so that I could see it better.

Unlike the other wrecks in 1904 and 1905, I recognized the names of the 1906 wrecks: The *Paso Rápido*, and the *Esmeralda*.

"The *Paso* is the one Papa and I salvaged with Ezra Asher," I said excitedly. "And the other—the *Esmeralda*," I said more softly after Striker told me to keep my voice down, "is the one Papa and I were going to salvage until we learned that Ezra was the wreck master. We didn't want to work with him again, and I know the feeling was mutual."

"C'mon," Striker said, closing the book. "Let's get out of here." He returned the log to Mr. Conway, who was busy trying to calm a young woman who was crying hysterically while holding a screaming baby in her arms.

Striker ushered us through the throngs of people and out of the building. He was walking fast and I struggled to keep up with him. He finally stopped halfway down the block, beneath a massive, leafless banyan tree. The storm had stripped away every bit of green on it. Placing one of his hands on his hips and running the other through his hair, Striker looked upward, as though trying to find one small leaf among the naked branches.

"Striker, what are you thinking?" I anxiously asked.

"The landmarks for every one of those five wrecks I pointed out to you were lighthouses," Striker explained. "And in every one of those lighthouses, either Owen Perry or Adam Wilson was the keeper at the time."

I was absolutely at a loss for words, but it didn't matter, because Striker wasn't finished talking.

"And if I had a hundred dollars left to my name," he continued, as the anger became ever more evident in the tone of his voice and the flashing of his dark brown eyes, "I'd bet every penny of it on the likelihood that Ezra Asher was the wreck master on every damn one of them, too."

Chapter 31

Chasing a Tiger

Striker and I started walking toward Duval Street, and as we did, a thousand questions filled my head; including what he planned to do with this newfound information.

"Nothing right now," Striker replied when I asked him. "I'll wait 'til we get back to Miami. They're overwhelmed down here. No one has the time to hear about some corrupt lighthouse keepers. But once we're back home, I'll contact the Secretary of the Department of Commerce, in Washington, D.C. I imagine he'll open some kind of formal investigation."

One question nagged at me. "Striker, was your parents' wreck listed?" I hated to bring up the subject, but if the wreck had been caused on purpose rather than the result of a structural failure, then the fault would not lie with Striker.

"No." He quickly replied, as though he'd checked for that very same thing. "Their wreck wasn't recorded. The boat was a small, personal craft. Nothing large went down that night."

Neither of us said anything for a little while after that. We were both lost in our own thoughts, though I had a feeling they were the same. The fact was the night Striker's parents wrecked on the reef, there'd been no storm to have caused them to slam into the deadly coral, and Striker's father knew the reefs well, so an error on the part of the captain was extremely unlikely. As a result everyone had assumed the wreck was caused by a structural failure.

We turned onto Duval Street, and the medical tents were the first sight that greeted us. "Striker, before we leave, I have to check them again," I said, pointing at the makeshift hospitals.

We checked there, and again at the private homes we'd been told were housing patients, but my parents had not been brought in.

"We need to start back, Eliza," Striker said quietly as we walked down Francis Street, after checking the last private home.

"I know," I whispered. Then, unable to hold it in any longer, I walked over to a tattered palm tree, rested my right arm high up on its trunk, buried my face against it and began to sob. Suddenly, I felt Striker grip my shoulder. He said nothing as I let my anguish out. He just stood behind me, patiently waiting as I released every last tear in me. Finally, after several minutes, I moved away from the tree, rubbed the wetness off my face, and firmly said, "Let's go." There was nothing else I could say or do. There was nothing more to be done.

We resumed walking and then Striker reminded me that he needed to get fuel. "I'm going to grab the cans from the boat and see if I can get them filled up. Instead of you coming with me, why don't you see if you can find some food for us? Anything'll do. More than that, though, we need fresh water. I'll bring the water jug back with me and I'll see if I can find a place to fill it."

Agreeing, I headed down Duval, towards town, keeping an eye out for anybody selling anything along the sidewalks, and peering down side streets when I intersected them. I found a woman selling coconuts, and bought a couple. A block or so down, I found a woman selling cookies. It was an enterprising move on her part, for people were buying anything edible that they could find, and making the cookies was a cheap and easy thing to do. I bought the four remaining oatmeal ones, and moved on.

Crossing the intersection of Catherine and Duval Streets, I saw a small table set up about fifty yards down on Catherine. From where I was, I couldn't tell what the young woman was selling, so I went to take a look. Fortunately, she had various sized jars of water. On the front of her table was a handwritten note that claimed the water had been drawn from her well. It looked clear, but before purchasing it, I took the top off of one of the larger jars, poured a small amount into my cupped hand and tasted it. It was fine, so I decided to buy it and ask her if we could pay her to fill up our water jug when Striker returned with it.

Pulling a dollar from my pants' pocket to pay for the water, I waited for the young woman who was selling it to finish up with another customer. As I stood there, I studied her face and decided that she must be about seventeen or so. With her blond hair and blue eyes, she was rather pretty, but there was something hard about her, too, even at that young age. She looked as though she'd not lived an easy life, but in Key West, that wasn't difficult to imagine. This wasn't the kind of place where women with delicate natures were often found. To live in this place required a certain amount of strength and determination that pampered ladies didn't possess. There was a hardness to the young woman's eyes, and around her mouth. Her neck looked as though it hadn't been washed in—

"*Where did you get that pendant?*" I asked the young woman in a near-panicked voice, interrupting her transaction with an older lady.

There, around the blond woman's neck was the mother of pearl pendant with the carved tiger's face that my father had made for my mother many years before. There was only one like it in the world, and this stranger standing before me was wearing it.

"What? Oh, *that?*" she replied, looking down at the pendant and then giving the older woman the change due her.

"Yes! *That* one! Where did you get it?" I cried. People turned to look at the ruckus I was beginning to make, but I paid them no mind.

"Someone gave it to me," the girl said dismissively. She started to turn away, to assist another waiting customer with money in hand.

"Wait a minute!" I shouted, grabbing her by the arm to stop her.

She pulled her arm out of my grasp. "I don't know who the hell you think you are, or who you think this necklace belongs to," the young woman said, clearly angry now. "But someone gave it to me, and I can't remember who!" Again, she started to turn away, but a hand shot past me and grabbed the woman's arm, stopping her once again.

"Where'd you get the pendant?" a low voice demanded. Though I recognized the voice instantly, I turned around and confirmed that Striker was behind me.

"Like I told her," the young woman replied, trying to pull free from Striker's grip. "It was a gift."

"You're lying," he flatly stated.

"I ain't!" she shouted.

"Tell you what," Striker said. "Let's get the sheriff over here and he can decide."

The young woman scoffed at that. "Yeah, you go find the sheriff! You think he's gonna give two rats' asses about a stupid pendant when he's got all the rest of this shit goin' on?" she laughed, referring to the bedlam around us. She had a point, and both Striker and I knew it.

"Yeah, you know, you're right about that," Striker agreed. "Which means he isn't gonna pay us much mind while I'm whippin' the hell out of you until you tell us the truth, is he?" That got the young woman's attention. "Now," he continued calmly, "here's what we're gonna do: I'm gonna give you ten dollars to stop what you're doin' right now, and take us to the place you got that pendant—specifically, the woman you got it from."

Striker finally let the girl jerk her arm free from his grasp, but instead of running off, she leaned in toward us so that only he and I could hear her. "I can't take ya there or I'll lose my job," she confided. "It's a house I clean a couple of times a week, and I need that money."

"Okay, go on," Striker encouraged.

"It's Mrs. English's house, and she took in a few folks who got hurt in the storm. She's got three of 'em there now, and I snitched the necklace off of an end table in one of the bedrooms. Please, mister, don't tell her. I gotta keep this job! I got a young 'un to feed, and no one helpin' me do it."

"What did the woman look like—the one whose bedroom you took the pendant from?" I asked, barely able to breathe. *God, please let the woman say she has red hair*, I prayed. *Sweet Jesus, please!*

"Well…" The girl's brows furrowed as she tried to recall. "I think she had red hair. Yeah, it was red!" She said with more certainty. "With a few bits of white in it!" she added.

My hope soared! "Where? Where is she? Was there a man with her? A big man with black hair—with bits of white in his, too?" My voice was shaky, just like the rest of me.

"Maybe." She shrugged. "Honestly, I wasn't much interested."

"Only in things you could steal," Striker sarcastically added.

I shot him a look. The last thing I wanted was for him to antagonize the girl.

Turning back to her, I said in a kind, soft voice. "Would you tell me where the house is?"

"On White Street," she said to me. "It's the big pink Victorian—the only one painted that ugly bright pink color. Just go four blocks up and turn right. It's the third house on the right. But please, I'm beggin' ya, don't tell Mrs. English I stol' it. Here," she said, slipping the pendant's chain over her neck and thrusting it at me. "Take it. Just don't tell her."

"Here," Striker said, holding the promised ten dollars out to her, plus another five. "Feed your baby with this." The young woman snatched the bills from his fingers. "And quit stealing," he added, before hurrying away to catch up with me as I headed toward White Street.

Chapter 32

Soundly Whupped

I repeatedly knocked loudly on the front door of the pink Victorian until a woman cracked it opened and peeked out. Seeing that it didn't look like anyone too threatening, she opened the door wider. The middle-aged woman was tiny. I guessed her to be less than five feet tall. She wore her hair pulled back in a tight bun, and she had broad hips and round rosy cheeks. She wore a cream-colored dress with small purple violets scattered over it, and tied around her ample waistline was a clean, crisp white apron.

"Lord, child, you got to give a body a chance to get to the door before you go knockin' it down," she scolded, but there wasn't any anger in her voice. "Now, how can I help you?"

"Are you Mrs. English?" I asked. When she confirmed that she was, I went on. "I was told you're caring for several people who were injured in the storm. My parents are among the missing, and I was wondering if they might be with you. Their name is Harjo—Eve and Max Harjo. Mama has red—"

I didn't have to finish describing them. Mrs. English beamed, and the smile made her soft brown eyes bright and her cheeks even rosier. She opened the door wide and stood aside. "Come in! Come in! Thank the good sweet Savior you're here! Lord, that poor woman has been worried sick about you and your brother. She's even been talkin' in her sleep about y'all."

"Is Papa with her?" I anxiously asked as I stepped inside the foyer.

"He is." She smiled even more broadly. "Come," she said, motioning for us to follow her up the stairway directly in front of us.

"Mrs. English, when did they come in, and how badly were they injured?" Striker asked as we followed her up. He'd taken the words right out of my mouth.

"Yesterday morning," she said, lowering her voice as she reached the second floor and turned left. I started to repeat the question about their condition, but she stopped in front of a door. She held her index finger up to her lips to quiet us, and then knocked softly. When there was no answer, she opened the door slightly and peeked around it. "Sweet," she whispered, apparently referring to the scene inside. Then, she stepped aside so that we could enter, but Striker said he'd wait out in the hallway to give me some privacy. Nodding at him, I stepped past Mrs. English, and into the room.

Lying on her back in a full-sized bed was Mama, and next to her was Papa, who was lying on his right side with his left arm draped protectively across her. Mrs. English was right; it was a very sweet scene, indeed, and, to my mind, the most beautiful thing I'd ever seen. However, their bodies were battered.

My mother had a bandage around her head, and there was a red spot on the white cotton material above her right eye where a wound was still oozing blood. There were also several cuts and bruises on her face, and an especially bad bruise on her right cheek. Papa's face and head looked uninjured. However, his entire torso and shoulders were bandaged.

I looked behind me and saw that Mrs. English was standing just inside the door. I assumed she had stayed to answer any questions I might have, or to be sure that my parents didn't further injure themselves by moving too much when they saw me.

"What's wrong with them?" I whispered, terribly afraid of what the answer would be.

"Nothin' that a little time and God's tender lovin' care won't take care of," she assured me. "From the little they've been able to tell me, your mother was thrown against somethin' on the boat. Said it happened when they hit a reef off Boot Key. The fact they were able to get to shore was through the grace of God, and the sheer determination of your father."

"What happened to his mid-section?" I reluctantly asked.

"Well, I think he's got a couple of broken ribs, or at least badly bruised, but it's his back that's a real mess," Mrs. English explained. "But what exactly happened, I couldn't tell you. Your father said the storm whupped him good, that was all. To me, it looked like someone had taken a cat o' nine tails to him and shredded him. But other than kind of makin' light of it, your father wouldn't say what happened. You go ahead and wake 'em now." She smiled and winked, encouraging me. "You'll be the medicine that'll mend 'em in no time." She stepped into the hall and quietly closed the door behind her. Turning back to my parents, I walked over to my mother's side of the bed and knelt down by her.

"Mama?" I said softly, gently rubbing the edge of her face with the back of my hand. "Mama, can you hear me?"

She let out a small, soft groan as though it hurt to have to come back to consciousness; then her eyes fluttered open and she turned her head sharply to see who or what was kneeling next to her. The grimace on her face told me she'd painfully felt that sudden movement, but, then, as recognition dawned in her eyes, all traces of pain were lifted, replaced with an expression of relief and absolute joy. She started to sit up, but I quickly stood and gently held her shoulders down. "Lie still, Mama. Lie still. I'm here," I whispered, leaning over her and softly kissing her lips. "I'm all right, and Dylan is fine, and I'm here. I'm here," I repeated, my voice cracking and the tears falling freely.

She said nothing, but took my hand, kissed it, and then held it to her cheek and closed her eyes. "Eliza," she whispered. "Oh, my Eliza." Tears escaped the corners of her eyes and slowly made tracks down her battered face.

"Don't talk, Mama. I'll sit here with you, but you just rest now. I won't go anywhere."

Just then, my father's eyes opened. Startled at hearing someone else in the room, he lifted his head off the pillow and turned toward me. At first, he looked a bit confused, but then he realized it was me and joy replaced the confusion on his face, just as it had on Mama's. "Ah, baby girl," he whispered, lowering his head and closing his eyes, but smiling as he did. "I told you she'd come," he whispered to Mama. Then, he drifted off.

I tip-toed to the door and opened it slightly. Striker was standing alone in the hallway, leaning against the gallery railing. "You want to come in?" I whispered. "They're sleeping, but at least you can see them."

"No. I don't want to take the chance of waking them," he said.

I walked out into the hallway and quietly closed the door behind me.

"How do they seem?" Striker looked deeply concerned.

"Well, they're hurt bad, but at least they responded to me. I want to sit with them for a while. Is that all right?"

"You stay with them for as long as you want. I'm gonna go get that fuel I keep trying to find. It might take me a while, but I'll be back."

I re-entered the room, closed the curtains a little more so that the sun wasn't shining directly in my parents' faces, and then sat down in a wicker rocker in the corner closest to them. I couldn't take my eyes off them, and I didn't, until the light of the day became the shadows of the night.

Chapter 33

Bound by Love

Mama and I sat on Mrs. English's porch waiting for Striker and Papa to return from the Port of Entry so that we could make the journey home. It had been three days since we'd found my parents but they hadn't been in any shape to leave before now. While we'd waited for some of their strength to return, Striker had returned to Alligator Light to let Dylan know that our folks had been found. His reaction was as expected; he was overjoyed that they were alive, but terribly worried about their injuries. Striker reassured him that they were being well cared for, and that the outlook for their recovery was good. And he also delivered Mama's message asking Dylan to keep the light burning brightly to help guide us back home again.

While Striker waited for my parents to heal enough to be moved, he helped with Key West's massive clean-up. There was nothing for him to do at Mrs. English's, so pitching in to help the community was a good way for him to pass the time until we were able to leave. He slept on the boat at night, while I slept in a small bedroom Mrs. English provided for me. I would have slept on the floor to be near my parents, but the kind woman graciously gave me a comfortable room, while also providing breakfast and supper for all of us, Striker included. Thanks to her good care, Mama was quickly recovering from her nasty head wound, and Papa's badly lacerated back was responding nicely to the salve which Mrs. English applied thrice daily. Papa had teased the good woman by asking her if she wasn't really a medicine woman who had run off from her tribe. With a twinkle in her eye, she assured him that she wasn't, and that what she lacked in training and skill, God had made up for with good common sense and stubbornness. "Ain't no one dying under my roof," she'd firmly said.

"Bad for business," she laughingly added. Now, as we sat on her porch on White Street, watching a neighbor hauling away debris from what had been a large shed, Mama wanted to know what was going on with Owen. She knew something was very amiss for I hadn't mentioned his name once, so I told her the truth, in all of its ugliness.

Mama was both stunned and furious, but I told her that Striker had had a little talk with Owen as we were leaving for the Keys, and that it was highly unlikely Owen would ever be a threat to me again. I also told her that Papa needed to know about Owen, Adam, and Ezra's ownership in the Florida Land Expansion and Acquisition Corporation, but that he didn't need to know about Owen hitting me. There wasn't any point in it and the consequences might be catastrophic.

"I thought I'd lost y'all once, Mama. We don't need to lose Papa to the penal justice system," I said with a small smile. Then, wanting to move on, I asked her, "How did you and Papa survive the storm? Do you remember much of it?" Mama said she remembered all of it until she was hit in the head, and from that point on, she could only recall scattered bits and pieces. It was bad, she said, but it could have been so much worse.

"We'd left Key West, and were making a mad dash for Alligator Light," Mama began. "That's where we wanted to be when we got hit with the brunt of the storm. We knew it was comin' in because we'd gotten word earlier in Key West, but we thought we had time to make it to Alligator. But just off Boot Key, a huge freighter making a beeline for Key West swamped our trawler, dousing the boiler. We were dead in the water. Soon as the next big wave hit us, we slammed into the reef, and I was thrown against the bait box, or somethin' on that side of the boat. Your father was slammed hard against the ship's wheel. He injured a couple of his ribs, and I got knocked out, but your father got us off the boat and onto Boot Key. I don't know how he did it, but he did. There was nothing around us but vegetation, so your father tied us to a red mangrove tree and we rode out the storm bound to each other and that tree."

"Good Lord, Mama! You mean you had no cover of any sort?" I asked, horrified.

"Well, I did, but your father didn't," my mother said, her eyes welling up.

"What do you mean?" I was confused. "I thought you said you were together."

"Oh, we were. Very much so," Mama said, smiling softly and pulling a handkerchief out of the pocket of a pair of my pants she was wearing. Mama wiped her eyes, gently blew her nose and went on. "Your father covered me throughout the entire storm. He kept his back exposed to the wrath of it. He had sand and shells, and God knows what all, tearing at his skin like he was being whipped by a cruel hand. And he didn't make a sound through it all, except at the end. Something fairly large must have hit him pretty good, and he let out a sharp grunt from the impact. Then he made no other sound for a long time. That was the scariest part of all. Oh, I knew he was still alive, 'cause I could feel him breathing against me. But I didn't know if he'd regain consciousness again."

Mama said no more, so we just sat there sipping our coffee and looking out beyond Mrs. English's front gate as I imagined the horrific scenes that my parents had barely lived through, while Mama relived them all over again. Finally, my mother broke the silence and returned to another painful subject; she asked me what I thought my plans for the future might be now.

"Well, the first thing I'm gonna do when we get home is to cancel all of the wedding arrangements," I replied. "I know it's going to cause our family some embarrassment and I'm so sorry for that."

"Oh, hogwash, Eliza!" Mama scoffed. "Nobody's gonna be embarrassed about anything! As far as calling off the wedding goes, why, the hurricane took care of that for us! It's a good excuse to cancel it, and no one will be any the wiser. Now, back to more important things, like how you're really feeling about all of this."

"Honestly, Mama, I know I should say I'm devastated over what happened with Owen, but I really don't feel all that broken up about it. I know that sounds strange. I don't know, maybe I'm just numb at this point, and the reality of it will hit me later. But I don't feel like I've received a crushing blow. Tell me the truth, Mama. Am I strange? Am I in denial?"

"Well, first of all, you're not strange." Mama smiled as she reached for my left hand, which was gripping the end of the rocker's arm. "And as far as denial goes, I don't believe you were ever in love with that man. Honestly, Eliza, I believe that the man you love is with—"

She didn't get the chance to finish. Mrs. English came out of the front door with a large bag and set it on the small table by Mama. "Here's some dinner for y'all to take with you. It's just some ham biscuits and a few chicken legs…and maybe some ginger snaps, too." She winked. Her cookies were wonderful, and we'd managed to eat every one of them up. "None of it's fancy, but it'll hold ya. I've also prepared some extra salve for you to take. Remember, you only need to apply it twice a day now."

"Bertie, what are we gonna do without you?" Mama said, taking the woman's hand and holding it against her cheek.

"Oh, poppycock!" Mrs. English exclaimed, but she looked pleased all the same. "You know I'm gonna miss y'all," she said.

"Well, there's no need to go missin' us, Bertie. You come to Miami whenever you want to. I've already told you that. There'll always be a room ready and waitin' for you. And you know we'll be back down," Mama assured her. It was obvious the two women had become friends for life.

Papa and Striker returned from the Port of Entry soon after, and both were in a pensive mood. While they were gone, I'd explained Striker's suspicions to Mama, and what we'd found in the Port of Entry log book. When the men walked onto the porch, no one said a word about what they had done at the Port of Entry. We all understood that this was something to keep among the four of us, at least for the time being. Thirty minutes later, after bidding a tearful Bertie English farewell at the front gate of her bright pink Victorian house, we boarded Striker's boat and pulled away from the salty mangroves of Key West. We wouldn't stop at Alligator, since we knew that Dylan was fine, and he knew that we were, as well. Instead, we set our course for North Key Largo. It was time to find Uncle James.

Chapter 34

Scattered and Shattered

Soon after we left Key West, we had a lengthy discussion about Papa and Striker's findings at the Port of Entry. We had to contact the Secretary of the Department of Commerce in Washington, D.C. once we returned to Miami. From that point, the Secretary would decide how to proceed. My father agreed with Striker that a formal investigation would likely ensue, and when I asked what they thought the punishment would be for something of that magnitude, neither one could say. Striker said that he'd never heard of a situation where a lighthouse keeper had been the cause of a wreck. That wasn't to say it hadn't happened before, but, if it had, no one had ever been caught.

As we approached North Key Largo, and specifically Angelfish Key, all talk about corrupt lighthouse keepers ceased while we focused our attention on the devastation that had occurred in this particular area. It was here that my uncle had built one of Flagler's hotels, and would soon start on a home of his own, as well as a second hotel for the railroad baron. It was also here that the railroad had been in the process of laying tracks down. Looking around, all we could see was an enormous amount of rubble. It looked as though a giant hand had reached down and simply ripped up buildings and train tracks. Metal and construction materials had been tossed about as though they were the tiny pieces of a child's dollhouse. There was little left to salvage in the scattered wreckage of so many people's shattered dreams.

Mama and Papa had visited Uncle James in Key Largo when he'd been in the midst of building the first hotel, and he had proudly given them the tour of what he expected would be his greatest accomplishment. Now, only half of it was standing. The building originally had four floors, but the top two were now gone. It looked as though they'd been sheared right off.

Drawing my attention away from the destruction, Striker told me to be ready to jump off the boat and tie us to one of the pilings at the dock. Once we were secured, Striker and I helped Mama and Papa off the boat. Not too far away was a group of men throwing things onto a heap of debris. "Maybe they'll know somethin' about James," Mama said anxiously, immediately heading over to them. One of the men, a tall lanky fellow, stopped working and met us halfway between the dock and the debris pile. It was obvious from the look on his face that he was curious as to why we were there.

"Can I help y'all?" the man asked once he was close enough to be heard.

"We're the Harjos from up Miami way," my father said. "James Stewart is my wife's brother." He nodded toward my mother. "We haven't seen or heard from him since the storm. Would you know him or his whereabouts?"

The hot Florida sun had tanned the worker's skin to the color of a nut, but upon hearing my father's question, the man literally turned a couple of shades paler. "Uh…Mr. Harjo—ya say yer name is?" The man removed his cap, and wiped sweat away from his forehead with a filthy handkerchief he pulled from his back pocket. "Might I speak with ya private-like?"

"If there's somethin' that needs saying," my mother said firmly, "then it needs to be said for all to hear."

The man walked closer. "Ma'am, my name is Patrick Wright, and I worked with your brother—have for a couple of years now. When the storm started comin' in, Mr. James made sure all of us workers were headin' out. A large barge was sent in to get us, and it got here early enough, but your brother decided to stay behind. We had a crew headin' back up here after takin' some lumber down to Tavernier, but they weren't back yet and the small window of time we had for gettin' out was closing. Mr. James said he wasn't leavin' without 'em, and that they'd try to get on another boat bound for Miami. Said if they couldn't then they'd ride the storm out in the safest part of the building. Last I saw of him, he was standing right on that dock there." He nodded toward our boat. "He was jus' watchin' us pull away."

I heard a small whimper from Mama, and I looked over to see Papa step up to her and wrap his arm firmly around her waist.

"Did they find his remains, Mr. Wright—or any of the others?" Papa asked.

"Found four of 'em, but we lost a total of nine men. The four we found was in the men's bathroom on the second floor of the hotel," he replied, nodding toward the sheared-off building. "The floors above just came down on 'em."

"Was James among those found?" my father quickly asked. It was unnecessary to hear any more gruesome details. Dead was dead. At this point, it didn't matter how it had happened.

"Yes, sir, he was," Patrick quietly confirmed, glancing over at my mother as he did. She said nothing, however. She didn't moan or cry or whimper. She looked frozen in place.

"Where'd they take his body, Mr. Wright?" Papa asked.

"We buried him over yonder. We tried to let the families in Miami know, but only one of the bodies was claimed, and it was gettin' too hot to try and keep—"

"Please just show us where he's buried." Striker said, cutting him off.

"O' course, o' course," Patrick quickly agreed.

We walked about fifty yards beyond the debris pile to a place that had three separate mounded graves. At the head of each was a rough wooden cross with the deceased's name, date of death, and the letters *R.I.P.* carved into it. Uncle James's grave was on the far left.

Mama fell to her knees at the foot of it. She leaned forward, placed her hands on top of the mound, and then she bowed her head and sobbed. I gave her a moment—we all did—before I knelt down beside her and rested my hand on her back. Striker and Papa came up behind us as if to guard the grieving, while Patrick Wright softly muttered his condolences. "He was one of the finest men I've ever known," he said softly as he stood there awkwardly spinning his cap in his hands. Then, unsure as to what else he could do or say, Patrick walked away and left us to mourn.

Chapter 35

Shadows

A certain darkness hung over our home, and though we tried to be strong and positive for each other, times of overwhelming sadness, grief, and anger came and went like stealthy shadows. We'd been home for nearly a week, and while we tried to return to some semblance of normalcy, we trudged our way through each day as though we were wading through mud, and found that sleep was an elusive comfort at night.

Mama was quiet and withdrawn as she struggled with the loss of her closest sibling. And Papa was frustrated and angry at himself for not having gotten to James in time to bring him home before the storm. He blamed himself for the death of his brother-in-law and close friend, and for the suffering that the loss caused Mama.

Meanwhile, I tried to process all the changes that had taken place in such a small span of time, not the least of which was my relationship with Owen. In reality, what bothered me the most was that I had been so blind to Owen's true character. I analyzed and dissected every day we'd spent together, which actually hadn't been a great many considering the fact that he spent the majority of his time at Fowey Rocks Light. And I rebuked myself over and over again that I hadn't been more attuned to the fact that what I had once considered to be Owen's ambitiously strong personality was, in truth, a downright conniving and deceptive one. But, as Mama was quick to remind me, hindsight was twenty-twenty, and the man had fooled us all with his charm and dishonorable intentions. While I was grateful for my mother's attempts to comfort me, especially since she was so weighed down with her own terrible sadness, I still blamed myself for being so easily deceived.

Knowing I needed to keep busy as well as make some money, since Papa and I hadn't salvaged any wrecks of late, nor had any plans to do so in the foreseeable future, I went back to work for Mr. Burdine. And I planned on talking to Paroh Monday about resuming my teaching position until the time the Seminoles were forced to leave. I just hadn't had the chance to go see him yet. The woman whom Mr. Burdine had hired to replace me hadn't worked out well at all. The wonderful expertise and skills she claimed never materialized, and the woman left the job one afternoon without giving notice. The shop was in complete disarray when I went to see him. New merchandise had arrived some days before, and other than Mr. Burdine and one part-timer, there'd been no one else to help inventory it, much less attractively display it throughout the store. So, I spent the majority of the first week back in Miami setting the retailer's business in order.

No matter how busy I tried to keep myself, the one constant thought that kept interrupting all others was Striker. There was no doubt about it: I loved him. I always had and I was quite certain that I always would. I knew that even if I was to fall in love with a good man and marry him eventually, there would always be a part of me that would be untrue to him. There would be feelings for Striker that would leave a shadow on my soul, but I prayed that the passing of time would quiet those torturous feelings, easing them into something I could tolerate.

I'd only seen Striker once since we'd gotten home, and that was the very next morning when he'd come by the house so that he and Papa could send a wire from the trading post to the Secretary of the Department of Commerce and Labor. Papa was gone for the rest of the day, but over supper that night he told Mama and me that the wire had simply stated that they requested a meeting with the Secretary, Warren Chaplain, to discuss evidence. Papa and Striker had stuck around the post to see if there might be a quick response, and within an hour one came in. Mr. Chaplain said that he took their allegations extremely seriously and would take a train from Washington the following week. Because Striker was due to report at his new job in St. Augustine in less than two weeks, he had just enough time to sit down with Secretary Chaplain before leaving. Until that time, he had to get back out to Fowey Light to relieve Owen. I wondered how the two men would react to seeing each other as one came and the other went. Hopefully, nothing more than a shift change would take place for it was vital that Striker keep his cool and allow an investigation to be conducted without anything else interfering.

I said nothing when Papa finished telling us what had transpired, other than that I would get started on the supper dishes. Afterward, I went out on the porch to finish my glass of tea and watch the sunset. Mama joined me a few minutes later, sitting down in the rocker next to me. She took my hand, and simply said, "There's a red sky tonight. Tomorrow should be a good day. We're due a few, ya know."

True to his word, Secretary Chaplain got off the train at the Fort Dallas station in downtown Miami eight days later, and Papa and Striker were there to meet him. It was in the middle of the evening when my father finally returned home. He said the day had been very productive, just longer than expected.

They'd started their meeting by giving the Secretary a detailed account of the correlation between the dates of specific wrecks and the lighthouse keepers who had been on duty, explaining that all of their information could be verified in the log books at the Port of Entry in Key West. But Mr. Chaplain had come prepared. He had copies of the logs with him, and the three men meticulously scrutinized dates, places, and keepers. In the end, the Secretary determined they had enough to begin a formal investigation.

Mr. Chaplain surprised them with the news that my brother would be considered for the Key West lighthouse keeper's job if charges were filed against Owen. But, even if they weren't, Owen could still be deemed incompetent to handle the job of light keeper at the end of the investigation. Though it would take Dylan farther from us, the job was a prestigious one, and the lighthouse was land-based, making it a far less isolated and dangerous place for him to work. So, we would keep our fingers crossed that the job would be offered to him.

The other bit of stunning news was not delivered by Mr. Chaplain, but by Striker: Owen had not been seen since right after the storm. When Striker had gone to relieve Owen the week before, he wasn't at the light. Jim Altman was the only one there, and had been since Owen departed. All Owen told Jim was that he had urgent business in town and would be back the next day, but he never returned. Now, with Owen missing, and Striker leaving, the Commerce Secretary would be actively seeking two new keepers to work alongside Jim at Fowey. Mr. Chaplain said he felt like Pandora's box had been opened because he wasn't just investigating the criminal conduct of Owen Perry and Adam Wilson—not to mention Ezra Asher—but he now had to file a report about the missing keeper, as well. We all wondered if perhaps Owen had sensed he'd been found out, and had taken off for parts unknown. However, there was just no way he could have known that an investigation was being considered, so we discounted that as a possibility.

Finally, after talking with my parents until well past midnight, I fell into bed, but once again, sleep was slow in coming. As I lay there, I watched the shadows on my ceiling cast by the avocado tree outside. Each time a breeze stirred the branches, the shadows moved like elongated abstract hands beckoning to me. I wondered where they might lead me if I was to jump through the ceiling into their light, ethereal realm. And if the pain I was feeling would be left behind or would follow me through infinite worlds.

Chapter 36

Ol' Blind Benny

I finally had the chance to go see Paroh the day after Warren Chaplain came in from Washington. As I made my way along the Miami River toward the village, I looked out at the disrupted, ever-changing landscape that was the result of the horrific dredging. Before too long, the canals would run the water out of the Glades and into the bay, but as of late, there'd been some problems with government funding. Those problems gave us hope that the project would take far longer than expected, and might possibly be snuffed out altogether if the price was too high to accomplish the enormous undertaking.

Not far from me was John Watson's farm. Newly arrived from Kissimmee, John was raising sugarcane, but I'd overheard him at the trading post telling a fellow farmer that if they drained the Glades, he wouldn't be able to raise an umbrella. And that was about the truth of it.

When I entered the village, the mongrel dog, *Fotcho*, appeared out of nowhere and barked at me until I gave him the piece of biscuit he equated with my arrival. "How you been, buddy, huh? I see you're still guardin' the place." I tossed him a second piece. I'd missed the little guy.

"Miss Eliza!" someone shouted. Looking off to my right, I saw Rose hurrying toward me with a broad smile and a small load of logs in her arms. Gathering wood to feed their ever-burning cooking fire was a never-ending chore. "Miss Eliza, we worried about you. No see since big wind."

"I know, Rose. I had a family emergency after the storm. How did you all do?"

"Everyone fine!" she said, smiling. The relief in her voice was evident. "The mangroves protect us real good."

"I'm glad," I said, climbing down from Sundae. "Where's Paroh? Is he around today?"

"He's over at Simon's chickee," she said, glancing off in the direction of his hut. "They kill big gator for gift to take to Chief Sam Church, in Immokalee. We go in four suns."

"How long will you be gone?" I asked. It wasn't unusual for the different tribes to gather together for festivals or celebrations, such as a marriage.

"Always," she responded matter-of-factly.

"What do you mean 'always'? I don't understand." My first thought was that she was confused about the dates.

"Paroh says we have to go before we have nothing to eat. Fish and animals don't like those machines that chew up our land. So, we go to place that still has plenty of food. Immokalee!" she stated again, as if doing so would clear everything up for me.

"My Aunt Ivy lives there," I said, my head reeling. Then, "Are you glad you're going, Rose? Does it make you sad?"

"Not so much," she answered honestly. "My people are used to running from the white skins and their bad ways." As if she realized she'd insulted my people, she hurriedly added, "Not all bad, Miss Eliza. But not so many good like you."

There wasn't much I could say in defense of my own race. Looking off in the distance at the encroaching dredging machines, I couldn't really argue her point.

"I'm goin' over to Simon's," I said. "I'll see you before I go."

I left her to her chores, and as I made my way through the village, I could see various tasks being performed that certainly indicated a move was imminent. Many of the household and personal items that usually hung from the beams of chickees' roofs had been removed and packed away. An unusual amount of clothing was being washed in anticipation of meeting their new extended family. These people had great pride and wanted to meet the Immokalee tribe as nicely dressed and neatly groomed as possible. Over on long racks, several beautiful large skins were being tanned. While that wasn't an unusual thing, considering what I knew about their upcoming move, I guessed that they were preparing these as gifts for some of the Immokalee elders.

When I reached Simon's chickee, he and Paroh were not in it, but I could see them about fifty yards away working on the gator. Actually, Simon was cutting up the meat, while Paroh stood by supervising. The meat would be salted to preserve it, or perhaps smoked, and the skin would be carefully preserved as a gift for Chief Sam Church.

"Greetings, Paroh and Simon!" I called from a short distance away.

Simon's knife stilled in the middle of cutting out a tenderloin as he looked up, while Paroh immediately turned to see who had called their names. Both men smiled so broadly that I realized they were just as relieved and happy to see me as I was to see them. These people had become family to me, and to think that they would soon be leaving stabbed at my heart as surely as Simon's knife had cut into the gator's.

The skin of the beast was hanging from a large rack, and it appeared to be about thirteen to fourteen feet long, making it one of the biggest alligators I'd ever seen.

"That's a big gator, my friends!" I exclaimed. "Did it take the whole village to kill it?" I asked, walking toward them.

"Believe it or not, Miss Eve, just Paroh!" Simon enthusiastically bragged about his chief's hunting prowess.

Paroh walked up to me and held me at arm's length, as though to confirm that I was indeed all right. "I see the storm did not chew you up," he said, smiling mischievously.

"No," I chuckled, "but it nearly did my mother and father."

Paroh's smile was instantly gone. "What happened?"

"Their boat went down off of Boot Key. Papa's back was cut up pretty badly and he cracked a couple of ribs, and Mama took a good hit on the head. But they're healing just fine, and nearly as good as new. I see y'all fared well," I said, looking around and seeing that the camp had already been cleared of any debris. "No one was hurt or lost, Rose tells me."

"We made it through fine," Paroh confirmed. "Simon," he said, turning to him, "finish the butchering and I'll be back in a while to decide what we'll eat now and what we'll preserve for gifts. The skin will go to Sam Church, of course, so care for it well. There can be no flaws in this one." Then Paroh invited me to his chickee to talk.

When we stepped into his dwelling, the relief of the shade felt wonderful. A gentle breeze blew through the large hut, making it comfortable enough in the midday heat. Paroh scooped up a dipper of water from a bucket, and graciously offered it to me before quenching his own thirst. Usually, the chief would have taken a drink first, but the fact that he offered the dipper to me was a sign of respect. I gratefully accepted and drank the entire dipper. Though it wasn't refreshing, it washed away the dry thickness in my mouth. The sun was still scorching hot, even in mid-October.

"So, you single-handedly killed that gator, Paroh?" The chief simply smiled at me as he tamped tobacco down into the bowl of his pipe. "I'm impressed," I said. "I don't mean to lessen your great feat any, but was the alligator sick, or very old?"

"Very *hungry*," Paroh said between pulls on his pipe stem.

"Why? There's still fish and game here," I pointed out.

"He was blind in one eye," Paroh said, sitting down in one of the two chairs and indicating for me to take the other. "Made it hard for him to hunt. So, I helped him. When he came in for the bait…well…that was the end of Ol' Blind Benny."

"And you're giving the gift of his hide to Sam Church," I finished. "Rose told me you're leaving." I couldn't keep the sadness out of my voice.

"We are," he said matter-of-factly.

"I have some news for you that just might change your mind," I said, praying it would.

"Oh?" he said, sounding doubtful.

"Owen Perry and the others who own the company that bought your land may not be able to drain it as planned," I began, resting my forearms on my thighs and leaning in toward him, as if I were sharing a big secret. "They're being investigated on some very serious charges. Nothing is going to happen while that's going on, and if they're found guilty, then they could be facing some lengthy prison time."

Paroh pulled the pipe from his mouth. "It won't matter."

"I beg your pardon?" I said, sitting upright in my chair. "What do you mean, 'it won't matter'"?

"Eliza, the white man is like ants on a grasshopper: What one doesn't eat up another will. It doesn't matter if one company doesn't dredge here. Another will dredge *over there*. What affects one part of the land, affects the other. The dredging is corrupting the flow of the water north of us, so it's affecting the hunting and fishing here. Why you think Ol' Blind Benny had such trouble? He still had one good eye, and he outweighed all the others, but he was slower than many of the younger ones. Fish are dying or heading to other places, so food is harder to come by for a poor ol' fellow like Benny. And when the animals don't eat, *we* don't eat. There's good land with plenty for all to eat in Immokalee," Paroh continued. "So, we go."

"Rose says you're going within the week," I said softly.

"In four days," Paroh confirmed. "We meet Sam Church and other tribal members at the halfway point between our camp and theirs.

"I'm glad you came today," he said, changing the subject and rising from his chair. "I want to give you something."

Paroh walked over to a small box sitting on the same table where he kept his pipe. Lifting the lid, he removed something, then walked back to me. I stood up as he did. Picking my hand up, he placed a beautiful simple gold locket and chain in my hand. In the center of it was an exquisite emerald.

"You aren't the only one to try to barter shipwrecked goods with us," he said, his mischievous eyes sparkling. "This is very old and very good. It comes from one of three ships that was wrecked in an armada from Portugal."

"Oh, Paroh," I whispered in awe as I examined the beautiful piece closely. It was oval, with the focal point being the magnificent solitaire emerald in the center. The gold was deep in color and heavy. "I certainly can't take this from you. I thank you from my heart and soul, but someone in your family should have it."

"You are part of my family, Eliza. You're a beloved *enhesse*—friend," he translated, laying his hand against my cheek.

Covering his hand with mine, I fought back tears as I looked at the proud Seminole chief standing before me. I'd grown to love and respect him in such a short amount of time.

"Thank you, dear friend," I said, grateful for his gift, but, more importantly, for his acceptance and love for me. "I shall wear it with pride, always." I slipped the chain over my head. "May I ask one thing of you?"

"Of course," Paroh replied.

"Would you allow my family and me to escort you and your people to meet the Immokalee tribe? It would be our honor to ride beside you as you begin your new journey. Also, if Aunt Ivy comes, Mama might be able to see her. And Papa has relatives in that camp, as well."

"We would be proud to have you with us," Paroh said, smiling.

"What time do we leave?" I asked.

"One hour after sunrise."

"My family and I will be here. I must go now." I kissed him on the cheek. "Thank you for this." I looked down at the locket. "Your gift is great, and my heart thanks you."

I turned to leave and as I did, something blue caught my eye up on one of the beams. There, nailed to it, was a navy blue cap, identical to the one Owen always wore. I slowly turned toward Paroh, who was watching me with a small smile that turned up just one corner of his mouth.

"Paroh, you didn't happen to see Owen Perry, did you? He's been missing for some days now, and no one can figure out where he's gone."

"Lots of men come and go," Paroh replied, shrugging. "They're always around here looking at the land. Guess they're trying to figure out what piece to chew up next. They don't hear when you tell them the swamps hide many dangers. They go in, anyway. But this Owen, I don't know if he was among them. I've never met him, so I wouldn't know what he looks like."

"But Simon and Turtle would," I said, squinting my eyes slightly.

"And perhaps Ol' Blind Benny would, too." He smiled cryptically. "But we'll never know for sure."

A chill crept up my spine, and I said no more. Neither did Paroh. Some things were better left unsaid.

Chapter 37

Collision Course

Two days after visiting Paroh, Papa asked me to go with Simon and him up to Jupiter. He needed our help, he said, but would tell us no more. Later that afternoon, as we approached the Jupiter Inlet, I could see the stately red brick lighthouse in the distance, standing out sharply against the backdrop of a brilliant blue October sky. It was the perfect day to be out on the water if one wasn't depending on the wind for sailing, which we weren't. Instead, we were test running a small tug boat that my father was thinking about buying. It was one he'd seen at the Standard Oil dock when it had come up for sale several days before.

After losing the trawler in the storm, Papa was in the market for a new boat, and he'd been longing for a tug. As he told Mama, there was a real need for them now that more and more visitors were sailing the waters of South Florida. With what he could earn from towing as well as salvaging, the rig would more than pay for itself within the first year. A tug boat was a fine commodity to have in waters as treacherous as ours were, he said, and Mama really couldn't argue that point. As a matter of fact, my parents did very little in the way of arguing in the days following their miraculous survival in the storm. Not that they had ever been ones to disagree very often with each other, and even when they did, it was always settled calmly and fairly. But, ever since the storm, I'd found them talking softly and intimately with each other on several occasions, speaking words that were only meant for each other. I realized that their horrific ordeal had only brought them that much closer, making them value each other even more, and I prayed that one day I'd have as strong and loving a relationship as theirs.

I was standing by Papa at the helm, enjoying my time with him. Because we were eighty miles north of Miami, we'd stay the night at the Inlet, and then return home the next day. "So, if you buy the boat, Papa, what will you name it?" I asked as I re-tied my ponytail which had come undone from being wind-whipped.

"*Raffee Kote*," Papa laughed. "Muscogee for 'Big Frog.'"

"Good name for it," I laughingly agreed. The tug boat's cabin was painted a handsome shade of beige, but the entire stern was a bright, flashy green.

"Eliza, would you yell down to Simon? Tell him not to add any more wood to the boilers and to come up here, please."

Once Simon was up on deck, Papa told us to get up on the bow and watch for the first sign of Jupiter's deadly reef. After a couple of minutes, Simon spotted it about fifty yards up, in the ten o'clock position off the port side. Papa immediately told him to drop anchor and shut the boat down.

"Before we head back in the morning," Papa said, "I need y'all to check something out."

"What are you up to?" I laughed, narrowing my eyes suspiciously. "I do realize that we've gone much farther than necessary to test this boat." Shielding my eyes from the sun so that I could better see him, I realized from the look on his face that whatever we were going to do in the morning was no joking matter. Papa looked extremely serious and focused.

I rephrased my question. "What do you want us to do, Papa?"

"I want you to dive a wreck," he said matter-of-factly.

"Which wreck?" I excitedly asked. "Are you thinkin' about salvaging it?"

"No," Papa replied, immediately squashing my enthusiasm. "It's nothing like that. Let's get some dinner and I'll tell y'all about it while we're eating."

Mama had packed plenty of food for us, so we pulled out some of the roasted chicken and cornbread, as well as mason jars of tea. Then we sat down at the table in the small cabin to eat.

"I need you two to go down to the wreck and tell me what you see; where the boat is damaged and how badly; if it looks as though the boat slammed up against the reef, as opposed to plowing into it head-on—that sort of thing."

"Okay," I responded, unsure what my father's thinking was at that point. "What wreck is it, Papa?"

"It's the Stricklands' boat, the *Strike One*," Papa grimly replied.

There was absolute silence in the cabin. No one said a word. Chills ran through my body as I realized what I was being asked to do: I'd be swimming into the place where Striker's parents had breathed their last.

Papa finally broke the silence. "Until I know more about it, let's leave it at that. Let's get dinner cleaned up and then call it a day. We'll get an early start tomorrow morning, so let's get a decent night's sleep."

I slept in one of the staterooms, while Papa and Simon shared the other. I was so tired that it didn't take me long to drift off to sleep, but that's when the nightmares started. In them, the Stricklands beckoned to me from their watery grave to come help them, but I was too frightened to do so. Instead, I turned to swim away only to come face to face with other victims of other wrecks swimming beneath the waves.

Right before first light, I was awakened by Papa gently shaking my shoulder. "Dawn's breaking," he said softly. Throwing back the covers, I slowly got out of the bunk, grabbed a cup of coffee Papa had already brewed on the small wood-burning kitchen stove and walked out to the deck. The dawn's light was turning the darkened sky into a breathtaking blue, and I was glad that we would have clear weather.

Once we were done eating, it was light enough to start diving. Papa reminded Simon and me what we were specifically looking for, so, after stripping down to my diving outfit, I dove in. A second later, I heard a splash to my right as Simon joined me.

We started to swim toward the reef, which was quite visible in the calm water, and as we did, I could easily make out the eerie sight of the ghostly wreckage of the medium-sized sailboat lying on its starboard side in about twenty-five feet of water. The mainsail mast was broken in two, with half of it still secured to the boat's deck so that it pointed off to the right, while the other half of it was lying on top of the reef. Once I got closer, I could make out the name, which was painted white on the transom: *Strike One.* I instantly stopped moving forward and could feel the rapid beating of my heart. Finally seeing the wreck affected me far more than I had ever thought it would. Treading water for a moment, I tried to calm myself while Simon swam along the exposed hull of the boat, carefully inspecting it, as well as the port side for any damage. Finally, I swam forward until I was within ten feet of the back of the boat.

Lying dead beneath the waves, the vessel looked as though it had been slain by some nautical beast. Part of the mainsail was twisted and wrapped around the broken mast like a useless bandage, but from this vantage point, I could see no other damage. Reaching out, I laid my hand against the ship's name, saying a silent prayer for Mae and Jerry Strickland, and then I moved on.

Just as Simon had done, I carefully inspected both the bottom of the boat and the exposed left side, but saw no damage, so I swam up toward

Simon at the bow. As soon as I joined him, he pointed to something. Turning to look, I was shocked by what I saw: There, where the lower part of the bow should have been, was a massive, jagged gaping hole. A front portion of the sleek, beautiful sailboat had been totally crushed and ripped away, and I was actually able to see inside the vessel's cabin. *The Stricklands aren't inside,* I reminded myself. *Thank God.* Their bodies had been washed ashore, and were buried in the Miami City Cemetery, on Second Avenue. My family and I had attended their double funeral. But, even without their human remains onboard, I could see small reminders that they'd been there.

Sitting upright on the floor was a small black pot, which was turning to rust. Behind it was a bait bucket with the word STRICKLAND hand-printed across it. But what affected me the most was the pair of gold, wire-rimmed glasses that had gotten caught up in some netting. They had belonged to Jerry. The netting gently flapped around as if in slow motion from the current moving in and around the boat, and the glasses were fated to move endlessly with it. The sight was too much, and I surfaced. Refilling my lungs with a great gulp of air, I swam away from the wreck as quickly as I could, vowing never to go back, and made my way to the tug. Grabbing the rope ladder hanging off the stern, I climbed onto the tug and sat down on a large equipment box. Looking over the side, toward the front of the boat, I could see Simon making his way back to us.

"What'd you see?" my father anxiously asked, handing me a towel.

"Lower section of the bow's gone," I said, toweling water out of my left ear.

"Any other damage?" he asked.

"None on the portside, but I couldn't see the starboard side. She's resting on it. From what I could tell, though, the front took the entire impact. But maybe Simon saw something I didn't."

A minute later, Simon climbed onto the stern. He confirmed what I had seen: The only damage visible was to the lower portion of the bow.

"I swam inside the cabin but I couldn't see any holes in the starboard wall," Simon said as he wiped his face with a towel my father handed to him. "It looks completely solid on that side. It was like Mr. Strickland got off course or somethin', and plowed head-first into that reef," he said, shaking his head. "But, still, even if he'd been off course, he shoulda been able to see the lighthouse. Odd," he said, his brows furrowed. Simon walked toward the cabin, looking as though he was trying to figure out a puzzle. "I'm gonna grab a clean shirt."

Once he was out of sight, Papa and I just stared at each other. There was no need for words. Both he and I knew that Jerry Strickland had been an accomplished sailor, completely at home in these waters; he wouldn't have made novice mistakes. The cause of the wreck was crystal clear to us: The Stricklands had intentionally been driven into that reef.

"Owen was on duty then," Papa said softly, but said no more as Simon reemerged from the cabin.

"Go ahead and fire up the boiler, Simon," Papa said. "We're headin' home."

As we made our way back to Miami, I racked my brain trying to figure out why Owen would have wanted to bring the Stricklands' boat down. They had no cargo on board to speak of, certainly nothing of such value that it was worth the risk of being caught extinguishing the light. So, what was the reason? The answers—if there were any—would have to wait until we got home, where Papa and I could talk openly. Until then, nothing more could be said. Striker and my family were the only ones who knew the investigation was going on, and until Secretary Chaplain made a decision about an indictment, it would stay that way.

Chapter 38

Battling Demons

When we got back to Miami after examining the wreck, Papa wanted to see the folks at Standard Oil about purchasing the tug boat. First, he dropped me off at our dock, then headed down river with Simon to drop him off closer to his little home near the fork. Fortunately, Papa's righthand man wasn't leaving with the rest of his tribe, but had elected to stay in Miami, where work was plentiful and the pay was good.

As Mama and I waited for Papa to get back, we sat on the porch shucking corn for our supper while I filled her in on what we'd found, and what we suspected had caused the *Strike One* to slam bow-first into the reef. Mama was just as anxious as I was to hear Papa's thoughts about it, and every time we heard the sound of a boat coming down the river, our heads quickly turned in that direction to see if Papa had returned. A little while later, as Mama finished working on an Apple Brown Betty, and I stirred sugar into a pitcher of tea, Papa walked into the kitchen.

"Looks good," Papa said, walking by the platter of chicken fricassee on his way to the sink to wash his hands.

"Did you get the boat?" I excitedly asked as I chipped away at a large chunk of ice in a bowl and filled our glasses with the small pieces.

"I did," Papa confirmed as he turned and dried his hands on my mother's apron.

"Get a towel," Mama laughed, playfully swatting his hands away. "Lord, you're a nuisance—you know that, Max Harjo?"

"Ah, but a nice one," he said, winking at me as he snitched a piece of ice from my bowl and stuck it in his mouth.

We sat down to eat, and after Papa said grace, we started passing food around.

"So, the boat's all yours, is it?" Mama smiled, handing my father a bowl of peas.

"All *ours*," he corrected her. "This is gonna be a good thing, Eve. She's a steady rig and she burns through fuel more efficiently than the trawler. I think we'll get a lot of use out of her."

I was trying to be patient about moving on to the subject of the *Strike One*, but my patience finally ran out. "Papa, I told Mama what we found today at the wreck; now tell us what you know about it."

"Let him finish his dinner first, Eliza," Mama gently admonished.

"It's all right," Papa said. The jovial mood immediately evaporated from the table. "I know y'all are anxious to hear.

"You know how Striker and I have been goin' over log books with Warren Chaplain, and such?" Papa began. "Well, I had a chance to spend some time with Chaplain, without Striker being around. I asked him if any real sizable ships had come into Jupiter Inlet, or even Hillsboro, the night the Stricklands wrecked. Don't forget, Adam Wilson was at Hillsboro Inlet then," he reminded us. I quickly glanced over at Mama and saw that she looked disgusted.

"Chaplain brought detailed copies of all the logs with him," Papa continued, "from each Port of Entry and every lighthouse, between here and Dames Point, on the St. Johns River in Jacksonville. They covered the last five years. It seems as though a steamer ship ported in Spain, named the *Mandori*, came into St. Augustine the same time every year, but would offload a small amount of its cargo at Jupiter Inlet while en route. Her cargo varied, but on her last trip, she carried silverware and fabrics, as well as beer and wine. The estimated value of her cargo was about a quarter of a million dollars. Have any guesses as to when the *Mandori* was due to arrive in Jupiter Inlet?" Papa sarcastically asked.

"The same night the *Strike One* went down," Mama said matter-of-factly.

"Right," Papa confirmed. "And that was why the Stricklands wrecked. We figure that the *Mandori* didn't take the last-minute turn into the inlet when Owen thought she would because there was just no cargo to offload at Jupiter like there usually was, or the captain thought the light was having problems and didn't want to chance it. The reality was the *Strike One* was in the worst place possible when the light went out. The *Mandori* did arrive in St. Augustine the next morning, and if it had cargo for Jupiter on board, it was either sent down via the train, or another ship coming back this way delivered it. Chaplain even suggested the possibility that Adam tried to snag the rig down at Hillsboro first, but when he failed, he sent a telegram to Owen, letting him know the ship was en route. Owen may have wrongly timed dousing the light 'cause he was jumpy about missing the *Mandori*, too, and if that was the case, then his bad timing saved the *Mandori*, but caused the wreck of the *Strike One*."

"How could Adam and Owen have communicated?" I asked.

"You forget that the Jupiter and Hillsboro lights are land-based. They have telegraph machines," Papa replied.

"Why wouldn't the captain of the *Mandori* have reported the lights going out?" Mama asked.

"Who knows?" Papa said. "Could be that Adam didn't try to catch the ship, but just alerted Owen that it was en route, and then Owen doused the light for only thirty or so seconds. Maybe the captain thought it was some kind of momentary glitch, or that he'd just lost sight of it for a moment. We'll never know, though, 'cause he died of consumption earlier this year.

"Look," Papa sighed, "the bottom line is this: The wreck of the *Strike One* was *not* due to a lack of nautical know-how, or because of substandard craftsmanship. From what Simon told me after we dropped you at the dock," Papa said, looking at me, "Striker's boat was exceptionally well made. After more than a year in the water, that thing is still solidly intact. It's a shame. What a terrible, terrible shame. It was a matter of the Stricklands being at the wrong place at the wrong time."

"As much as I hate to say this," Mama said, reaching for my hand, "I think that Owen wanted to marry you because you could help dive the wrecks they were causing, and having someone as well-respected as your father helping on some of them would keep people from taking too hard a look at Ezra, Owen, or Adam. I'm sorry, honey. I really am."

"Don't be, Mama," I said, covering her hand with mine. "I was a fool to trust him so quickly. So what now?" I asked, turning back to Papa.

"Chaplain is going to question Adam out at Carysfort, and Ezra Asher will be detained at the next Port of Entry he walks into. Obviously, Ezra's making a ton of money salvaging those wrecks. And," Papa added, "they're gonna be lookin' for Owen. My guess is warrants will be issued for all of them, and the indictments will include murder charges. The Stricklands will be among those they're being prosecuted for."

Mama and I didn't say anything for a moment as we digested the news. Even though the truth was terribly upsetting, we were all relieved that the answers to things that had plagued us were finally coming to light.

"Now," Papa said as he slowly rose from the table. He suddenly seemed tired. "I'm gonna go see Striker and tell him what we found. He's leaving first thing in the morning, you know."

I did know. And I also knew that the Seminoles were leaving in the morning, too. My heart felt as though it was breaking; one half going with Striker, and the other half with the tribe.

Without saying anything more, I carried my half-eaten supper to the sink and began to rinse the plate. I wanted to go with Papa to talk to Striker about his parents' wreck, but it would be better if Papa went alone. If Striker wanted to hit a wall, or cry, or use every uncouth word in the world, he could do so without holding back, and without feeling shame or embarrassment that a woman was standing there to witness it.

As Papa headed out the door, Mama gave him an extra Brown Betty she'd made for Striker. "Tell him we'll miss him and to come see us when he's in town again." Papa said he would and was almost out the door when Mama called to him.

"What time we leavin' to meet up with Paroh and the tribe tomorrow?" she asked.

"He said they were going to leave an hour after sunup, right, Eliza?"

All I could do was nod yes. I didn't trust my voice at that point.

"Let's head out about seven o'clock, then," Papa said. "That should make our timing about right." I heard the screen door slam behind him.

Suddenly, I felt Mama come up behind me and wrap her arms around my waist.

"Sometimes life is awfully hard, isn't it?" she said, laying her head against the back of my shoulder.

"Lately, it's been hard all the time, not just sometimes," I said, trying to make light of it.

"It'll get better," she assured me.

"Will it, Mama?"

"It will, and in the meantime, the good Lord will see to it that our skin gets a little thicker," she quipped.

"At this point, Mama, I think I need more than thicker skin. A suit of armor might serve me well."

"You don't need that, darlin' girl," Mama said, releasing me and going back to the table for more dishes. "Think about what wearin' that would be like on a hot July afternoon in Miami!"

We laughed and it felt good; then we fell into a comfortable silence as we became lost in our own thoughts. After the dishes were done, I went to my room to pack for the trip to Immokalee, but my mind was on Striker.

I wondered how he was reacting to the news from Papa, but I didn't have to wait long to find out. About an hour later, while Mama and I were sitting on the porch having some Brown Betty, Papa got home. Before he even reached the top step of the porch, Mama asked him how Striker had taken the news. Papa said that he got real quiet, and other than saying he was relieved to hear it and grateful to us for finding out, Striker didn't say much else. Papa also said that when he told Striker how Owen had caused the wreck, an absolutely murderous look crossed his face. Who could blame him, my father said. Silently, I thanked God that Ol' Blind Benny had gotten to Owen first, otherwise we might be taking Brown Betty to Striker in one of the prison labor camps.

Late in the night, while staring up at the avocado tree's shadows, I decided to go see Striker. I wanted to check on him, to see if he needed someone to talk to. Plus, I'd never really said good-bye to him. After quickly throwing on some clothes, I quietly left my house and made my way through people's backyards to Striker's place. His shed door was closed and the windows were dark, but one window in the second story of the house was illuminated. It was Striker's bedroom. I stared up at it from the corner of the house, and as I did, I heard deep wrenching sobs come through the open window. As much as I wanted to go to him and comfort him, I knew that I couldn't. A battle was taking place, and it was strictly a private affair between Striker and the inner demons that had tormented him for so long. Quietly, I stepped back into the shadows and went home.

Chapter 39

H, as in…

It was mid-morning on the second day of our journey, and the humidity and heat of Florida's interior were already starting to wear on everyone. The breeze—if it could even be called such—was stingy and hot, and only added another layer of grit and grime to our skin. Wearing us down even more was the fact that a heavy rainstorm had erupted soon after we'd made camp the night before, turning our site into a muddy mess. Finally, after settling down in another area that was just as wet but a little less muddy, a vicious squadron of mosquitoes had made a midnight meal of us. No one could sleep; we spent the entire night either slapping at the biting insects, or nearly succumbing to heatstroke while seeking refuge under a blanket. Now, as we rode the last seven miles of the fifty-mile journey to meet the Immokalee tribe at the halfway point, I let my mind wander wherever it would to distract myself from my sore back and bottom.

Looking over at Mama on my left, I saw that she looked about as trail weary as the rest of us. Her lightly tanned skin was covered with a thin layer of dust, as was her hair. But she still sat tall and proud in her saddle, which made me sit up a little straighter in mine. She was the one I measured myself to in all things. Once again, I thanked God that in His infinite wisdom, He'd seen fit to put my earthly life in her hands. I also uttered another prayer that Aunt Ivy and Uncle Moses would be among the Immokalee people rendezvousing with us. Mama had no way of knowing if they'd come, and no way of letting them know in such a short amount of time about our plans, so all we could do was hope and pray they'd be there.

Turning my head to the right, I looked at my handsome father. Set against the backdrop of his deeply tanned Creek Indian skin, his eyes looked like blue sapphires. But it wasn't just the color that made them so striking, it was the wisdom and kindness behind them. There was integrity and honor there, as well, which made me want to be nothing short of all that he expected me to be.

Next, my mind wandered where it always did, even when I tried to detour it: Striker. I never did get to say good-bye. I thought that perhaps I'd have a chance when my parents and I were leaving, but Striker was already gone. It was probably just as well that he was. I hated good-byes, and it would have been especially hard with him.

I wondered what he was doing at the moment, but figured he was probably getting settled at the St. Augustine lighthouse. Though he'd taken the train, he'd brought Odie along, which made me smile as I pictured the poor animal riding in one of the cattle cars, wide-eyed and wondering what hellacious beast had swallowed him whole. I was glad that Striker and Odie had each other, and could spend more time together again. It had been hard on them both when Striker worked offshore at Fowey.

I wondered what Striker had had for breakfast, and if anyone had taken the time to clean the lighthouse well before he got there, just as I had done in preparation for...*Stop it!* I told myself. *That chapter is over now. You've got to let it go, or it'll eat you alive worse than last night's mosquitoes!* But telling myself to do something was far easier than getting myself to do it.

Suddenly, Papa's voice startled me out of my thoughts. "There they are," he said, jutting his chin slightly toward the left as he raised his hand in greeting.

There, waiting in a long line to meet us were the Immokalee Seminoles. Craning my neck to see if my aunt and uncle were among them, I suddenly caught sight of a long silver-haired Caucasian woman sitting regally upon a spotted black and gray horse. Next to her was a tall black man, looking equally regal sitting atop an enormous Palomino horse. My Aunt Ivy and Uncle Moses had come.

Mama saw them, too, but respectfully waited for both village chiefs to ride out ahead of everyone else and warmly greet each other. Then the first of many gifts were exchanged between the two men. Paroh presented Sam with a beautiful walking stick. It was made from rich oak that had the exquisitely carved face of an owl at the top, where the hand would grip. And Sam gave Paroh an intricately carved ceremonial pipe inlaid with various hardwoods. The men spoke for a moment or two, then turned to their respective tribes and held up their right arms, indicating their people should join them.

Mama and Ivy did not have to be told twice. Both sisters dug their heels into their horses' haunches and raced toward each other. When they were about ten yards away from each other, they pulled their horses to a hard stop, jumped from their saddles and ran into each other's arms. Papa and I slowly rode up to them, as did Uncle Moses and my three cousins, Charlie, Martha, and Isaac. As the women continued to hold each other, cry, and talk over each other, Papa and I embraced the rest of our family. Finally, Mama and Aunt Ivy turned their attention to the rest of us. My aunt held me at arms' length, running her eyes over me. Then, my stately, silver-haired aunt said, "You are magnificent. You're a warrior." If she'd told me that I had just won all of the gold in Fort Knox, I could not have been more pleased.

"Come. Let's sit together before you have to start back," my aunt said to all of us. Looking around, I saw that people from both tribes were sitting in small groups wherever they could find shade.

We went to a scrub oak tree that offered enough shade to shelter my family. Uncle Moses and my cousins began to gather up wood for a small fire so that they could make tea, while Papa and I took our horses over to a creek to water them. When the tea was ready, Mama pulled out a sack of sweet biscuits she'd made, and we ate together as a family for the first time in ten years. There was so much news to catch up on, we decided to go one by one and give a small overview of what we were each doing. But, before we could start, Mama told Ivy the news she'd dreaded giving her, that Uncle James was gone.

"At least he was doing what he loved to do, Ivy," Mama said, holding her sister's hand. My aunt, too stunned to do any more than nod, tried to smile reassuringly at Mama, but her tear-filled eyes gave away the depth of her sadness. My mother patted her hand, comforting her. "His life was too short, but he was happy in it, Sister. And that's what matters most. I know that if James had had a choice of living for another forty years without accomplishing the things he had, or enjoying the great satisfaction of his accomplishments during a life short-lived, he'd have chosen the latter."

"I know," Ivy whispered, tears falling into her lap as she sat cross-legged on the ground across from my mother. "You're right."

Mama pulled her twin sister into her arms, and the two of them cried softly together. I knew there had to be regret on Aunt Ivy's part that she'd seen so little of James in recent years. And I knew that there had to be regret on Mama's part that James would not be there to share the years ahead. Our time with our Immokalee family was so limited that we couldn't dwell on James's death. So we moved on, instead, to what was happening in each other's lives.

Uncle Moses, handsome and dignified in his middle years, was still busy acting as liaison between the world outside the Everglades and his Seminole family. Often acting as a negotiator in business dealings, he was respected and trusted by both sides. Aunt Ivy was now the most revered medicine woman in the area, and was often sought out by people of all races to help treat their many afflictions. Charlie, their first born and two years older than Dylan, was managing a turpentine camp about ten miles north in Felda. Their youngest son, Isaac, was working construction in the town of Immokalee. But what really got my attention was when their middle child, Martha, told us that she was teaching the children in her village, just as I had been doing.

"Eliza has been teaching Paroh's people," my mother said, and I could hear the pride in her voice.

"Oh?" Martha said, turning to look at me. That revelation had gotten her attention. Smiling at my cousin, I confirmed it was so. Looking at the girl, I couldn't help but admire her unusual beauty. Being of mixed race, she had skin the rich color of burnt butter, and her hair was as black as mine was. But her eyes were her most striking feature. They were light blue like Aunt Ivy's. Set against her darker skin and black hair, they were truly glorious. Neither of her brothers had inherited those eyes, so it set Martha apart.

"I guess you wouldn't consider living here so that you could work with us, would you?" Martha asked seriously. "There're only two of us teaching all grade levels and with Paroh's tribe joining us now, we could use at least another teacher or two."

"You should, Eliza," both Mama and Aunt Ivy said in unison, causing them to laugh. It was good to see them smiling again. However, I looked hard at Mama to gauge if she was truly serious. Honestly, it surprised me she would suggest such a thing, and I was a little hurt that she would urge me to leave home. But she was a smart and unselfish woman who knew that nothing much awaited me back in Miami.

These Seminole people I had grown to love so deeply would no longer be there. I wouldn't have the pleasure and fulfillment I'd had from hearing Rose read aloud, or hearing her younger sister recite her ABC's by memory. From now on, I'd spend many of my hours at Burdine's, and while I was grateful to the good retailer for giving me employment, I never planned on making it a career. I supposed I could ask for a teaching job in the elementary school in Coconut Grove, but they didn't seem to have trouble keeping teachers on, and with more and more people coming into the area, including teachers with years of experience, it wasn't likely I'd get a job there.

I could continue to dive wrecks with Papa, but with the reef lights alerting ships to the jagged rocks' exact locations, fewer and fewer vessels were going down, and there'd be even fewer now that reputable lighthouse keepers would be dutifully burning their Fresnel beams. The one thing that might have kept me in Miami was Striker. But he was gone now.

"We'd have to check with Paroh and Sam," I said quietly, unsure whether this was the path I really wanted to be on.

"Oh, don't worry about Sam," Aunt Ivy assured me. "He'd be only too happy to have you join us."

"And I don't think you'd have to worry about Paroh," Mama said, gently fingering the locket on my chest to remind me of his acceptance and love for me.

"Baby girl," Papa quietly said, while looking me directly in the eye. "Follow the path your heart sets you on."

"Let me think about it, all right?" I replied, looking around at everyone. "Even if I were to accept the position, I'd need to go home first and get more of my things. I'd also need to give Mr. Burdine a little notice. Just let me think about it for a little bit."

We got home a day later and found an envelope by the front door with Papa's name written on it, and the key to Striker's motorboat inside. A note was with it, gifting the boat to my father for finding out the truth about the death of his parents. I knew then that there wasn't a chance that Striker was coming back. And I also knew it was time for me to move on. Two weeks later, Papa escorted me to the Immokalee village, where I picked up teaching exactly where I'd left off the last day in the Everglades village, on the letter *H*—as in *heartbroken*.

Chapter 40

Winds of Change

December 1907

"There is absolutely no reason why you can't use a cypress tree for a Christmas tree, Thomas. If Bettie wants to use a regular old pine tree...well, that's her choice, but you use the one you think is most beautiful to celebrate Jesus's birthday." Squatting down, I dried my six-year-old student's eyes and made him blow his runny nose into my handkerchief before sending him back to his seat. "Now, children," I said firmly. "The good Lord saw fit to plant a whole bunch of different types of trees, and He gave us the freedom to pick which ones we like the best. There's no right or wrong in His eyes about it, so there shouldn't be in your eyes either. With that said, y'all are dismissed—oh, and don't forget to take a peppermint stick from the bowl by the door!" I hurriedly added, but it wasn't necessary. The children were looking forward to their little Christmas treat from me. As they made their hasty exit, they had to run by Paroh, who stood patiently aside at the door.

"How long have you been standing there?" I asked, surprised he hadn't just interrupted class if he needed something.

"Only a moment. You handled the battle of the better Christmas tree quite well." He looked amused.

"Lord knows, I love the holidays," I said as I erased their homework assignment from the blackboard. "But with half the class telling the other half that there's no such thing as Santa, or that a cypress makes a better Christmas tree than a pine, it seems that we've lost the old 'goodwill to man' Christmas spirit."

"I think you need a break," Paroh chuckled.

"And I think you're right," I agreed.

"When are you leaving?" he asked as he helped me collect the Christmas songbooks on the desks.

"I told Mama and Papa that I'd be home by the sixteenth, which is day after tomorrow. I'll be heading back the day after Christmas.

"Were those planks I saw the men bringing in on the wagon about midday?" I asked as I threw a dark brown shawl around my shoulders and took one last look around the room before we walked out.

"Yes. Sam's been complaining ever since this school was built in the spring that a chief should have a wood and concrete home, as well. So, he's finally getting one."

"And are you going to build yourself one, too?" I smiled.

"Not if I can help it," he laughed. "I like the breeze blowing through a chickee, and being able to look all around me. Not just through a tiny slot of a window."

"You can have big windows, you know," I pointed out.

"Having no walls is better. Come," he said, directing me in the opposite direction from my own chickee. "I have something to show you."

"What?" I asked, intrigued. "You haven't gone and bought another goat, have you? Lord, that thing ate poor ol' Nollie's garden all to pieces!"

"I know. She keeps reminding me," he said, rolling his eyes. "I've come very close to telling her that the worms ate it up long before the goat ever did, but…"

"But you're far better mannered than that," I finished for him.

As we worked our way through the village, I marveled at how much had changed in the year I'd been there. It had grown with the addition of Paroh's tribe, of course, but it was more than that. The two tribes had worked together as one and within the first few months had built a nice little schoolhouse. But they'd also increased their fields of tomatoes, strawberries, and beans to three times the size, so that they could sell what the tribe didn't consume. Now, they were in the middle of building a larger corral for holding some cattle they had purchased. It was just a few head, but it was a start.

"Look," Paroh said, pointing to the old small corral just ahead of us. Inside was a massive bull.

"You did it!" I said excitedly. I was thrilled that they'd finally been able to procure one. Without the bull, the cows were useless, unless they were good milkers.

"He's a fine one, no?" Paroh said proudly. We walked over to the corral to inspect it. "He's young, too, so we should have him around for many years to come."

"Oh, he *is* a fine one, Paroh! Truly fine!" I was absolutely tickled that another small goal had been reached by the tribe.

"Who's going with you to the halfway point tomorrow?" he asked, turning away from the bull to look at me.

"Charlie and Martha," I replied. "Isaac was planning to come, too, but he's working on that new church in town, and they're hoping to have it completed for Christmas services."

"That doesn't give them much time," Paroh said with raised eyebrows.

"And that's why Isaac isn't riding with us," I chuckled.

"We'll miss you while you're gone," Paroh said kindly.

"The children will miss the candy," I quipped.

"Yes, they'll miss the candy, but they'll miss you far more," he assured me.

I smiled humbly, though I knew he was right. I loved the children, and I felt that the feeling was mutual. "A lot has changed over the months, hasn't it?" I rested my arms on the top rail of the corral and looked out at the growing herd.

"A lot has, yes," Paroh agreed, resting his forearms on the railing next to mine. "It always does—whether we want it to or not. But it sure is nice when the winds of change smell sweet instead of fishy."

"Ain't it the truth," I softly but wholeheartedly agreed.

Chapter 41

A Time to Heal, a Time to Grow

The main hall at the Royal Palm Hotel was elaborately trimmed with Christmas greenery, ribbons, and bows, transforming the room into a scene not unlike one found in some fantastical snow globe. In the center of every table was either a red amaryllis or white roses, while poinsettias lined the baseboards of every wall. Garlands of berries were threaded through the massive chandeliers, their bright color reflected in the crystal prisms. And in the center of the room was a massive Douglas fir tree, which had been shipped in from Banner Elk, North Carolina. As couples on the dance floor swept past it, they craned their necks around, trying to catch a glimpse of the various ornaments hanging merrily from the many branches. It was Christmas in the tropics at its finest, and my family and I took in the breathtaking opulence through child-like eyes as we dined on the Royal Palm's most decadent dishes. After numerous courses, which included crab cocktail, consommé à la Royale, roasted turkey, sweet potato croquettes, creamed onions, sautéed mixed greens, and cranberry punch, our Christmas dinner was topped off with a stunning Nesselrode pudding. Looking around at my family as I enjoyed each luscious bite of the roasted chestnut and rum-laced candied fruit concoction, I admired how handsome each one of them was.

Mama had outdone herself in designing both her dress and mine. And though I'd felt a little awkward when I'd run into William Burdine because I was wearing a dress that had obviously not come from his store, I couldn't help but enjoy the fact that it had been designed just for me. My gown was made from a deep gold silk that hung down to the floor in straight lines. Per the latest styles coming out of Paris and New York, bustles were a thing of the past, and corsets were optional, much to the delight of women the world over. Finally, we were able to breathe normally without restrictive binding, and we were far cooler without them, too. While women didn't have hourglass figures any longer, they looked the way God intended them to look. And, as I overheard one man say to another one morning at Burdine's, at least they could see the truth of what they were getting in a wife *before* the wedding night. I'd laughed to myself at that. They were right; corsets and bustles had been false advertising.

My gown had elaborate scrolled beadwork on the scooped-neck bodice and capped sleeves, but other than that, it was unadorned. The magnificence of the golden silk was statement enough. Mama's dress was a deep green satin which played beautifully against the red of her hair, and Papa was wearing a handsome navy suit. Mama had tried to get him to wear a light gray waistcoat with it, but Papa said that he'd made enough of an effort wearing the suit and dark gray four-in-hand tie without the added layer of the vest. With or without it, my father was strikingly handsome, and Mama was beautiful.

Sitting to Papa's right was Dylan, who had arrived nearly two weeks before. I hadn't been told he was coming home, and I was thrilled to see him when he showed up along with my parents to meet me at the halfway point between Miami and Immokalee. Another surprise addition to our Christmas gathering was Kathy Baker, who sat to my brother's right. When Striker and I had stopped at Alligator Light following the storm, she was the one who had told me about Dylan's heroic efforts in saving her and her sister, as well as many of the other passengers from the ship that had hit the reef near the lighthouse. Since then, she and her sister had been living with their aunt and uncle in Miami, and Dylan and Kathy had kept in touch through letters. They'd even seen each other on a couple of occasions when Dylan had come home during leave from the Key West light. True to Warren Chaplain's word, Dylan had been given the position there, and was now the fulltime keeper. Though we wished he was closer to home, we were glad he was no longer hopping from one reef lighthouse to another, and was permanently placed at a land-based light. Watching the looks that were exchanged between my brother and his lady friend was both amusing and endearing, and I couldn't have been happier for them both. But Christmas and Kathy weren't the only reasons that Dylan had come home; the trial of Ezra Asher and Adam Wilson had brought him back to Miami as well.

Now, as we finished our dessert, our conversation turned back to the final verdict: Twenty-five years of hard labor for Ezra at Aycock Labor Camp, in Chipley, Florida, and life without parole for Adam Wilson, at the Chattahoochee Penitentiary in Florida's panhandle. The only reason Adam didn't receive the death penalty was because he'd turned state's witness on the still-missing Owen Perry. He had also testified to Ezra's complicity in the wrecking scheme. Ezra had helped to determine which ships should be targeted, and then made enormous gains from them as wreck master. There was much speculation as to where Owen might have run to, but I knew it was a mystery that would never be answered, at least not by me.

"Well, it's a blasted shame Owen hasn't been brought to justice," Mama said, after swallowing a sip of coffee. "But whether he is or isn't here on Earth, the good Lord will certainly get His shot at judgin' him. And you couldn't give me all the treasure in the world to be standin' in Owen's shoes when he is." Murmurs of agreement were heard around the table.

"Has anyone seen or heard from Striker?" I asked as nonchalantly as I could.

"He came in just a few days ago, near the end of the trial, to testify about watching the light go out at Fowey," Dylan said.

"Did he go back to St. Augustine?" I asked. Just then, the band began to play, and people started making their way out to the dance floor.

"Uh, apparently not," Papa replied, looking past me with a bemused smile on his face.

"Evenin', Harjo clan," an all-too familiar voice said from behind me. Turning halfway in my chair, I looked up into the handsome face of Paul Strickland.

Striker was elegantly dressed in an ink-black wool suit. He wore no waistcoat, but with his black jacket contrasting so sharply against his stiff white shirt and maroon striped tie, he didn't need one. Finishing off his attire were beautiful gray star sapphire cufflinks.

"Striker! Why didn't you tell us you'd be stayin' around?" Mama exclaimed.

"I wasn't sure how long I'd be here." He smiled. He and Mama had always liked each other.

"Well, I wish we'd known," Dylan said, standing and shaking hands with him. "You could have joined us for dinner. Have you eaten yet?"

"I did, with some friends in the bar," Striker confirmed. "I'm sorry to interrupt y'all, but I wanted to see if I could borrow Eliza for a minute," he said, looking down at me. Placing his left hand on that tender area between the shoulder and the neck, he squeezed ever so slightly. "Will you dance with me?" he asked.

"Uh, yes...yes, of course," I stammered, finally finding my voice again. He pulled my chair back for me as I stood up, and when I turned around, our faces were within inches of each other for the first time in over a year. Still keeping his eyes on mine, he took my hand and then led me over to the dance floor, where gently but firmly, he pulled me into his arms and we began to waltz. Unfortunately, the tune the band happened to be playing was "Love Me and the World is Mine."

"How've you been?" I asked, breaking our gaze and looking past his shoulder, but not really seeing anything.

"I've been well," he replied. "And you? I hear you're over in Immokalee teaching."

"I am—doing well *and* teaching," I clarified, looking back at him.

"That's good—that you're doing well *and* teaching," he teased. Slowly, the smile faded as his eyes traveled over my face, slowing ever so slightly at my lips before moving on.

The countless number of candles in the sconces on the walls washed the room in soft light, giving Striker's thick wavy hair a deeper golden hue, but nothing could soften the intensity of his dark eyes. They showed every bit of his emotion. They always had, and tonight was no exception.

"You look beautiful," he said in a soft, husky voice.

He pulled me even closer, and I breathed in his scent as we danced our way around the room. He smelled of spice and the sea. The smell was clean and masculine and alluring. Forcing my mind to move on, I pulled away from him slightly so that I could look at him. "So, when are you returning to St. Augustine?" I asked.

"Tomorrow morning," he replied. "On the 8:05. Let's walk outside for a few minutes, okay?"

"All right," I agreed.

Taking my hand, Striker led me away from the dance floor and out the side door, leading to an open-air promenade walkway that ran the length of the massive hotel. To the north was the main entrance, complete with an enormous circular driveway, great columns and a deep portico. Lying to the east was Biscayne Bay, and to the south, overlooking the river, were perfectly manicured gardens. Different areas designed for sitting and talking had been carved out among the vast numbers and varieties of flowers and plants, and surrounding all of it was a perfectly maintained high hedge that afforded the hotel's guests some privacy. Though it was late December, the weather was relatively mild, but there was enough of a breeze that I was chilly without my shawl, which was uselessly keeping the back of my chair warm in the dining room.

"Here," Striker said, slipping off his jacket and draping it over my shoulders. "If you're too cold, we can go back in."

"No, no." I assured him. "I'm fine now, thanks."

We continued into the garden, where we took one of many paths. This particular one led to a break in the hedge with a picket fence-style gate that allowed people to walk out to the river. Going no further than the gate, we looked out at the shimmering water that reflected a full moon and millions of twinkling stars.

"Nice, isn't it?" I said, if for no other reason than I had absolutely no idea what else to say.

"It is," Striker said, turning away from the river and facing me. "Are you sure you're not too cold?" He pulled his jacket closer around me.

"I'm fine," I laughed, touched by his concern. It was good seeing him again, and I told him that.

"It's good to see you, too, Eliza," he replied, his eyes locking onto mine. "I stopped by your house a couple times to see you, but no one's been home."

I was surprised that'd he'd done so. "I guess with the busyness of Christmas, we've all been out."

"How long are you here?" he asked, before turning back toward the river again.

"I leave tomorrow," I replied. "Just like you."

"And you like Immokalee, and being with your aunt and uncle, I guess?" he asked, though it sounded more like a statement than a question.

I looked up at him and smiled. "Not really and very much."

"Explain." He smiled, confused.

"I don't much like Immokalee—the place, I mean. I miss the water, and being right on the coast. And I miss my parents. Things like that. But getting to know Aunt Ivy and Uncle Moses better, not to mention my cousins, has been wonderful. They're special people, and they've watched over me like I'm one of their own children."

I didn't want to talk about me anymore. "How 'bout you?" I said. "Do you like working at the St. Augustine light?"

"I do. But I won't be there much longer," he replied.

"Why's that? Have they transferred you to another lighthouse?" I asked.

"No, no," he said, shaking his head. "The keepers at the land-based lights aren't moved around nearly as often as the ones who work offshore. Unsurprisingly, the keepers who work on land are more content. They have a life."

His statement made me wonder how much of a life he'd been living. Before I could stop myself, I asked, "Have you been seeing anyone?" I could have kicked myself.

He looked at me for a couple of seconds and smiled slightly as if trying to decide how much to tell me. "I've gone out some. Yes. How 'bout you?"

"Well, if you're asking me if anyone is courting me, no, not really. Listen, enough about me. You said you wouldn't be at the light in St. Augustine much longer. What will you be doing?"

"Building boats," he said matter-of-factly.

"Striker, you don't mean it!" I cried, thrilled that he'd be putting his wonderful talents to use again. "What changed your mind?"

"Several things," he said. "One of them was time." Suddenly, he looked very serious, almost pensive.

"Listen, Eliza, finding out what really caused the death of my parents lifted a weight off me that I pray you'll never be able to fully understand. Living with the guilt of thinking you killed two of the people you care most about in this world is enough to break you for the rest of your life. It about did me.

"There's nothing worse," he continued, "than being out at some isolated lighthouse while you keep telling yourself over and over again that if you'd designed the boat more like this, or if there'd been a little less of that, then the outcome would have been entirely different. Staying alone out there, with nothing but guilt for company, does things to a man's head—and heart. That's why keepers come and go so quickly.

"Anyway," Striker said, taking a deep breath, "I drew up some designs and sent them over to my old bosses at Merrill-Stevens boatyard in Jacksonville. They got back to me right away and said that if I'd build two of the boats I designed under both my name *and* theirs, they'd pay for me to open and run another boatyard for them anywhere I wanted."

"And you took 'em up on the offer, of course," I said, unable to imagine him not jumping at such a wonderful opportunity.

"No, I didn't," he corrected me, smiling. "I want to build boats under my own name, but I need capital to do that. So, I sold Merrill-Stevens one of the two designs and gave up all rights to claim it as my own, as well as the rights to profit from it."

"But couldn't you have figured out another way?" I asked, aghast that he'd give up his design so easily.

"Eliza, if I told you how many zeros were on that check, you'd understand that I made a very nice deal for myself. I have a lot more designs I'm working on that will be mine alone. In the meantime, this has given me more than enough to open my boatyard and marina."

"So, where are you thinking about building it?" I asked as nonchalantly as possible.

"Here—in Miami," he said, watching me closely as he did. "And I was hoping you'd be by my side when I do. I was hoping maybe we could start all over again, building a life together and—"

"How can you say that to me, Striker?" I angrily interrupted. "Did you really think you could show up after all this time and expect me to throw my arms around you, like I've been pining away for you since you left for St. Augustine? Did you just assume that I'd wait around until your head cleared and you were finally able to feel something other than guilt again? Well, I'm sorry to disappoint you, but I didn't stop living just because *you* did. I've moved on!"

Striker's eyes flashed like dark shards of fire. "All right, Eliza. That's fine," he said in a controlled voice, but I could hear the anger mounting anyway. "But understand this: I never assumed anything. I never assumed that you were pining away for me, nor did I assume that you would wait around for me."

"You're absolutely right. I stand corrected. You wouldn't assume that since you made it perfectly clear I could never expect anything from you. *Ever*!" I cried.

"What the hell are you talking about?" Striker looked at me as though I'd lost my mind.

"In the Keys, Striker! What you told me then!"

"What, Eliza? What was it I said?" He didn't just sound angry now, he sounded frustrated, too.

"You told me to stop trying to make you love me!"

"Eliza!" Striker said, grabbing me by my upper arms and holding me in place so that he could look me in the eye. "You never had to try to make me love you! *I always did!"* He lessened the grip on my arms, and repeated more softly, "I always did." Then he let go of me and turned away. Planting his hands on his hips, he looked up to the sky as if searching for guidance or patience, or both. Finally, he turned around and studied me for a few seconds before calmly saying; "What you couldn't see was that I needed time to heal. And you needed time to grow up, Eliza."

I felt like I'd been slapped. Narrowing my eyes, I said, "You know, it's a funny thing about time; sometimes it causes people to drift apart from each other, instead of pulling them closer together." I glared at him for a second or two. "Here's your coat," I said, pulling it from around my shoulders and thrusting it into his hands. "We're leaving early, so I need to go. Merry Christmas," I said as I started to walk away.

Saying nothing more, Striker let me go.

Chapter 42

The Direction of the Heart

"You sure you got everything you brought? Your Christmas gifts, too?" Mama asked as we headed out the front door the next morning just a little before eight. After I assured her for the third time that I did, we walked down the porch steps to Papa, who was waiting patiently in the yard with all three of our saddled horses.

"You ladies ready?" he said, helping Mama secure one last thing to her horse, Gracie.

"As we'll ever be." Mama smiled.

All three of us mounted our horses and started walking west along the river. At the same time, the wind picked up. "Looks like we might get a shower or two," Papa said, looking up at the heavy gray sky. "Wind's comin' from the north, too, and it's got some chill to it. Y'all have enough warm things with you?"

"Lord, Max, you sound like our mother!" Mama teased. "But we're much obliged to you for keepin' an eye out for us, aren't we, Eliza?" Mama said, winking at me.

I knew she was just trying to lighten my mood. I'd been quiet all morning. She knew it had something to do with Striker because when I'd returned to the dinner table after walking in the garden with him, I only stayed for a short while. I'd excused myself as soon as I could without being rude, saying I needed to get home to pack. They'd offered to leave with me, but I assured them I was fine, and that a little quiet would do me good. Mama had seen my light on when they got home, but I didn't feel like talking any more then than I had when I'd returned from my walk in the garden. All I did say was that Striker seemed to be doing well, and had come to terms with his grief. I also added that the old humble Striker seemed to have been replaced by a much more arrogant Paul Strickland, and that he and I no longer saw eye to eye on things.

"I see," Mama said. Her expression looked a little doubtful; as if she wasn't sure she really did see. Then she wished me a good night and left the room. For the remainder of the night, I watched the avocado tree shadows play across my ceiling.

"Who's meeting us at the halfway point?" Papa asked, but before I could answer, a sharp whistle broke the early morning quiet. It was the 8:05 train's first signal for departing passengers to board.

"Train's fixin' to leave," Papa said matter-of-factly, though I saw his eyes cut over toward me.

No one said another word until a moment later a second shrill whistle ripped the air, causing me to jump slightly. This whistle was the train's second and last call for all to get onboard who were going.

Mama was looking at me hard, and I noticed that nobody seemed to want to move.

"Eliza!" Mama said sharply, almost as though she was reprimanding me. "You're as pale as a sheet. Now, you listen to me! I'm gonna ask you one question, and it may be the most important question you ever answer in life, so you think hard: Does your heart belong to the man on that train?" She waited for a second or two before adding, "Don't you dare lie to yourself!"

I looked straight ahead toward the west, the direction we were riding in, and then I heard the train's shrill whistle for the third time. It was a final farewell as the train slowly pulled away from the station to begin its trek north.

Suddenly, all doubt was gone. Pulling Sundae's reins sharply to the right, I spun her around and then dug my heels into her sides. The horse exploded forward, racing east along the river through people's backyards, including my own, and then I steered her to the north and across the bridge that spanned the river just beyond my house. We ran past the Royal Palm Hotel, and I glanced over at the gardens where Striker and I had been just hours before. Next, we flew through downtown. Fortunately, it was still early, so the streets were quiet, with the exception of Mr. McNamara, who was sweeping the sidewalk outside of his tannery, and shouted for me to slow down. Leaving the main business district behind, we cut diagonally across a brand new area where both residential and commercial buildings were being built, and then we finally came to the railroad tracks. After crossing over them, I immediately pulled Sundae to the left so that we were running parallel to the rails. Fortunately, the train's pace had been slow as it traveled through the more populated area, but it was nearly clear of it now and black steam poured from its stack as it was preparing to pick up speed. Urging Sundae to do the same, I leaned low on her to cut wind resistance and slapped her haunches smartly with the ends of my reins. Faithfully, my horse answered with magnificent effort and we made up some ground.

Just as I was about to reach the caboose, a few raindrops began to fall. Swirling winds whipped my hair across my face, but I kept riding hard. As I came upon the windows of one of the rear cars, passengers stared out at me as though I was playing some crazy game, while others waved at me as if I was giving them some grand escort out of town. Finally, I pulled alongside the next car, and saw a profile I knew and loved well. But then it was gone almost immediately and the train began to pull away from me.

"*Striker!*" I desperately shouted. "*Striker!*" I knew he couldn't hear me, but it was a cry from my heart, a shouting of my soul. I called his name again and again as the train pulled further away from me, but at that point, I knew I couldn't ask any more of my loyal horse. Pulling the reins back, I brought her to a stop. Both of us were shaking hard, and as she heaved for air, I lowered my head and sobbed. I kept my head down, unable to watch the retreating train, but I couldn't silence the sound of the torturous clacking as the wheels rotated faster and faster, taking Striker further and further from me.

Suddenly, there was a terrible screeching and my head snapped up. Sparks flew from the wheels as they locked up and metal slid against metal as the train strained to slow down. At last, it came to a complete stop, and smoke hissed out of the top as if in protest to the deviation from its strictly adhered-to schedule. For a moment, nothing happened; then, suddenly, a man jumped from the train with a satchel in his hand. Standing there, staring at me was Striker.

For a second or two, he seemed frozen in place, just as I was. Then we both moved at once. Dropping his satchel, he started to walk toward me, and then he began to run as I walked toward him on wobbly legs. As soon as he reached me, he placed his hands on either side of my face, then began to kiss every inch of it—over and over again. He pulled away slightly while still keeping my face cupped in his hands, and looked into my eyes as if to confirm that this was indeed what I wanted. To confirm that it was, I brought my mouth up to his. Then, at last, we experienced the familiar taste of each other again, deeply and urgently. Nothing else in the world mattered at that moment. All sight and sound ceased to exist, including the chugging of the train as it slowly pulled away, leaving us to find our own way back home. But we already had.

Epilogue

March 1908

I looked from one family member to another as they waved to us from the dock at the Royal Palm Hotel, and, for the hundredth time that day, I thought about how very blessed I was. How very blessed *we* were actually, for my family was officially Striker's now, too, though we'd always felt like he belonged to us. Looking away from the dock and back at the man who had been my husband for all of two hours, I couldn't help but think I had married a man who'd played different roles in my life depending on what we were doing, and what I needed at the time. On the one hand, he could be like a brother when we were competing against each other as to who could land the biggest fish. But he was also my best friend, as he had proven when we were hunting for my missing parents in the Florida Keys. Now, we were on our way to Key Biscayne, specifically the Cape Florida lighthouse, where he would become my husband in every sense of the word. I was excited about that, but also a little nervous, though I knew that I would be fine in his hands. The bottom line was that Striker had played all of these roles in my life because he was my soul mate. And I was his. He'd said as much after he'd jumped off the train that morning Sundae and I had chased him down, and he'd sworn that neither of us would ever leave the other behind again.

Early on, both of us had known our souls were intertwined, but it had taken a while for that understanding to go from our hearts to our heads. But once the connection had been made, Striker and I were finally free to move forward together. Our story wasn't unlike that of my parents, who'd had to overcome their own obstacles in order to see what was right in front of them: each other. Now, looking back at my mother and father standing on the dock, I realized that I had never loved them more than at that very minute. Their understanding of what Striker and I truly meant to each other had helped me to finally see it clearly, as well.

Standing next to Papa was Dylan, and next to him was Kathy Baker. In the late summer, she would be leaving her Aunt Halcyon's home in Miami, and joining my brother as Mrs. Dylan Harjo, down at the Key West Light. He had finally found the person who could anchor him, and the place, as well. I asked him if he was still writing, and he said that he was. Of particular interest to him was the wild life he saw down in the Keys. My brother was a sensitive, gentle man, with the soul of a poet, and I knew he would make a fine husband to the gentle girl from the north.

Beside Mama on the dock was Aunt Ivy, and Uncle Moses and Martha were there as well. Both Charlie and Isaac had had to work, but I was grateful the other three had come. Mama sorely missed Uncle James, and never more so than on this day, but Aunt Ivy's presence helped lift that sadness. I wished that their oldest brother, Joseph, could have made the trip down with his family, but it was a long trip from New Orleans, where he still worked as the main engineer on one of the massive paddlewheel river boats.

My eyes came to rest on Martha, and I couldn't help but smile. The night before, my cousin and I had had the chance to talk well into the evening, and I learned that she and Paroh had grown very close over the months. In one of life's sweet ironies, they planned to be married in the upcoming Green Corn Ceremony, just as my Aunt Ivy and Uncle Moses had done so many years before. I couldn't have been happier for Paroh and Martha, and I would miss them both. I would miss everyone in Immokalee, but none more so than the children.

Leaving my students had been the hardest part about returning to Miami, however, the good Lord saw to it to find a replacement for me. Rose had studied hard, and had excelled quickly; quickly enough that during the two months I remained there after Christmas to tie things up, Rose stepped into the new position of helping Martha and me as an assistant teacher. Once I was gone, her duties would increase, as would her responsibilities. It was a role she was ready for, and I couldn't have been prouder of her. As I'd walked down the aisle toward Striker just hours before, I wore the beautiful blue sea glass bracelet that Rose had made for me to use as my "something new" and "something blue" in my wedding. Rose had become a good friend and I would carry that friendship close to my heart always.

I gave one last wave to my family before turning back around and looking out over the bay as we made our way in our newly christened motorized sailboat, the *Eliza Jane*. It was one of Striker's wedding surprises for me, and the other waited for me on Key Biscayne. I'd tried to pry it out of him, but he said I had to see it instead of hear about it. Now, as Key Biscayne began to grow bigger in the distance, the butterflies in my stomach flew around in a frenzy.

"How long do we have permission to use the lighthouse?" I asked, coming up to stand next to Striker.

"We can use it as long as we want," he replied. "I figure we'll stay a couple of days, and then head on over to the Bahamas. There's a lot to show you there. I particularly want you to see Eleuthera. I think it's one of the prettiest islands in the chain, and you'll love diving the reefs. Speaking of which, is your father going to keep salvaging the *Paso Rápido* while we're gone? Or is he going to wait 'til you're back to continue?"

"I told him to keep working it with Simon and Turtle. Finding that gold bar a few weeks ago is enough to keep me happy even if I never dive the wreck again."

"It was good the courts awarded your father the rights as wreck master."

"Well, we were pretty happy about it, too." I smiled. "There's still a lot to be found in and around that wreck. Papa said that whatever he salvages from the sea, he's puttin' back into the land now. He bought twenty-nine acres of land on Miami Beach, on some new road they put in called Collins Avenue. It's kind of rough right now, he said, but he also said that any road that's called an avenue is bound to be worth its weight in gold. I hope he's right since I bought eight acres too from the money that gold bar brought in. We're gonna use the rest of it to help you build that large marina."

"No, you're not, Eliza. We already talked about this. That's your money, to do with as you choose."

"The marina is what I choose," I retorted. "Listen, Striker, if I'm going to be your partner in life, then you've got to let me help you when I can, with what I can."

He said nothing more, but just smiled at me, and I could see the love and gratitude in his eyes.

We slowed way down as we approached the beach on Key Biscayne. "Okay, toss it over now," Striker instructed, and I heaved the anchor off the bow. Once Striker was certain it had caught bottom, I discarded my canvas pants and shirt, and stripped down to my diving outfit, while Striker stripped down to his denim shorts.

When I'd changed out of my wedding dress and into my shirt and pants following the reception at the hotel, the minister's wife looked shocked. "I do declare, Eliza," the woman had said, aghast. "You're the first bride I've ever seen who looks like she's headed for a day of scrubbin' instead of a night of lovin'!" Everyone had laughed, including me.

"I can assure you, Mrs. Granger," Striker said, overhearing her comment, "the last thing she'll be doing is cleaning tonight." Everyone laughed again, while I blushed profusely.

Striker and I began unloading the few things we were bringing ashore. Holding everything high over our heads, we waded through waist-deep water to the beach and then we continued up to the keeper's quarters, which was a small cottage next to the lighthouse. Striker found a loose stone in the walkway, and lifting it slightly, removed the key that was hidden there.

"How'd you know that was there?" I asked.

"Keepers know how to get into most every lighthouse within a hundred mile radius. We move around so much, we have to know."

Instead of being musty-smelling and cobweb-covered, the cottage had been spotlessly cleaned, and was cozy and bright. Fresh flowers awaited us on the table, along with a large basket of food, courtesy of the Royal Palm Hotel Management. And the current caretaker of the lighthouse, Mr. Pullam, had kindly left a bottle of wine for us on the small kitchen table.

"Okay, before we get too settled in, I want to show you something."

Striker grabbed the bottle of wine, glasses, and an opener, and we left the cottage. We walked about a quarter mile down the beach until we came to the place where we'd boiled crabs on the shore and shared our first kiss. A fire had been laid and was ready to light, and sitting next to it was a large bucket of live crabs, as well as a blanket with a loaf of fresh bread, butter, cheese, and fruit.

"Who left this?" I asked, amazed. It had to have been done shortly before we arrived.

"Simon and Turtle," Striker replied. "Didn't you notice how quickly they left the reception?"

We'd not eaten much, so we were hungry. We got the fire started to boil the crabs, and then opened the wine. Thirty minutes later, we dined on a fine feast.

"Eliza," Striker said, taking a sip of his wine. "Look to your left. You see that point, where the land juts out about a hundred yards down?" I told him I did. "Now, look to your right. You see that sea grape tree drooping down? It's got a bright red ribbon tied to it." I confirmed that I did. "From that point to the other, is yours. This is your beach now."

I was too stunned to say anything for a moment. My head swiveled back and forth, looking from one end to the other. "It's ours? Truly?" was all I could manage after a moment.

"It is. Listen, Eliza, Miami is growing fast, and once roads are built, allowing folks to travel down here by automobile, this place is going to explode. We're going to have a hell of a tourist industry, and not just made up of wealthy people. Folks who have less to spend, but as much desire for a taste of the tropics are gonna come down here in droves. The way I figure it, the more land we invest in, the better. But, even more important than that, I want us to have a place where we can bring our children that's a little quieter than a city; a special place that's all ours, where we can show them how to catch crabs and cook 'em on the beach. The more land the developers scoop up, the less there'll be to do those kind of things. We'll still keep our home on the river, but I think we should build a small cottage on this piece of land, too. At least that's the way I see it. But what about you?"

"What I think is that I'm very glad I married you. Before we leave for the Bahamas," I said, gently pushing him back onto the blanket, and looking down into his warm brown eyes, "we're going to figure out exactly where we're gonna put that cottage." I leaned down and kissed his mouth, and just as I did, I felt the first rain drops land on my nearly bare back.

"Let's go back to the cottage," he said, emotion evident in his deep voice.

Leaving the remains of our meal behind, we ran up the beach to the keeper's house, but the rain caught us anyway, and by the time we made it through the front door, we were thoroughly drenched. The cozy cottage was no longer bright and cheery, so Striker lit the gas lamp in the middle of the table, as well as a small fire in the wood stove. This early in March, it was still chilly, especially on the beach in a storm. Once the flames were licking the wood, Striker turned to me as I stood there drying my hair with a towel and dripping on the braided rug in the center of the room.

Walking over to me, he took my face in his hands, brought his lips to within an inch or two of mine, then whispered that he loved me before kissing me deeply.

When he pulled away, the look in his eyes was unmistakable: There was a confidence there, a knowing, and I knew that he was about to play teacher to a very willing but uneducated student.

Keeping his intense eyes locked on mine, he pulled my soaked bandeau top over my head. Then, drawing me to him, he lowered his head, and his tongue sought out my taut nipples. The hot moisture on his tongue felt good on my rain-chilled skin. I held his head close to me, but he pulled away a moment later to finish undressing me. Then, as I worked at the buttons on his shirt and then his pants, he gazed down at me, smiling, obviously pleased with my eagerness to feel his naked skin against my own. Finally, after much kissing and touching, he led me to the bed. I lay down on my back, and he lay beside me, looking down at me as he gently brushed aside some wayward strands of hair from my face.

"Eliza, am I the first man you've ever been with?" he asked.

I was surprised at the question, but, at the same time, I respected him for assuming nothing and for realizing that my life might have involved others before him. I nodded, unable to trust my voice.

"Good," he whispered in my ear. He licked the outside of it, and then explored the inside. "That's good," he whispered again. I knew he was making me ready for him, and he was accomplishing it, to the point that I began to squirm against him, encouraging him, wanting him.

"Eliza, look at me. This is going to hurt for a moment, but only for a moment, then never again after that."

I trusted him and gave myself over to him completely. And throughout our love making, Striker watched me, gently guiding me and encouraging me, while letting my excitement build and then relax a little so that he could build it up again. I felt as though I was riding a wave, rising and falling as it undulated. Finally, when he knew we both needed release, he let me crest the wave, and then we rode it all the way in together.

At first light, I slid out of bed and put on a pair of pants and a flannel shirt. As I did, I looked down at my husband sleeping peacefully, and thought about how different I felt today. Something within me had been changed in the night, and as I looked down at the reason for the shift in me, I felt a depth of love that I'd never known before. Now, I understood how deep love could be, and I leaned over and softly placed a kiss on his slightly parted lips.

Putting the coffee on, I sat out on the porch waiting for it to brew. Once it was ready, I filled a big mug, then walked down the beach, listening to the palm trees as they began to stir in wakefulness. Finally, I came to that place I'd remembered. It was a perfect spot to look across the bay at Miami and see her silhouette against the brightening sky. There upon the shore she stood, rising higher every day, and becoming a glistening, radiant jewel on the sand. Nestled within her were the people I loved, and together we would watch this glorious town grow; helping her to rise to magnificent heights, and helping her to stand up again if she fell. Through every season, for all time, we would be there, permanently weaving the stories of our lives into Miami's beautiful tapestry.

**Read on for an excerpt from the fascinating
conclusion to Janie DeVos's trilogy of old Florida,
The River to Glory Land, coming soon!**

Preface

Eden in Ruins
September 18, 1926
Miami, Florida

The roof blew off at exactly 3:17 a.m. I knew that because the violent winds that instantly invaded our home tore the kitchen clock off the wall, and shot it across our living room, where it barely missed Mama's head before shattering at my feet. The roar in the room was so deafening that I couldn't hear the clock's wood and glass case explode. But I could see the time, and it was 3:17.

Suddenly, Daddy grabbed my arm and pulled me into the kitchen, with Olivia and Mama right behind us. We made our way out the back door, which was hanging precariously by one hinge, and into the yard. Making a human chain, we clung to avocado and mango trees as we made our way through the backyard, paralleling the rising river, to Howie Weiss's house. It was dark out, but the sky was an eerie cement-gray color, which only blended into the gray curtain of rain pelting us hard enough to skin us alive. Glancing up for a second, I caught a glimpse of Howie's silhouette cast by the illumination of his lamp as he stood in the doorway urging us to hurry in. Thank God, he knows we're coming, I thought.

At last, we made it up the porch steps and into his kitchen, then Daddy and Howie used their shoulders to force the door shut. Once it closed, the muffled noise was a relief, yet oddly unnerving in its own way.

"How'd you know we were coming?" Daddy breathlessly asked as he wiped the wetness out of his eyes with the back of his drenched sleeve.

"Part of someone's roof hit the side of our house," Howie replied as his wife, Ellen, handed towels to all of us. "Looked out the back door to see what the dickens had crashed against our east wall and saw y'all comin'. Glad I did because I wouldn't have heard you poundin' on the door."

"That mighta been our roof," Daddy said. "It's completely gone."

"Well, thank God, you're not," Mrs. Weiss replied. "C'mon. Let's move in to the living room. We'll more comfortable in there."

We all got settled and I noticed that everyone had found someone to sit close to, closer than usual. I was sitting by Mama on the couch, while Daddy was sitting next to Olivia on a loveseat. She'd not said a word since she'd let out a blood-curdling scream when our roof started to peel back. Even in the weak lamplight, I could see that my younger sister was as pale as a ghost. Obviously, she was scared to death—we all were—but with Olivia's quiet nature, I was never quite sure what she was thinking.

Just then, something hit the house hard. "Lord God, this is a bad one," Mr. Weiss said quietly, almost to himself. Fortunately, the sound of windows breaking did not accompany the loud bang, for if it had, it was likely the Weisses' roof would go, too.

The quiet in the room was heavy as we all continued to listen to the storm's relentless rampage demanding entry. Each time the wind would rise into a high-pitched wail, I held my breath, and then let it out as the gale calmed down. Everyone gripped the arms of whatever piece of furniture they sat in with white-knuckled readiness as though we knew that at any second, we might be forced to make a mad dash out of the house. The only trouble was there was really no place to go. The neighbor between the Weisses' place and ours wasn't home and the house was boarded up tightly. And the neighbor on the other side of the Weisses was quite a distance down. Finally, my mother broke the silence.

"Poor Mama said she got harassed all day by folks sayin' that the headline about the approaching hurricane was just an attempt at sellin' more papers."

She was referring to my grandmother, Eve Harjo, who worked at the Miami Herald. My mother said that Grandma had told her that by noon she'd heard enough malarkey about overblown stories, and so she'd left the paper and headed home.

Home for my grandparents was the ten-storey Spinnaker Hotel they owned on Miami Beach, and the Weisses' home actually belonged to them, too. It was the house where my mother and her brother, Dylan, had been raised, and Olivia and I had spent much of our childhood there. Our home, which was probably completely destroyed by now, was where my father had grown up. Living practically next door to each other, my parents had been childhood sweethearts.

"I'm surprised your folks didn't come stay with y'all," Mrs. Weiss remarked. "It seems like it'd be safer here, than right on the beach in a building that tall."

"Mama and Papa wanted to keep an eye on things at the hotel," my mother explained. "Besides, some of the employees asked if they could ride out the storm there since their own places aren't much more than shacks. Worries me, though, 'cause most of the windows on the upper floors don't have protection on them. But all we can do is pray they'll be fine."

And I was praying. I prayed that my grandparents and the hotel would both be standing after the storm. For without those two people I adored, I'd be completely devastated, and without their hotel, I'd be unemployed.

Throughout the remainder of the early morning hours, we made small talk as we continued to watch the ceiling, praying the roof would hold, and listening to the storm's wrath pound us with a fury unlike anything we had experienced before. Finally, as we sat at the kitchen table eating some of Mrs. Weiss's guava jelly donuts, the rain stopped battering the house and the winds died down. Opening the kitchen door, we cautiously stepped outside to look at a new Miami awaiting us. In the course of just one night, she had fallen, leaving much of the city completely flattened and still submerged after a river of water from Biscayne Bay had surged inland. No one said a word as we surveyed the absolute destruction around us, though I could hear Mrs. Weiss and Olivia softly crying.

"Well, I swear, would you take a look at that?" Mr. Weiss exclaimed. Everyone turned to him and saw that instead of looking around at all of the destroyed homes and buildings, he was gazing up. Our eyes followed his to a sight I was sure I would never forget if I lived to be a thousand. There, caught up in the splintered and leafless branches after being carried in on a tidal wave from the bay, were fish, hundreds of them, looking as though they were some kind of peculiar fruit hanging in a ruined Eden.

About the Author

Photo Credit: Barbara Kahn

Janie DeVos is a native of Coral Gables, Florida. She attended Florida State University, then worked in the advertising industry for over a decade, including radio, cable television, public relations and advertising firms. Though her career changed over the years, one thing didn't— her love of writing. She is an award winning children's author. *The Rising of Glory Land* is the second book in her Glory Land series. Learn more at www.janiedevos.com.

Made in the USA
Middletown, DE
27 July 2018